WANTING MR. CANE

CANE #1

SHANORA WILLIAMS

NOTIFICATIONS

To get notified about new release alerts, free books, and exclusive updates, join my newsletter at
www.shanorawilliams.com/mailing-list

WANTING MR. CANE PLAYLIST

Water - Jack Garratt
Fetish - Selena Gomez ft. Gucci Mane
Now Or Never - Halsey
Naive - Laura Welsh
Love Lies - Khalid ft. Normani
The Ways - Khalid ft. Kendrick Lamar & Swae Lee
Terrified - Childish Gambino
Not Afraid Anymore - Halsey
Atomised - Laura Welsh
Perfect - Selena Gomez
Devil In Me - Halsey
Redbone - Childish Gambino
Unforgettable - French Montana ft. Jeremih
PCH - Jaden Smith
Give Me Love - Ed Sheeran
Don't Forget About Me - Cloves
What Goes Around Comes Around - Justin Timberlake

1

KANDY

I remember the very first day I met Mr. Cane.

I was only nine years old, but I remember exactly what I saw and how I felt when I first laid eyes on him.

A shiny black car pulled into the driveway of our two-story home, parking less than a yard away from where I was. I sat on the tire swing of the big tree on the front lawn, wearing dingy-white chucks with rainbow laces, jean overalls, and knee-high pink socks. I was covered in grass stains after playing hide-and-seek with Frankie earlier that day.

I squinted my eyes and watched as the car door swung open and the sole of a shiny, black dress-shoe planted itself on the pavement. My eyes shifted over to the navy blue suit pants he wore, then up to the white button-down shirt that was rolled at the sleeves, revealing strong, inked forearms. And then I found his face. He stood tall, shoulders broad, a pair of sunglasses covering his eyes. His skin was a rich bronze, like it'd been kissed by the sun his entire life. He rolled his neck, and I swear I could hear the crack of it from where I sat.

I don't think he saw me right away, but I saw him. He was too busy looking at the house, probably impressed by it. I really liked that house, too.

The man shut the door behind him, and when he took a step to the side, I noticed a tattoo on the curve of his neck. *RISE.* I could see the word in bold script from the short distance away.

His jawline was sharp, the barest trace of stubble on his face. There was ink on his hands and all over his arms, some of it dark, some colorful. His dark brown hair was tapered on the sides and in the back, the lengthier part at the crown gelled back. If I were to guess, I would have assumed he was no older than thirty. Maybe twenty-six or twenty-seven?

He inhaled and then exhaled, taking off his sunglasses, and when he finally turned his head to the left, his eyes landed right on mine.

His face didn't change.

He almost seemed unbothered by my presence, or like he already knew who I was.

I didn't know him at all.

He walked toward the hood of his Chrysler still eyeing me, head in a slight tilt, a hint of a smile tugging at the corners of his lips. Reaching into his back pocket, he pulled out a pack of cigarettes, plucked one out, and then stuck it between his lips. A lighter was in his other hand, and he lit the cigarette in a flash, taking a hard pull from it.

I frowned at him. "You know you probably shouldn't smoke," I said, pushing back, lifting my feet, and easing into a light swing. "It's bad for you."

He continued puffing, sitting on the hood of his car. "You should mind your own business."

I stopped swinging, planting my feet on the ground. "Are you supposed to be here? I don't know who you are…"

"I'm a friend."

"I've never met you. How can you already be my friend?" I challenged.

5

He shrugged. "Don't know, but what I do know is that you ask a lot of questions."

Okay. This guy was being a real jerk. I stood up, narrowing my eyes at him. "My dad is a cop. I'll tell him you're out here."

At that, he smirked and stood tall, looking at me beneath thick eyebrows. He waved his free hand at me. "Go on, then. Tell him."

My heart was pounding now. I'd never had an adult talk to me that way. I panicked, running for the house before he could do something crazy, like stop me, or trap me, kidnap me, or something. I didn't know who he was. For all I knew he could have been here to kill my entire family.

"Dad!" I screamed, bursting through the front door. The soles of my shoes pounded into the wooden floorboards as I ran down the hallway. "Dad!"

Dad popped his head around the corner of the kitchen, brows heavily stitched. "What, Kandy? What is it?" he asked, concern etching his face.

I clung to him, throwing my arms around his waist.

"Kandy, sweetheart, what's wrong?" Mom asked from the fridge, rushing my way as soon as she shut it.

"There's a-a man standing out there. He's smoking a-and he told me to mind my own business!"

"What?" Dad immediately pulled away, handing me over to Mom, who cupped my face and then reeled me against her.

The doorbell rang, and Dad looked at her, worry creasing at his forehead. "Stay in here," he told us both, and I was really scared then.

My instincts were right. He was a bad guy. Good thing I ran.

Mom pulled me even closer as Dad stepped around the corner to get to the living room. I heard things rustling around and then he came back out with his service pistol, tucking it in the waistband in the back of his pants.

"Oh, no," I whispered. Daddy was going to hurt that man. He didn't like anyone messing with me. He'd always threatened that if someone ever hurt me, physically or mentally, he would make the person pay for it.

Dad had his hand wrapped around the gun the entire time, even as he looked through the peephole. But when he peered out, a soft chuckle escaped him, and he immediately lowered his guard.

Wait. What?

"Jesus, Kandy." Dad looked back at me, letting out a heavy sigh.

"Who is it?" Mom asked, still worried.

Dad reached for the doorknob and pulled the door open. And there he stood, the strange, tan man with the tattoos and cigarette.

"Cane!" Dad let out a hard, coarse laugh. "What the hell, man? I almost pulled my gun on you, thinking you were some stranger messing with my daughter!"

Cane?

The stranger, Cane, laughed. "Did I scare her, really?" He stepped into the house, and I held Mom tighter. "I was only kidding, Kandy. I know who you are. I know all about you. We've actually met before, but you probably don't remember."

"Yep, she was about six, right?" Dad said, smiling. "It was brief though. Dropped something off for him after picking you up from school. You waved at him and everything when he said hey."

"I don't remember," I mumbled. My eyebrows were pinched. I was still mad at him.

Cane held up a bottle of wine in his hand, looking at Dad. "I brought you guys something to go along with dinner."

"Oh, Cane, that was sweet, but you didn't have to," Mom said, pulling away and walking over to grab it. She smiled at him, and he returned it.

No, Mom! What are you doing? Stay away from him!

"Please. It's not like me to show up for an occasion empty-handed. It was the least I could do. That's our number one selling label, too. You'll love it. Not too sweet, not too bitter. Derek has told me all about your love for wine."

Mom blushed. Seriously, she blushed. Why was everyone falling for his charm but me?

Cane dropped his gaze to me again. "I even brought something for you, little one."

"I don't want it," I muttered back, crossing my arms.

"Kandy—" Mom started to scold me, but Cane shook his head, smiling softly.

"It's okay. I scared her. She just has to warm up to my twisted sense of humor."

He walked my way with slow, measured steps, and when he was about an inch away, he knelt down on one knee, digging into his pocket and pulling out a red bag with a sticker that said *Tempt*. There were tattoos on his hands as well, the same word *RISE* on his knuckles.

"Can you guess what it is?" he asked softly.

I blinked down at the bag. I was more curious than angry at that moment. "No. What?"

"Chocolate." He handed me the bag. I gladly took it, but still stared down at it like it was puke in my palm. "Your father told me you love chocolate. There's lots more where that came from, Bits."

"Bits?" I questioned, nose scrunching as I met his eyes. I noticed they were a mixed shade. Gray and green. Pretty. They reminded me of the marbles I collected with the colors inside, clear all around with the color in the middle.

"Your name is Kandy, but all I'm getting is bitterness. Bits for bitterness," he said.

Dad laughed behind him, and I felt my face turn hot.

"What do you say, Kandy?" Mom asked, tucking loose strands of blonde hair behind her ears.

"I don't know his name, Mom," I groaned.

"Mr. Cane," she replied.

I sighed, trying hard not to roll my eyes. Yes, I was glad about the chocolate, but I was still upset with him. "Thank you, Mr. Cane," I mumbled.

Mr. Cane stood up straight, and Mom and Dad walked around him, Mom announcing, "The steak is still grilling but should be done soon! I'll put the wine in the fridge to get cool!"

"Get settled in and meet me out back for a few beers," Dad said to him, pointing toward the deck.

"All right." Mr. Cane walked past me, tossing a wink my way. "Don't worry. You'll warm up to me soon enough. Enjoy those chocolates, Bits."

I smashed my lips together, my face burning hot again.

My heart fluttered in my chest.

My palms were sweaty.

I was afraid for my life out there, the stranger-danger bell chiming in my head, but not anymore. No, now it was just a weird, bubbly sensation running through me. One I couldn't fully describe or comprehend.

I'd never known what having a crush felt like before that day. I didn't understand the tingle in my chest, or the tumbling in my belly. I couldn't understand why I was constantly struggling for words, or why my face suddenly felt so hot. I didn't know what the hell I was feeling, and that freaked me out.

But there was one thing I knew for certain: this man was no good. I knew he was bad. He didn't make good first impressions—well, not with children anyway.

He was overly confident, and he was a smoker, which Mom always told me was a bad habit. He was a jerk—no, if I was being honest, he was a straight-up asshole. I knew he probably cared more about himself than anyone else—he just gave me that sort of impression.

And despite knowing all of that, I still developed a crush on Mr. Cane.

And I didn't like it one bit.

2

CANE

I hadn't seen my buddy Derek in eight long months. Work had me slammed, and he had a busy schedule himself. He had a family he was taking care of, and I had a business to grow. We'd finally stopped making excuses for ourselves and agreed to do dinners.

I was glad.

It was nice to hang out with his family. I'd met Mindy before, when she came to pick Derek up from the bar because he was too drunk to drive back. She was a nice woman, a perfect match for D. Kandy was a sweet girl, with an attitude just like his.

I hadn't spent a lot of time around kids, so it was funny to see her run away from me one moment, and then blush the next when I gave her the chocolates. I guess I needed to work on my manners. I was a bit rusty, but was glad they understood.

She was a smart, sweet girl. Derek wasn't kidding about how brilliant she was.

"Kandy has straight A's right now," Derek bragged after chewing his steak. "She's a smart girl. Her teachers love her."

"Dad." She glared at him, and her cheeks turned rosy as she tried to avoid looking at me.

"What, Kandy? It's true! You're a smart girl. You don't have to be ashamed of it."

When she finally looked at me, her face was red as a beet. I smiled at her, which made her neck flush, too. She ducked her head down, chewing her food.

"You know, I've been meaning to ask how you came up with the name 'Kandy' anyway?" I looked at Mindy.

"Oh, gosh!" She wiped the corners of her mouth with a napkin. "I'll let Derek tell you. He's the one who insisted we name her that, after what happened."

I focused on Derek, who answered right away. "Oh, damn! I've never told you this story before, have I? Well, two days after Kandy was born, Mindy was feeding her and Kandy start choking out of nowhere. There were two nurses in there with us when it happened. One of them kind of froze up a bit, while the other took action and saved our girl. Pretty much saved her life. Milk was coming out of Kandy's nose and everything. The coughing and sputtering was too much. It was bad."

My eyes stretched. "Oh man."

"Seriously? I've never heard this story either," Kandy said, lifting her head a bit.

"That's 'cause it hurts my heart every time I think about it," Derek stated. "I panicked too. I wasn't sure how to handle a choking newborn. It was my first kid—I freaked."

"Neither of us knew what to do," Mindy admitted.

"The nurse that saved her was so focused and attentive. Saved my baby girl's life. Mind you, we didn't have a name for our baby yet. We were still thinking of options. After everything had calmed down, I asked for the nurse's name, and she laughed and told me she hated her name. Her name badge was flipped backwards and everything. Like, she seriously hated her name," he chuckled. "Eventually, she caved and told us. Her name was Kandy. Mindy and I agreed that day to name her after the woman that'd saved our daughter's life."

SHANORA WILLIAMS

"Wow," I huffed. "That is insane!"

Mindy smiled and shrugged. "Worst thirty-seconds of my life, but she's here now." She rubbed Kandy's head. "So, how does it feel being the owner of Tempt?" she asked with a big smile. "Must be a nice feeling to have a company that big and to own all of it."

"Oh, it is. Thank you for asking." I picked up my water. "I love my job. Investing in it at a young age was the best decision I've ever made."

She nodded. "That's great, Cane. It has obviously paid off."

"Well, I'm proud of you, man," Derek added. "I really am. I remember when you told me you were going to school and everything. How you kept saying you felt like you were never going to get out of there."

We both laughed.

"Oh, yeah. I remember. Those were tough days, man. But I got out of there. Graduated and went straight to work. It was a struggle at first to build it, but I wouldn't trade it for the world."

"Amazing," Mindy said, elated.

During the rest of dinner and even through dessert, Derek's little girl was still trying not to look at me. She'd fail every time I glanced her way. There were moments she would cave, and when I felt her eyes on me, I'd wink at her, just to get under her skin. She'd either snatch her eyes away really quickly, or poke her tongue out at me with a slight grimace.

I had a feeling it would take her a while to warm up to me as a person, but I didn't mind. I planned on making many more trips to the Jennings' home in the future. Derek was my best friend, and I couldn't forget to mention that Mindy was a wonderful cook. Having good talks and great food always made for the perfect Saturday night.

It had taken a while for Derek and I to find time to hang out with so much going on in our lives. I was glad that we finally did.

Being around them made me feel like I belonged.

It was a nice feeling—a feeling I never wanted to go away.

12

3

KANDY

September 8th, 2007

Hey diary,

My birthday was today! Turning eleven is cool. I don't feel any older, but it's okay, I guess. I'm closer to being a pre-teen, so that's pretty awesome! Anyway, I don't have much to talk about today. Mr. Cane came over again. He looks at me funny...like he knows about my crush but doesn't want to say anything. I hope he doesn't. That's really embarrassing.

Anyway, gotta go. I have softball practice in thirty and have to pack up!

Bye,

Kandy

January 12th, 2008

Hey diary,

He gives me chocolates a lot. Like every time he sees me. Is that weird? Mom says he's just being nice and thoughtful, but he doesn't bring her chocolate or anything. Maybe when he picks it up, he's thinking of me? Maybe he likes me too!

Hahahahahaha! That's so stupid. He's too old for me.

Talk later,
   Kandy

September 8th, 2009

   Diary,

   I turned 13 today. I also got my first period. It's so weird having something wedged between my legs!! Is this how it feels when a baby wears a diaper??? Yuck! It's so gross. Mom said I'd get used to it, and she also promised not to embarrass me by telling Dad about it right in front of me. She gave me some painkillers and told me I didn't have to do dinner and cake with them tonight if I didn't feel like it. She said I could bring some cake to my room and eat it here, but I stayed for dinner. Mr. Cane visited again. I like seeing him. He always smells good too, and on top of that, he brought a birthday gift for me. I thought it would be chocolate again, but it was an iPod. I've got it hooked into Mom's computer right now while my favorite songs download to it. I can't wait to listen to it!

   Even though I don't want him to know it, he's a really cool guy. Why can't cool, nice guys like him be my age? :/

Bye, diary.
   Kandy

4

KANDY

My love-hate relationship with Cane grew in size, dwindled, and then blossomed again with each passing year. It was like watching cycles of clothes washing inside a washing machine, the same routine over and over again.

He came around at least once a month for dinner, always with a new bottle of wine his company had created, some Belgian chocolates—some caramel-filled and some not—and his smart-ass mouth.

The only reason it wasn't a full-blown hate-hate relationship was because he brought me sweets every time.

By age thirteen, I felt I was getting too old for the gift of chocolates. I'd finally hit puberty, had gotten my period months ago, and like all teenage girls assumed when they were thirteen, I was pretty much a "woman" now.

I remember the day he came to our home with two bags instead of one. After getting the iPod for my birthday, the chocolates could hardly compare.

"You can keep it. I won't eat them," I told him when he offered them. "They'll screw up my diet." My parents were nowhere in sight, both in the kitchen preparing the food while I sat in the living room reading.

"Bits, I brought this chocolate for you, just like I always do." He tossed them onto my lap. "Don't break the tradition. Take them."

"And if I don't?" I challenged.

He rolled his neck, and it cracked. I was so sick of that damn neck roll. Then again, a lot of things annoyed me at this age.

"Give it to a friend for all I care." He turned his back to me and started to walk off. It was interesting. He would only act that way when my parents weren't around, but around them, he was practically a saint, and *oh-so-sweet*, as Mom would say.

"God, you're so annoying," I muttered.

"Right back at you, Kandy Cane," he said, never looking back.

I was pretending to be the snotty teen—you know, the kind where nothing ever fazed her, and she just shrugged everything off? Yeah, that definitely wasn't me in that moment, and it wasn't working.

Every time he called me Kandy Cane, I wanted to squeal. I wanted him to say it over and over and over again. His voice was like silk, smooth and delicate. It was deep and somehow hypnotizing. He constantly joked with me and my parents about how my name matched so well with his. To be honest, I liked it. Probably a little too much.

When he walked out back with my parents, I went up to my room, storing the chocolates in the drawer of my vanity, like I always did. I would eat some of them at night before bed, or I'd take some to school and share them at lunch with Frankie—but I was never going to tell him that.

These chocolates were too good to pass up, and when I did some research online and saw they were $15 a bag...well, I couldn't be that much of a bitch by wasting them.

I found out a lot about Cane during my research on Tempt, too.

He'd launched Tempt, a wine and chocolate company, when he

was only twenty-five years old. By age twenty-seven, he'd won many awards for his wines, and his brand was ranked first place in a popular magazine, which boosted the Tempt name and its sales even higher. Celebrities began posting images of his wine, and it quickly became a household name.

He was featured in an entrepreneur magazine for Atlanta, his face all over the cover, and there was even an article about how he got started. There was nothing about his personal life though, or his family, which left me curious because, even with us, he hardly spoke about anything personal. He'd mentioned a sister who lived in California because she wanted to be an actress, but not much else.

I started warming up to Cane several years later, though. He was a great person and also a great friend to my family. He attended several of my softball games after I'd shamelessly begged him. He cheered me on right along with Mom and Dad, and of course I always played my hardest when he made an appearance. My crush on him was still present, but I began to appreciate Cane for more than that. He made my family happy, especially my Dad. I couldn't count how many times Cane showed up at our place with tickets to a local basketball or baseball game.

There were times when he'd take me out for milkshakes, even when I knew he had a busy schedule. He told me I was a champ and had no doubt that I would get an athletic scholarship for softball. I hoped so.

By age seventeen, I'd gotten over most of my premature, hormonal nonsense, and he began bringing me pens and notebooks from his job, along with the delicious chocolates. They all had the word Tempt on them. I loved to write, and I loved collecting pens, so getting them was a true pleasure, even more so than the chocolates.

He surprised me with Tempt's latest branded notebooks and pens during several of our dinners, and I thanked him in the sarcastic way only a teenager can.

The very first time he gave me a notebook set and pens he'd said, "I noticed you're always writing in notebooks."

"They help me express myself a lot better. I don't think I'd be able to live without my journals."

He smirked. "Well, good. I'll keep that in mind." That one smirk made my belly go haywire. The butterflies had been unleashed, and I couldn't control them.

I still pretended I didn't like him, which was my own version of flirting, and somehow it worked. Pretending not to like him, but really admiring every single thing about him. I couldn't ignore the way my heart raced when he sat beside me at dinner, and his arm or knee would accidentally brush against mine. I couldn't forget how I'd rush to the window and watch him get out whenever I heard his car pull up.

I would intentionally wear skirts and dresses whenever he was around, but he would never notice. I kind of wished I was older so I could tell him just how I felt. Unfortunately, he was seventeen years my senior. That was a lot of years.

I liked him a lot, and even though he teased and taunted me, I still *wanted* him.

I enjoyed his company, and so did my parents. They trusted him. They loved him. He was like family to us.

One day, I was getting ready for dinner when I heard a car door shut. I smiled as I stood in front of my bathroom mirror and fluffed my straightened brown hair. I knew it was him. I heard another door shut, though, and my smile immediately collapsed.

With a slight frown, I rushed to my window, spotting Cane walking up the sidewalk that was scattered with orange and brown leaves. My heart nearly failed me when I saw a woman at his side, her arm linked through his.

Straight, slick brown hair.

Rosy red lips.

Tall and thin, but not so thin that she didn't have curves.

She was stunning, from what I could see.

I stepped away when I heard the doorbell ring, my heart racing. I was too nosy to stick around in my room.

I walked down the stairs as casually as possible, the hem of my frilly pink dress flowing around my thighs.

Mom and Dad were introducing themselves, and then I heard laughter and the woman's shrill voice say, "Wow, I love your dress!"

I finally stepped around the corner as all of them chatted and greeted each other.

Cane looked at me first.

And then Mom.

And then *her*.

She was even prettier up close. Silky, beige skin, green eyes, and perky breasts. They weren't fake either. I instantly envied her.

"You must be Kandy," she said, stepping toward me. She even had manners. Wow.

"I am," I said, tipping my chin. She pulled me into a hug, and my eyes stretched wide. I found Cane's gray-green eyes, and a smile twitched at his lips.

I avoided a frown.

"So nice to finally meet you! Quinton has told me all about you! I'm Kelly." *Quinton.* She used his first time? *Intimate...*

She pulled away, and I smiled at her. It was forced and tight. "It's nice to meet you too, Kelly."

"So, dinner is ready! How about we pop open that bottle of wine you have there, Cane, and let's eat!" Dad declared.

"Oh, that sounds amazing," Kelly chimed. "I've been saving my appetite for tonight's dinner. Cane has told me all about how wonderful your cooking is, Mindy."

Mom beamed and thanked her graciously. Great. She knew how to kiss Mom's ass, too.

Mom wasn't an easy woman to please, but she loved compliments about her cooking and clothes the most. After all, she worked hard trying to perfect her look and her delicious dinners.

She'd scroll through Pinterest like a madwoman, asking me constantly if something looked good enough to wear or cook.

Kelly walked with Mom to the kitchen, Dad following after them to most likely help. Cane was unbuttoning his suit jacket, about to put it on the coat rack, when he glanced over his shoulder at me. "What do you think of Kelly?" he asked.

"She's pretty," I admitted.

He smirked. "I know." He hung his jacket on the coat rack. "Jealous?"

I narrowed my eyes at him, my heart slowly thudding now. *Asshole.*

He was only kidding, but he had no idea just how jealous I really was.

Kelly was charming and witty. She was simple and practical. She knew when to laugh and when to appear concerned, shocked, and so on. She was everything I was not, and I wanted to hate her —I really did—but I couldn't.

She didn't deserve my hate.

She didn't know about the hardcore crush I had on my dad's best friend.

She only knew me as Kandy Jennings, Derek and Mindy Jennings' eighteen-year-old daughter.

So instead of directing my hate toward her, I passed it over to Mr. Quinton Cane himself.

Yes, it was childish of me to no longer accept the chocolates he brought to our dinners, and to not say more than two words to him whenever he happened to drop by. It was beyond childish of me to hurry and finish my food and excuse myself from the table, just so I wouldn't see him and Kelly holding hands, or kissing, or sharing an inside joke. It was dumb of me to think he even cared how I felt, when he didn't even have the slightest clue.

Well, I thought he didn't care, until one day I was leaving school and his car was parked in front of the building. It was April in Decatur, Georgia, and the sun was beaming down, no clouds in sight.

Cane was leaning against the passenger door of his Chrysler 300 wearing gray suit pants and a black button-down shirt with the sleeves rolled up to his elbows, a pair of Ray-Ban sunglasses covering his eyes. I couldn't tell behind the dark tint of the lenses, but I was pretty sure his eyes were fixed on me.

"Oh my gosh," Frankie gasped as we walked out of the building. "Who is he?"

I stopped walking, focusing on him. "My dad's friend. The one I've been telling you about," I mumbled. I had no idea why he was here right now.

"Oh—the hot, rich guy!" she said, almost loud enough for him to hear. I wanted to strangle her. My face flooded with heat and embarrassment swept through me.

I stopped and held Frankie's wrists, looking her deep in the eyes. "Play it cool. Is he still looking at me?"

"Uh, yeah," she laughed. "He took his sunglasses off. Looks like he's ogling you to death."

I looked back with furrowed brows, and Cane had indeed taken his sunglasses off. His head was tilted now, and he flicked his fingers twice, a silent demand for me to come to him.

"I'll call you later," I told her.

"Please do! I want to know everything!"

She twirled around, meeting up with her boyfriend, Troy, by the flagpole.

Unease swept through me, a bundle of nerves building up in the pit of my stomach. I walked to him, and my heart was slamming down on my ribcage. My mind was screaming a million different thoughts.

Thoughts like: *He's so fucking hot. Why does he have to be so damn hot? I hate him, and his stupid, cocky, sexy face.*

"What are you doing here?" I asked, finally meeting up to him. I looked around, meekly tucking a strand of hair behind my ear.

Everyone was staring at me. I felt exposed, like everyone knew how I felt about this hot, older man.

"Your dad called and told me your mother had a last-minute meeting and wouldn't be able to pick you up today," he said. "He's on duty, per usual, and since I don't have any meetings for the rest of the day, I told him I would come get you."

"Why?" I asked, apprehensive. "I could have caught the bus to my friend's house."

He pushed off the car, grabbing the door handle and pulling the door open. "I wanted to."

I ran my tongue over my dry bottom lip, peering around. People were still watching our exchange. I guess if I saw a handsome man like Cane parked in front of our school with an expensive car, I'd be staring too.

I knew getting into his car was the only thing that would spare me from the gaping and gawking, so I slid my backpack off, handed it to him when he extended a hand for it, and climbed inside. He shut the door behind me right away.

The scent of leather and sandalwood surrounded me, as well as a small trace of tobacco. The car was clean and practically empty, like he hardly spent any time in it. There was nothing in the cup holders but a silver Zippo lighter.

Cane slid behind the wheel after putting my backpack in the trunk and started the engine. It pulled off, smooth and easy, and he drove with his left hand, checking his wrist for the time.

"You have a clock in your dashboard, you know," I said.

He glanced sideways. "Shut it, Bits."

I rolled my eyes, but my heart doubled in speed. It was already starting. The bantering. Teasing. The inside jokes. My own twisted little version of flirting.

"Where are we going?" I asked.

"Since I have you, I thought I'd take you to a late lunch before taking you home. I have reservations. You'll like it."

I sighed, twisting in my seat. His brows dipped when he

glanced my way again. "Put your damn seatbelt on, Kandy. I'm not about to get my ass handed to me by your parents if something happens."

When he cursed at me, I felt good and bad all the same. He only cursed when we were alone, and it gave me a thrill. Like it was a secret thing only we knew about. Like he considered me older and at his level of maturity.

I clicked my seatbelt into place and then threw my hands in the air. "There. Happy now?"

He smirked, but said nothing.

We were quiet for a few seconds, a song by Elton John pouring out of the speakers, barely discernible.

"I know why you're upset with me," he finally said. "Why you've been treating me like shit the last couple of months."

I looked at him. "I'm not upset with anybody. I only see you when you come to the house. How can I possibly be mad at you?"

"It's because of Kelly," he said, merely ignoring my comment.

My pulse skittered. He stopped at a red light and looked at me. "When I asked if you were jealous of Kelly, I didn't think you really would be, Kandy."

My heart dropped to my stomach. *Shit, he knows.* "I'm not jealous," I lied, palms clammy now. I snatched my gaze away, fire building in my throat. I had the urge to open the car door and roll out—anything that would spare me from the shame and truths right now.

"You are. You like me. It's obvious by the way you treat me. Cute, honestly. A little crush that I'm sure will pass soon."

I sucked my teeth, fuming at his dismissal. "Is that why you picked me up? So you could rub it in my face while my parents aren't around?"

A grin tugged at the corners of his lips. "No. I'm just being a good friend and feeding you before dropping you off. That's all, Kandy Cane."

"Don't call me that," I snapped.

SHANORA WILLIAMS

The light flashed green and he drove, taking the freeway. "You are really bitter, you know that? I have no idea why your parents went with naming you Kandy. They should have named you Sourpuss instead."

"Whatever, asshole."

He glanced at me through the corner of his eye. "You feel good when you curse at me, don't you? Your dad would have a fit if he knew about your potty mouth," he chuckled, and the deep rumble of his laugh made my spine tingle, and not in a bad way. "What other names have you called me behind my back?"

"Jackass. Dipshit. Fucker. Asshat. Jerk-face—just to name a few."

"Amusing." By his tone, I figured he'd found it anything but. "You really know how to break a man's heart, Kandy Cane."

We were quiet again, only for a few seconds this time.

"I'm not mad about Kelly," I finally said. "It just caught me by surprise when she showed up. " I admitted.

"Why did it catch you by surprise? Am I not allowed to date anyone?"

I avoided looking at him. Would it have been selfish to say he couldn't date while I had a raging crush on him? Probably. "I can't tell you what to do."

"You can," he said, simply. Blatantly. "But it doesn't mean I'll listen."

"Exactly, so why should I even bother?"

He laughed. "Because you're Kandy Jennings. A feisty little shit who doesn't know how to hold her tongue."

I laughed at that, only a little. "Yeah, whatever." I ran the tip of my thumbnail over a cuticle. "She's not even your type."

"Oh, yeah? And what is my type, exactly?"

I thought on it, chewing on my bottom lip. "I don't know, but it's not her. You seem too...*harsh* for her. She's all proper and prim and chipper, and you're just...Quinton Cane. You need someone who can stand up to you when you're being illogical and unfair.

24

After meeting Kelly, I highly doubt she's the kind of woman to do that."

"Harsh?" he repeated, seeming delighted. "You think I'm harsh?"

"I don't call you jackass for nothing."

He laughed, a smooth warm, rumble that made my body feel warm and gooey, despite the frosty air conditioning. His voice always did that. "You make me laugh, little one." He made a right turn. "Try working for me. Then you'll see what harsh really is."

"Are you kidding? I would *never* work for you."

His eyes twinkled with amusement when he looked at me. "Never say never."

We spent an hour and a half at a seafood restaurant in the heart of Atlanta. Cane told me to get whatever I wanted, so I went with the lobster and clam chowder. He ordered lobster as well, with a baked sweet potato.

"There's something I want to ask you," Cane said after taking a sip of his water.

"What?" I asked, digging into my house salad.

"Your mom was telling me there's a guy you've been texting. She said you've been very secretive about him and not giving up too many details." Cane quirked an eyebrow. "Who is this mystery boy?"

I laughed. Why did he even care? "I don't think that's any of your business!"

There was a guy, but it wasn't that serious with him. His name was Carl Ridley, and he was a running back for my school. We would text here and there, kiss on the cheek when we saw one another in the hallways, but nothing more. His father was a pastor and his mom was the assistant pastor, so he refused to kiss on the lips until he actually loved a girl, but I didn't want love with him so I didn't mind it. He was nice and kind of funny.

"Does your dad know about him?" Cane asked.

"I doubt it. I'm sure he would have asked me more about him by now if he knew. I'm surprised Mom hasn't told him anything. She put me on birth control and everything because of it. I doubt I'd ever do anything with him though."

His eyes expanded a bit. "Birth control already? What the hell? That's insane."

"What's so insane about it?" I laughed. "I'm eighteen, which is way past puberty. I should have gotten it long ago, don't you think?"

He slightly shook his head. "It's just crazy that you're growing up so fast. I still remember when I first met you as the little girl with pigtails and rainbow socks, running away from me because of stranger-danger."

I fought a smile. "Well, I'm not nine anymore."

"I suppose not." He shrugged. "Well, yeah, she told me about the guy you're supposedly talking to when your dad wasn't around. She thinks I'm a good listener. Good at keeping secrets, too." He sat back in his chair, smirking while focused on me.

"What?" I asked, suddenly nervous. I dropped my gaze to my plate, but still felt him looking at me.

"Just make sure he treats you right," he said after a brief silence. "Last thing any of us wants to see is you get hurt."

I picked my head up and met his gaze. Our eyes locked, and when they did, my tongue ran over my bottom lip. I wasn't sure if it was in my head, the way he stared at my mouth and hardly blinked, but it almost seemed like he couldn't pull his eyes away from me either.

In fact, he didn't look away until his cellphone rang on the table. I happened to catch a glimpse of the screen before he picked it up, and Kelly's name was on it. *Figures.*

I sighed, shifting my ranch-dressed lettuce around in the bowl with my fork, pretending her name alone didn't bother me. Cane answered, trying to keep the conversation quiet. And when he said, "Yeah, I'll be there in an hour," my heart dropped to my stomach.

"Sorry about that," he murmured after he disconnected.

I shrugged like I didn't care. "It's okay. I have a lot of homework to get done tonight. You should probably get me home anyway."

He nodded. "Sure. Let me get the bill."

After Cane paid, we were out of the restaurant in a heartbeat. He opened the car door for me again, and I forced a smile up at him, sliding into the passenger seat and clipping my seatbelt.

What was my deal? I couldn't believe I was so upset about this. Kelly was his girlfriend, and I was his best friend's daughter. He didn't see it any other way—couldn't see it any other way—so how could *I*?

Cane finally got behind the wheel, started the engine, and drove away from the restaurant. "Did you like that place?" he asked.

"Yeah. It was pretty good," I said with another small smile.

"Good. I'll have to take you to this other spot nearby. Not seafood, but they have *amazing* soul food." He turned the radio on, most likely to avoid the awkward silence, and when a song by OneRepublic came on, I settled in my seat, putting my feet up on the dashboard. I had to loosen up—pretend I didn't care too much. This was Cane, the only person other than Frankie who allowed me to be myself.

I never felt judged around Cane. I knew I could get away with things with him that I would never be able to get away with when it came to my parents. Mom was right about Cane—he could keep a secret, and he was a good listener. I needed to appreciate that a lot more.

I didn't want things to become awkward. It was my first time being alone with him, and I couldn't blow it, so I teased and said, "Hope you don't mind me kicking my feet up in your fancy car."

He chuckled, and his eyes softened like he was glad I wasn't making things too weird. "Get any dirt up there, and you'll never set foot in my car again, Bits."

I laughed, collecting my hair in hand and placing it all over one shoulder. When he stopped at a stoplight, he looked at me briefly before sighing.

"I wasn't kidding about what I said earlier." His voice was soft, sincere. "Make sure the guy you're talking to treats you right, Kandy. I'd hate to have to come after anyone who breaks your heart."

"That's what Dad is for," I teased with a giggle. "I'm sure he'd go after the guy in a heartbeat."

He smiled a little, but it quickly slipped away. "Not if he doesn't know about him. From what I gathered, your mom doesn't plan on telling your dad about the guy until you decide to bring him up."

I shrugged. "He's a good person, Cane. He's nice, and he doesn't force things. He's different."

"Yeah," he scoffed, foot pressing on the gas pedal when the light turned green. "That's probably what he wants you to think. He's a teenaged boy, and I know what all boys that age think about."

I broke out in laughter. "Just for that, maybe I'll make him my boyfriend. That will really bug you, huh?"

He side-eyed me with furrowed brows. "You don't need a boyfriend," was all he said, but I could tell he wanted to say more.

"He won't be my boyfriend. Don't worry. Just like Kelly isn't your type, he's not my type either. Maybe it's just a phase for both of us."

"Yeah." He fought a grin. "I never said she wasn't my type. Now you're just putting words in my mouth."

It didn't take long for us to get home. He parked in the driveway, and Mom's car was already there.

"Would walk you in but I have to get across town," he said. "Want to beat the traffic before it piles up."

"I understand. Hanging with Kelly." It was a statement, not a question. "At her place?"

He nodded.

"Oh, okay. Cool." I pushed the door open when he unlocked it, and he popped the trunk before stepping out of the car. He took my backpack out and handed it to me, smiling when I hefted it over one shoulder.

"Tell your mom I said hello."

"I will," I murmured. "See you later."

He stopped me with a hand on my shoulder before I could get away. "I'm only a phone call away if you ever need me, little one. Just know you can talk to me whenever you need to."

"I'll pass," I joked, and a faint smile graced his lips. I turned my back to him and walked away before he could notice how bothered I truly was. "Thanks for the late lunch," I called over my shoulder. "It was awesome."

"Anytime, Kandy Cane."

He said that silly nickname again, only this time, I didn't just feel the tingle in the pit of my belly. I felt it between my thighs, on my bare neck, and on my full lips. I felt it everywhere I shouldn't have.

I reached the door and watched Cane drive away. I watched until I could no longer see him and then I went inside.

Mom was on a call in the kitchen, so I kissed her cheek as she patted my head, and then I went up to my room, shutting the door behind me, tossing my bag on the recliner, and flopping facedown on my bed.

I thought about Cane and Kelly—how he would greet her when he walked through her door. How he would probably kiss her, so passionately her toes would curl in her tall stilettos. How they would eat dinner and drink wine together, and he'd tell her it was a great meal. They'd hold hands and chat for a while, and then afterwards, they'd fuck on the table or in her kitchen.

Thinking about it made my heart ache in indescribable ways. And before I could process what I was feeling, I realized I was crying. I cried softly, for less than five minutes, and then I rolled over and stared at the ceiling, realizing I didn't just have a crush on Mr. Cane anymore.

I had fallen hard for him, and it hurt so much to want a man I couldn't have.

5

KANDY

May 14th, 2017

Hey diary!
It's been a while since I last wrote to you!! Well, I guess it makes
sense. I only write here when Cane comes around. It's weird, I know.
Kinda sucks too, because I feel like I'm using you to vent. lol! I guess
that's the point of having you. Writing here also makes me feel good.
Anyway, let me fill you in about what happened today. So, I got out
of school and Cane was waiting for me. It was kind of embarrassing
because I felt like, literally, EVERYONE was staring at me, but now that
I think about it, I don't know why I cared so much. He's really hot, and I
want some of the girls to know that I get to hang out with a guy like him.
Maybe they'll think I'm cooler somehow? I don't know. I guess that's
dumb. I'm a senior now and have a one-year ride to Notre Dame. I
shouldn't care that much about popularity anymore. Dad says I should
be super proud of myself and all I've accomplished!
Okay – I'm getting off track. So, Cane picked me up and took me to
a late lunch for seafood because Mom and Dad had to work late. The
food was UH-MAZING and we shared nice conversations. I always feel

so good around him. We could have stayed there longer, talked forever, but of course Kelly called and ruined everything.

He had to go to her...and ugh. I don't know... It kind of hurt to know he was leaving me for her. Why does it feel this way? I shouldn't care that he goes to her, right? She is his girlfriend and I'm just Kandy to him. Plus, he's my dad's only real friend. Dad loves him like family. Shouldn't I love him like family, too? My heart shouldn't pound so hard whenever he's near me. I shouldn't like him or have this whopping crush on him.

Ugh.

This sucks.

Not going to lie, I cried earlier, right before coming to you and writing this. My heart hurts. It hurts because it's longing for the wrong things. I wish I didn't feel this way about him.

I think about Cane so much and I want him soooo bad...but I know that I can't have him. He doesn't want me. To him, I'm just a little girl. His best friend's daughter. He wouldn't even bother.

Talk later,
Kandy

6

KANDY

Despite my feelings for him, I couldn't fail to appreciate Cane for all he did for my parents and me.

I loved the little trips he would plan—well, I think he'd planned them. He had an assistant he talked about often, who he mentioned maintained his schedule and booked his personal appointments, like the massages he got every Thursday. I remembered because I'd always wanted to get a massage.

It was a warm, spring day of May when Cane showed up at our house. I was sitting on the stool at the kitchen island, talking to Mom about how tough softball practice was. I didn't hear a knock, just saw Cane coming into the kitchen with two Atlanta Braves baseball caps in hand.

I immediately stopped my blabbering when his throat cleared, peering over my shoulder to find him. He wore a half smile, his eyes sparkling from the sunlight that was bouncing off the marble counters.

My heart sped up to full-throttle, my throat thick and tight.

Mom greeted him, and he gave her a hug. Around the corner came Dad, who was wearing jeans and an Atlanta Braves T-shirt, along with a baseball cap.

"Come on, kid. Get dressed." Dad met up to me, clapping my shoulder. "Cane booked a private booth for the Atlanta Braves game tonight for his employees. Said there's room for us to join them. Your mom has to work, and we all know you'd rather spend time alone, but what do you say? Wanna come hang out with us and watch the game?"

In that moment, I could have squealed until the glass shattered. Of course, I wanted to go! Cane was going to be there, and in a private booth? I had always wondered what those private suites were like, so being in one with him was going to make it the best night ever.

But I played it cool. "Sure. I'm not doing much else tonight. A Braves game sounds fun."

"Good." Cane took a step forward and tossed one of the hats my way. "Bought this for you. You don't have to wear it. Just figured you'd like it." He smiled and shrugged as I held the hat to my chest.

"I'll consider it," I teased, but deep inside I was beaming like a ray of sunshine. I headed upstairs as Dad started talking about the game and the rival team. That would spare me a good twenty minutes.

I washed up quickly and changed into a pair of jean shorts and a white shirt. I looked at the hat on the bed that Cane had just given to me. I wasn't a huge hat person. The only time I'd worn them was for softball practice or games, and I hated them because they made my head hot and my hair would always get a matted ring where it pressed against my head.

But this, like the notebooks, pens, and chocolates, was a gift. And, whether he knew it or not, I cherished his gifts. So I brushed my hair until it was smooth and put on the hat.

When I went downstairs, Dad and Cane were standing by the door waiting. Cane saw me first, and his eyes lit up, like he couldn't believe I'd actually worn it.

"Wow. I'm surprised you didn't trash it," he laughed. I blushed and tried to hide it. "You all set?"

"Yep. I'm all good." I met up with Dad who was clearly chomping at the bit to get going. "Let's get out of here. Love you, Mom!" I shouted toward the kitchen.

"Love you, honey! Have fun!"

We were in Cane's Chrysler and on the way to the game in no time.

The traffic was madness, dimming the spark of my excitement just a bit, but Cane had an assigned parking spot, so that was a bonus. We didn't have to walk a mile just to reach the stadium. With a few steps, we were in an elevator and going up.

Dad talked the most. He loved baseball games—well, let me rephrase that. He loved *any* sport, really. He was a die-hard sports fanatic. If there was a game on of any kind, he knew all about it and would talk about it for hours. Even tennis. He loved it all.

The private suite was a dream, spacious and equipped with comfortable chairs and cocktail tables.

It was interesting meeting the people that worked for Cane. He was clearly the star—many were eager to shake his hand and thank him for the tickets. I could tell they hardly got the chance to see him, and now that they had it, they weren't going to pass it up.

I enjoyed watching him interact with his employees. It gave me even more reason to fall for that man. He laughed and showed interest in their families. He offered them drinks and food and didn't mind hugging or patting them on the back. He was far from stuck-up or rude. He was the kind of boss an employee wished for. Understanding, compassionate, dedicated, and easy to talk to.

Oh, and I can't forget to mention his charisma. His personality was made of gold, but sometimes I wondered if it exhausted him, having to be on top of things all the time. Having to stay uplifted and motivated and happy, just so everyone else in the room had the same energy. That kind of extroversion seemed absolutely draining.

While Cane mingled and chatted, I sat with Dad on the front

row, right in front of the window. We watched the game together for the most part. Dad made bets with me, and told me who was the best and who needed work.

"Watch him," Dad said. "The batter. They have to keep a close eye on him. He has a strong arm on him, and he's as fast as lightning, I swear. He's had three home runs already, and the season just started three weeks ago. Isn't that crazy?"

"Three already? Holy crap."

"Right." Dad sipped his beer, leaning forward as he watched the batter wiggling his hips and adjusting his stance.

My eyes wandered to the left, where Cane was standing at the bar, ordering drinks for a couple. The woman was mindlessly chatting. I think she was nervous. She was probably an employee. Her face turned beet red when Cane placed a hand on her shoulder and said something. She gave a simple nod, and I saw him mouth the words, "It's okay. Really." He said something else and then he excused himself.

When he did, his eyes locked right on mine.

His smile came naturally, and my pulse quickened as he crossed the room to get to me. "You guys having fun?" he asked, sipping the amber liquor in his glass.

"Hell yeah, man," Dad answered, not even looking at Cane.

I snickered. "He's really into this game."

Cane laughed. "I see that. Glad you're enjoying yourself, D."

Dad didn't respond, and Cane and I fought grins. I expected Cane to turn and make conversation with more of his employees, but instead, he sat down in the seat right beside me, placing his drink in the cup holder. His arm brushed mine as he ran his palm over the thigh of his slacks. A hard breath poured out of him, and I kept my gaze ahead, unable to deny my body's reaction.

My spine straightened, and my heart was beating even faster. My neck and hands felt hot all of a sudden, so I picked up my Mountain Dew and took a big gulp.

"I love my employees and my job," Cane started, "but if I don't sit down, they'll talk my head off all night."

At that, I looked at him and smiled. "Two hours of talking is good enough, I think."

"Should be." He sipped from his glass while looking ahead, not really watching the game, more like staring off in the distance and thinking about something else entirely. "I'll never admit this to them because I don't need anyone around here taking a position with my company for granted, but it's nice to hear how much Tempt has helped their families, and has even allowed some of them to achieve their goals. A few of them are interns, and since they're working for free, the least we could do is give them a ticket for the game." He looked to his left and pointed at one of the boys sitting at a table with a can of soda. He was talking to a really pretty blonde-haired girl. "He's with the graphics department. From what my assistant tells me, he loves it. The girl sitting with him is with our modeling agency. She's grateful for her position. Being a Tempt model has apparently gotten her a big following on Instagram. "

My brows dipped. "Modeling agency?"

"Oh, yeah. I have a modeling agency for our adult line. Things you shouldn't be worrying yourself about right now." He fought a smile, picking up his glass and swirling the ice.

"Damn right you don't need to be worried about it," Dad said, pushing to a stand. "Going for a beer. You guys want anything?"

"I'll take another Mountain Dew," I told him.

Cane simply shook his head and pointed to his glass. Dad took off, and I waited until he was out of earshot before asking, "You mean the adult line for the lingerie and edible body oils?"

His eyebrows shot up, nearly touching his forehead. "How'd you know about that?"

I stared at him. "There's this thing called the Internet. I wanted to know more about the chocolates. Then I saw the lingerie tab. It's cool, honestly. It all fits into the same thing—wine, chocolate, and lingerie. I'm eighteen, Cane. I've shopped for lingerie before."

He seemed uncomfortable with where the conversation was heading, shifting in his chair and loosening his tie with his free hand. "You've shopped for lingerie. For what?"

I shrugged. "It makes me feel pretty, I guess."

"I see."

We were quiet a beat. Damn it, I'd made it awkward.

"How are the models chosen?" I asked. He was clearly uncomfortable, and as badly as I wanted him to picture me in some of his lingerie, I wanted him to stay here beside me just as much.

He relaxed, only a little, shoulders dropping. "We do auditions by doing photo shoots. The person auditioning has to be at least twenty-one because in some of the shoots, the women are using other Tempt products, like the wine, depending on the set."

"Oh. That sounds cool." I fought a laugh.

"What's funny?" he asked, tilting his head to try and catch my eyes.

I focused on running my thumbnail over my cuticle instead of looking at him. "I don't know. It's stupid."

"I'm sure it's not."

"I don't know," I paused. "I always used to think I wanted to be a model. My best friend, Frankie, always tells me that I'm tall enough and pretty enough to be one. I guess it takes confidence to do that kind of modeling though. Like being half naked in front of so many cameras and stuff?"

Cane blinked quickly and cleared his throat, making a choking noise right after. "Kandy, you are too damn blunt for your own good, you know that?"

I shrugged. "Mom tells me to always express myself however I want. She doesn't think it's a bad thing, being this blunt."

"That blunt mouth of yours could get you into some serious trouble one day." He finished off his drink and then sighed. "Say the wrong thing to the wrong person and they may take it as something else."

"Well then I'll clarify myself for them so they understand." He focused on my face for a few seconds, slightly shaking his head with that same smile. "What?" I threw my hands up, trying hard not to smile with him.

"You," he murmured. "You're just too much sometimes, Kandy Cane."

Those words. His voice. I probably shouldn't have taken it as much, but they made me feel untouchable. On top of the world. Was I too much for him? Did he like that I was too much? Was he tempted to test my limits, my boundaries?

"Do you know why you're really here tonight?" he asked.

"No. Why?"

"I wanted to congratulate you on your softball scholarship. It's not easy getting an athletic scholarship at the college level. You have to be extremely good at your sport to get one."

"Yeah. People kept saying I was the best pitcher in our district. It's only a one-year athletic scholarship, though. The coach probably wants to see how I play before putting me on a full ride."

"Doesn't matter. You got one, which is more than a lot of people your age can say. I felt bad I couldn't take off for your signing day, hence the reason I brought you double the notebooks and the gel pens you like."

"Thanks for that," I laughed, my gaze dropping to the smile that had taken over his face. As much as I enjoyed our conversation, it felt wrong to keep thinking about how beautiful his smile was or how great he smelled. He was close enough for me to kiss him, hold his hand, even. My hand itched, dying to caress him, but I stayed in control. "I have a question for you."

"What's that?" he inquired.

"You always take my dad or me with you to little outings like this. Why don't you ever take your family?"

His lips smashed together, and if I weren't mistaken, his nostrils even flared up a bit. He looked away for a moment, and then released a heavy sigh. "They're busy people," he answered. "Plus, hanging with you and D is much more fun." With that, he flashed his charming white smile, but I could tell it was forced. I'd struck a nerve, and felt bad for even asking the question. Cane never talked about his family. There was hardly any mention of them when you researched Tempt or Quinton Cane. It's like he had no real family, just his good friends, the Jennings.

"I'm proud of you for getting that scholarship though, Kandy. I really am." He was creating a diversion, escaping our conversation. It was cool. I didn't mind. I didn't want things being weird, especially after how the lunch ended with us not even two weeks ago, when he had to drop me off to go to Kelly. He didn't see it that way—would never see it that way—but I did. Cane was mine, whether he knew it or not. He was always going to be mine. I just wished I could tell him.

"Kind of sucks you'll be so far away though, huh?" His voice pulled me out of my cloudy thoughts, and I sat up a little higher with a nod.

"Yeah. It will suck. I'll miss getting chocolates and notebooks and being invited to baseball games in VIP boxes."

He laughed at that. "Well, I'm not sure if you'll want to go to baseball games while you're in school, but I can always have notebooks and chocolates shipped to you. As a matter of fact, now that we're talking about this, what do you want as your going-away gift? I want to give you something better than chocolate and pens."

"Um..." I chewed on my bottom lip, giving it some thought. I wasn't really sure. Mom had a list of everything she was going to get, and I had added to that list. She said she would get all of it, despite Dad's griping about the things that were desires instead of necessities. "I'm not sure, but I have all summer to think about it. I'm sure there'll be something that comes up that I want."

"Well, whatever you want, it's yours, Bits. Nothing is too much or too pricey. Got it?"

"Even a MacBook?" I asked.

"Even a MacBook," he chuckled.

I nodded, still chewing on my bottom lip. "Got it."

The game was tied and had shifted into another inning. Dad was pumped. Of course the Braves won. After the game, we were back in Cane's car. He took us home and bid us a goodnight. Dad was pretty hammered, so I helped him to the couch. He was lucky he didn't have to work until the next night. He crashed on the couch and I went upstairs, giddily reliving the conversations I'd had with Cane.

I'd even dreamt about him that night.

The dream was so vivid that it lugged me out of my sleep. I woke up with a gasp, my panties damp, and my core tight and raw. My nipples were taut, prodding through the white camisole, and I don't know why, but I was working hard to catch my breath.

Holy shit. I'd dreamt of Cane using his mouth on me. Everywhere. Sucking. Licking. Tasting.

I had a hard time going back to sleep. I was so wound up.

The next morning, I felt the weight of my secret crush hit me hard as Dad made me coffee, whipped up some pancakes, and cut up some fruit for me, despite his obvious hangover. I felt awful because there I was, crushing on his best friend, dying to do things with him that would have sent my father over the edge if he knew.

What was wrong with me? Why couldn't I get over this stupid crush already? It was almost like the more time I spent around Cane, the more I craved him.

Maybe it was a good thing I was going to college. I would be away from him for months, and would probably forget all about the crush when I had an entire university of hot guys to choose from.

I told myself I would forget Cane eventually, but deep down, I knew it wouldn't happen. When someone is on your mind day and night, how do you possibly forget them?

It didn't help that there was a delivery the day after my guilt trip. Mom brought the box up to my room and left me to open it.

SHANORA WILLIAMS

It was packaged nicely, wrapped in purple and white tissue paper, and was made out to me, but didn't say whom it was from. Inside was a stack of notebooks, pens, and...a MacBook. *A fucking MacBook!* At the sight of the laptop, I knew it could only be from one person.

I couldn't believe it.

I'd been using Mom's computer for most of my research and schoolwork, but a laptop? I squealed. I squealed so loudly that Mom rushed back to my room to ask what was wrong. When I showed her, she couldn't believe it herself.

"Well, I guess we can scratch that off the list, huh? And look, it's the rose gold one you wanted!"

"I know!"

"It has to be from Cane. He spoils you, you know that?" She pursed her lips. "He'd better put a lid on that before he ends up broke!" She laughed on her way to the door. "Make sure you call him and thank him!" When she left me to it, I grabbed my phone and called right away."

He answered after the third ring. Yes, I counted. I always counted the rings, the minutes, the hours, and the days—especially the days when he wasn't around. The longest he'd gone without visiting was three weeks.

"Hey, Bits," he answered.

"Hi, Cane. So, um...I got a delivery today. Judging by how expensive it is, I'm pretty sure it's from you."

"Really? Hmm... I don't remember sending a package. What was in it?"

"Oh my gosh, don't play dumb. I know it's from you, Cane! The MacBook? Dad refused to get me the Mac, so I know it wasn't from him. I'm so excited right now!"

Cane chuckled, and I swear it made the tightness at my core even tighter. I wanted to drop the phone and run to him. Run as fast as I could, jump into his arms, and kiss him. "I'm glad you're excited about it, Kandy. It's the least I could do."

"The least? Are you kidding me? This is…it's so great, Cane. Thank you so much. Seriously."

"You're welcome. I still want you to think about a going-away gift you'd like before you go. This was a gift from me because your parents were talking about how badly you wanted one and how they didn't want to spend so much money on your first laptop. They agreed to let me get it for you as a gift, but I'm sure there will be something special you'll need more. Just let me know, all right? Also, don't forget to thank them."

"Okay. I won't." I sucked on my bottom lip before releasing it. "You're the best, Cane." Something possessed me to say that. I shouldn't have because it made me seem desperate and lame, but I was glad he took it with a grain of salt.

"Nah, I just like to see you guys happy. That's all."

Something he'll never know is that I spent all night using my new laptop to write about how thankful I was to have him in my life.

Cane was a great man—a blessing—and he didn't even realize it. He underestimated his love and even the goodness in his heart. I could tell by the way he carried himself, almost like he felt something was missing and wanted to fill the void.

Maybe something was missing, and that something was his family. He never spoke of them, and I had a feeling there was a reason for it. I also had a feeling they were still around. Was he hiding them? Was he ashamed of them?

I noticed a lot about him—things he didn't want people to catch on to. His giving ways were a good distraction for the people around him, but they could never fool me.

I knew Cane cared about me. I knew he loved to spoil me, as well as Mom and Dad, and even his employees.

But at the end of the day, I always wondered why?

Why did he feel the need to give so much to the people who simply enjoyed his presence and his time?

What was he trying to change or run away from?

7

KANDY

June 7th, 2018

Diary!!! I'm back!

Today was SO AMAZING! Oh my gosh! I'm trying to figure out how to form it all into words. So, today was a big day. I GRADUATED! No more high school for this girl! Gah, I'm so glad to be done with it, and not only that, but I have a scholarship in my back pocket. I feel like a freaking boss!

Today was super busy, and I'm so tired writing this (it's like 1 a.m. right now) but I need to get my thoughts down before I lose the high.

So, Cane told my parents a few weeks back that he wasn't sure he would make it to my graduation ceremony because he had important business in San Diego the same day. I was bummed to hear it, but I understand how busy he is so I couldn't be too upset. There I was, standing by the stage waiting to be called, wishing he was there. My mind kept circling back to him and I don't know why. I should have been thinking about my future and the memories I'd made, but instead I was thinking about him.

Well, I walked the stage, right? And I hear my dad's EXTREMELY loud voice (even though they tell you not to cheer too loudly when the names are called – lol) and I see Dad with Mom sitting right beside him, and on the other side of Dad is Cane. I'm so glad I didn't trip in my heels while staring. He looked so amazing. He wore a tan suit with a sky blue tie and handkerchief to match. I mean it—amazing. Probably cleaner than I'd ever seen him before.

After graduation, I hugged the hell out of my parents when I realized that I'd be gone soon and would be far away from them. Of course Dad gave a pep talk, which only started up the waterworks for Mom and me.

Cane gave me a hug next, and he also gave me this beautiful bouquet of flowers. I asked him how he'd made it to the ceremony—that I thought he would be away for business. He told me he wouldn't have missed my graduation for the world. I'm sure it's safe to say that I cried even more hearing those words leave his mouth. I couldn't help it. It was an emotional day.

Cane had dinner with us at a nice restaurant in Atlanta. Mom and Cane had drinks, Dad didn't.

I loved everything about today. But you wanna know what the best part of it was? Cane didn't check his phone or watch once. Not once, and I know because I watched him. There were no calls from Kelly, and if there were, he'd clearly ignored them. He laughed with us. Drank with us. Teased and smiled at me. He put my big day first, and let business come second. That makes me unbelievably ecstatic.

I guess what I'm saying is that I can't believe I'm this important to him. Really not sure what I'd do without him.

I'm so happy, diary. My life is good. Seriously. What could go wrong?

8

KANDY

I truly didn't know why I wanted Cane so badly. There was something about him—something that made the pit of my belly flutter with frenzied butterflies and my blood pump with fiery desire.

He was irresistible, and I loved that he didn't treat me like a child. I loved that he was always there for me. I loved when he teased me. I loved his gifts and his presence. Everything about him pushed me into hyperawareness.

His touch.

His smell.

His laugh.

Everything.

There was so much joy in my life and so many good things happening between him and my family, that I began to take most of it for granted. I hate that I did.

I had slept over Frankie's house for a girly sleepover. I normally did the sleepovers with her when Mom and Dad had to work late on the weekends.

We'd graduated three days ago and were ready to take on the world. It was funny—in school, we didn't care too much about popularity or fitting in. At the end of the day, we were our own crazy duo, and we loved it.

I will admit that Frankie was boy crazy. She had a new boyfriend every month. If I thought I was a rebel, she put me to shame. She'd dyed her hair a bright green, even when her mother had told her not to. She didn't have a father figure in her life, and her mom traveled for work often, which may have played a big role in why she wasn't very disciplined. She grew up spending a lot of time on her own, had set her own routine. She was smart and sweet when she wanted to be (had to be with a full-ride scholarship to University of North Carolina), and she loved her mother to death but, well, most of the time, Frankie just didn't give a fuck.

I opened my MacBook, going to YouTube to watch a new music video by Laura Welsh. "I still can't believe he bought you that expensive-ass Mac!" Frankie flopped down beside me, belly flat on her twin-sized bed.

I looked over at her. Her dark brown, almond-shaped eyes were pinned on the screen, the naturally tanned skin on her face covered with a green organic facemask.

"It was a gift," I laughed.

"Well, next time he's feeling gifty, tell him to buy me one too!" She bumped my arm.

"Have you asked your mom for one?"

She gave me a dull glare. "You know my Mom isn't going to buy a damn Mac, K.J."

She had a point. Her mom ran a popular traveling and food blog and had articles featured in magazines and popular websites. Didn't matter that her mother made thousands monthly, she was still deep-rooted and refused to drop big bucks on expensive devices for an eighteen-year-old.

Frankie was the only person to call me K.J. She'd been calling me that ever since fifth grade. She claimed she didn't like the name Kandy, because it was too sweet for my bitchy personality, so K.J. it was.

"How did Cane make it to your graduation anyway?" she asked. "You never filled me in about that."

I stopped scrolling, crisscrossing my legs and sliding the laptop back a bit. Frankie sat up with me.

"I don't know. He might have wrapped up early on what he was doing or had someone else handle it." I shrugged.

"I think he's fucking into you," she guffawed. "Why else would he just magically show up? Graduations are important, yeah, but business is business."

I rolled my eyes, fighting a smile. "He was being nice, Frank. He told me he wouldn't have missed it for the world. He ate dinner with us, didn't rush the evening or act like he had to be somewhere. He wanted to be there for all of us." I said that, but deep down, I felt he was really there to make *me* happy more than anyone else.

"You should have told him to kiss you. A graduation kiss. Totally harmless." Her tone was nonchalant as she shrugged and then climbed off the bed. She walked to her bathroom and turned on the faucet.

"You are crazy!" I busted out laughing, climbing off the bed and following her, pressing a hand to the frame of the door. "Ever since that night, it's worse, though. No matter what I do, I can't get him out of my head, Frank. It's been like this ever since I was a little girl. I've always been attracted to him. It's fucking weird because he's supposed to be, like, family to me."

"He's sex on a stick, K.J. He's super successful and handsome and he gives you chocolate and notebooks. It's also hot as fuck when a guy shows up unannounced. That is any woman's dream. There's nothing weird about liking someone like him."

Hmm...yeah. When she put it that way...

Someone pounded on the door and Frank turned quickly when her brother, Clay, barged in. Clay was tall, well-built, and shirtless. His blond hair was damp, like he'd just gotten out of the shower. If Clay wasn't such an asshole and always grabbing his crotch to show off, I would have found him hot.

He wasn't really Frankie's brother. They had been adopted siblings since she was six and he was eight. She was the adoptee.

"Where the hell is the charger for my Beats Pill, Frank?" Clay snapped, tossing her pillows off the bed. He turned for the stuffed animals on her recliner next, snatching them up and throwing them on the floor.

"I don't have your stupid charger, Clay, now get the hell out of my room!"

"You do have it! I know you do. It goes missing every time I have a girl over, and then it magically appears the next morning. I know you keep taking it!"

Frankie marched his way, pressing her hands to his chest and shoving him backwards until he was out of the door, slamming it in his face right after. Of course, she struggled—she was half his size—but she managed. I could tell she'd done this way too many times before. They always fought and bickered. It was hilarious sometimes.

I broke out in laughter. "You guys are nuts, you know that?"

She locked the door and rolled her eyes, huffing as she went back to the bathroom to finish washing her face.

While she did, I sat in the middle of her bed and busied myself with my laptop again. A whisper crossed my mind, and I went to the browser to type in *Quinton Cane*. The first page to show up was Tempt's website, so I clicked it.

There were many pictures of new wines, more awards the company had won, and even Instagram images of people eating the chocolate, but then one image appeared as I scrolled further down and it stopped me.

It was Cane, holding one of his bottles of wine in the air. It was typical Quinton Cane fashion *not* to smile for a picture, but nonetheless he still looked breathtakingly amazing. He wore a navy blue suit with a silver tie. His beard was trimmed neatly, the lengthier part of his tapered hair combed in perfect, smooth waves.

He looked so handsome.

A sprinkle of the caveman mentality and a dash of gentleman.

The look fit him well.

I clicked through more pictures as Frankie ranted on about how annoying Clay had been lately, and how she had to break it off with a guy because Clay kept threatening him.

Her voice was mostly a buzz while I scrolled though. I was stuck on stalking Cane, loving how clean and handsome he looked in suits. Loving the times he rarely smiled, and how he took photos with his employees, like he truly cared and appreciated them. I'd witnessed his love for his employees. It was genuine.

Later on that night, I couldn't stop thinking about him. I kept going through my phone, scrolling to his name listed in my contacts.

"I'm only a phone call away if you ever need me, little one."

I knew he'd answer, and I had the urge to call, especially when Frankie fell asleep with reruns of the Kardashians on...but I didn't do it.

I wasn't that bold. Plus, what was I going to talk to him about? My pajamas?

9

KANDY

Around 3:00 a.m. in morning, there was a buzz beside my head. My phone was ringing. Foggy-minded and bleary-eyed, I picked it up with a groan. Mom's name and our favorite selfie was on the screen.

"Mom?" My voice was thick with sleep as I answered.

"Kandy, honey?" I was so tired I didn't even realize her voice was laced with worry and heavy with emotion. "Baby, I need you to wake up and listen to me."

I rolled onto my back, running a hand over my face. "What's going on?"

"Y-your father has been shot."

With those words alone, my back was off the bed, the fogginess clearing and the bleariness vanishing.

"What! Shot? How?"

"It was while he was on duty. H-he's being taken to the hospital. One bullet hit his thigh and the other pierced his neck. They said he bled a lot. I'm on my way to the hospital right now so I can't get you, but I called Cane. He's on his way to pick you up. Just be calm and stay with him, okay?"

"Okay. I'll get ready." I climbed off the futon, and Frankie groaned, popping one eye open to glare at me. She pushed up on one elbow and rubbed her eyes. "Dude, what the hell are you doing?"

I grabbed my sweatpants and tugged them on with haste, snatching up my bag next. "That was my mom. She said my dad was just shot on duty."

"Oh, shit!" Her eyes stretched wider. She climbed off the bed too. "Is he okay?"

"I-I don't know. She said one bullet hit his thigh and the other pierced his neck. She sounded worried." I don't know how I was still so calm. My heart was pounding now, beating like a drum in my chest. My chest felt like it'd been crushed by the foot of an elephant and all oxygen seemed to have been sucked from my lungs. Still, I kept moving.

My phone vibrated in hand. I looked at the screen, and it was Cane calling. I rushed to the window and saw his black Chrysler parked at the curb.

"I'll come back for my things later," I told her.

"Yeah, babe. It's fine. Go," she insisted, watching me rush to her door. I hurried down the hall and hustled down the stairs, swinging the front door open to get outside.

I don't remember if I closed it behind me or not. I just remember Cane standing by the passenger door of his car, holding the door open for me, his face pale, and eyes wide with worry. I'd never seen him that way.

I jumped in and the door was immediately shut.

He was behind the wheel before I could even give myself a moment to take a deep breath. He pulled off, gripping his face with his free hand and dragging his palm down.

"Damn it," he hissed beneath his breath.

"Why are you driving so slow?" I frowned at him and then checked his speedometer. The speed limit was 45, but he was going 35.

He kept quiet, not looking my way.

"Cane!" I shouted. "Hurry and get me to the hospital! I need to make sure my dad is okay!"

He stopped at a light.

"Drive through the light! This is an emergency, and he's a cop! If you get pulled over you can tell them who my dad is! I know most of the cops here! Just go!" The tears were like fire in my eyes as I tried to fight them off.

I wasn't in the mood for his asshole-ish ways that night. I wasn't in the mood to pretend-argue, or bicker, or do anything fun and exhilarating with him right now. I just wanted to be with my dad.

He was shot twice. He needed me right now. His only child. His little girl.

"I'm not taking you to the hospital, Kandy. Your mother told me not to."

"What?" I snapped. "Why the hell not? I deserve to be there! He's my dad—"

"Which is exactly why you *shouldn't* go," he stated, voice harsh. "He's already at the hospital and going straight into surgery. You'd just be sitting there. Your mother has to be there for him when he makes it out." He let out a tight breath. "You'll wait at my place until we hear from her. She wants you with her, trust me, but she knows you'll be better off waiting outside the hospital. I'll take you there as soon as I get the say-so."

I scoffed, blazing hot tears sliding down my cheeks. "This is so fucking stupid. I want to be there with him!"

Cane kept driving, not even responding, and when he went past the exit to get to the hospital, I wanted to fucking wail. I bit hard on my bottom lip until I tasted blood. The tears continued falling, landing in my lap, my heart still drumming.

"You can hate me and be mad at me all you want, Kandy. I'm doing what's best for you right now," he murmured.

"You don't even know me. How could you possibly know what's best for me?"

"I know more about you than you think I do."

The speed of his car decreased, and he took a left turn, pulling into a gated community. He said something to the security guard at the box, something I didn't bother listening to, and the gates drew apart.

He drove until we reached a creamy white home with a black roof. Gold lights illuminated the exterior of the house, as well as the trimmed rose bushes in the front. If I hadn't been so distressed, I would have admired how elegant it was, but in that moment, I didn't care about any of it. I didn't care that I was being selfish. I didn't even care about the fact that Cane and I were alone again. I needed to be with my father.

Cane killed the engine of the car. "Coming?" he asked softly.

"No."

He breathed heavily through his nostrils. "You can't sit out here all night, Kandy." He was agitated now. I didn't care.

"Then take me to the hospital! I don't care what she wants! I don't care if I have to sit there all night! This is what I want!"

"You know I can't do that."

"Well screw you, then," I snapped.

"Are you fucking kidding me?" he bellowed, like he was truly fed up. "Derek wouldn't want you there, Kandy! Your mother told me to keep you here with me, so stop being a fucking *brat*, get out of the goddamn car, and come into the house already!"

My eyes stretched wide as I turned my head to focus on him. He'd never spoken to me this way before. Yes, he was arrogant, and yes, he cursed often, but not *at* me. Not like this.

Frustrated and honestly embarrassed, I gripped the door handle and pushed out of the car, rushing for his front door with the same stupid tears still burning the rims of my eyes. I refused to cry in front of him right now.

He followed right behind me, unlocking the door and opening it.

Pressing a hand on my shoulder, he ushered me inside his

home, but I jerked away, still burning with fury. He pulled his hand back, nodding slightly, and led me down the corridor and into the living room.

Creamy leather furniture was set up inside, the room neat and hardly worn-in, set up like a home out of an interior design magazine. The electric fireplace was burning, and a glass with ice in it was on the coffee table, along with some papers, like he'd been sitting in this very room when he got the call and had dropped everything to come get me.

"Sit, Kandy. Please." He extended an arm, gesturing to the biggest sofa. I noticed his voice was softer, like he felt bad about his sudden outburst in the car. But Cane wouldn't apologize. Not for speaking his mind and telling the truth.

I avoided his eyes, walking past him and sitting down. I kicked off my shoes and drew my knees to my chest, resting my forehead on them.

I tried to fight the wave of emotion that shook me, but it was impossible. I couldn't bite back the tears anymore. My body shuddered. The tears clogged and thickened in my throat. The saltiness finally ran over my lips.

The whimpers and cries I'd made that night, just thinking about my dad in pain, were foreign noises. I'd never heard myself cry like this before. So hard. So desperately.

"Damn it, Kandy." The couch dipped beside me, and a hand ran through my hair. "He'll be okay. Stop crying. You know he wouldn't want you crying."

"I don't care what he wants right now," I sobbed. "I just want to see him. I want to know he's okay."

Cane's fingers stroked the back of my neck, the pads of them feathery-light and caressing my skin. "He'll be okay."

His touch electrocuted me, awakening my soul, even through the thick layers of emotion. I picked my head up and looked over my shoulder at him, tears clinging to my lashes. "You don't know that," I whispered.

"Yes, I do." His eyes latched with mine. He sighed softly, like he wanted to say more to make me feel better. He obviously didn't have much else to say because he clamped his mouth shut instead and pulled away, standing up. "Can I get you something to drink?"

I shook my head.

"Then I'll go make one for myself. Let me know if you change your mind." He walked away, glancing back once at me. I dropped my chin on top of my knees, staring ahead into nothingness.

All I could think about was my daddy. What if he didn't make it out of the hospital alive? What if he'd bled out on the way there?

I could picture Mom's reaction when they told her the bad news. She'd bawl and break down—fall to her knees and weep into her palms. I prayed he would pull through.

I was pissed off, but I knew they were right. They were *so* right. I wouldn't have been able to handle waiting at the hospital. Every ticking second would have felt like centuries. Plus, I hated hospitals. I didn't like being surrounded by pain and misery.

The sound of ice clanking in a glass a short distance away pulled me from my trance, and I heard Cane talking.

"Yeah, I picked her up already. It's fine. She can crash here for as long as you need her to." He was talking to Mom.

Cane stepped around the corner moments later. He sat beside me again with a short tumbler in hand and a half-empty decanter of amber liquid in the other. He placed the decanter down on the coffee table and then swirled the ice in his cup, causing it to rattle in the glass.

After taking a small sip, he let out a long, weary sigh. "He'll be okay," I heard him say. It seemed he was trying to convince himself as much as me.

I looked up at him, a sudden thought crossing my mind that escaped me vocally before I could stop it. "You love my dad?" I asked, but it was a juvenile question. Men like Cane didn't tell other men he loved them, even if it were true. It was just...not in his nature, I supposed.

His response took me by surprise. "He's my best friend. Love him like a brother."

"How long have you known him again?"

"Since I was twenty-one. He saved my mother's life."

"How?" I asked, intrigued.

He side-eyed me, probably debating whether to tell me or not. "From a domestic abuse dispute. He got a call about it, showed up in less than five minutes since he was nearby. I was on my way home from college and still an hour away."

"Domestic abuse?"

His lips pressed thin. "Between my mother and my father."

"Oh. I'm sorry."

His nostrils flared, head dropping, eyes focused on his lap instead. "Thanks to Derek, my mother wasn't killed that night. My father had pulled a gun on her. He was drunk and accused her of cheating, but he was the cheater. We all knew it. Derek came at the right time and took care of it, sent my sorry-ass father to jail, and I haven't seen him since. I was only twenty-one then. Derek was twenty-eight and new to the job. I haven't been able to thank Derek enough for it. He put his life on the line for hers. He considered it his duty—said he was just doing his job—but I respect that much more than he will ever be able to imagine. She could have been seriously hurt or dead if he hadn't shown up when he had. After that, I invited him to meet me about once a week, whenever he was free, so I could repay him with cheap beers and hot wings at this late-night bar a short drive from downtown. As we got older, and when I finally kick-started Tempt, we got a little busier. We still kept in touch with phone calls and texts, but didn't get to see each other as often. He was raising a child, taking care of his family, and I was building my career."

"That's cool," I said softly. "I'm glad he saved your mom."

"Me too."

I lowered my gaze to his glass. "What are you drinking?"

"Macallan scotch. Strong stuff. And expensive."

"Can I try it?"

He cocked a brow, looking from me to the glass. I could tell he wanted to say no, but instead he lifted it up and handed it to me. This was my pity drink from him to me. I didn't care. I wanted it.

"A little," he said, "and only because I don't know how else to make you feel better right now."

I accepted it, taking a sip. It was strong and burned my throat, but also seemed to soothe the fire in my veins. I took another big sip, and then two bigger gulps.

"Kandy, come on," he grumbled, taking the glass away from me. He looked at the nearly empty glass, sighing and picking up the decanter of scotch from the table. He topped off his glass again, keeping it to himself this time.

"I'm scared, Cane," I confessed after a brief silence. "I don't want him to die."

"He won't," he said, cut and dry.

I laughed a little, but it hurt, and my eyes welled up.

"What?" he murmured.

"I don't know. It's just...funny. I always saw my dad as this hero, you know? Like a man who could take on anything, even bullets. Kind of like my own superhero. Nothing is ever supposed to hurt him. In my mind, he's this indestructible man who will always protect and save me. Live forever."

Cane huffed a small laugh. "Yep, I know. He talked about that a lot. He told me once that he used to have you call him Mr. Strong-O."

A giggle bubbled out of me. Cane chuckled.

"Yeah...I remember that."

We both went quiet again. It was a long silence, but far from uncomfortable. I dropped my legs and pressed my back into the cushion, shutting my eyes. I felt tears building back up again, burning behind my eyelids.

"Can you distract me, please?" I begged, voice cracking. "I can't

—I mean, I just don't know what else to do—*shit*." The tears dripped, despite my eyes being sealed.

"Stop crying, Kandy. Please," he pleaded when I pressed my palms to my face. "I'm not good with tears. Never have been."

"Yeah," I huffed, swiping hard at my face. "I can see that."

He reached up and ran the pad of his thumb over my cheek, brushing a teardrop away. I avoided his eyes.

"Look at me," he murmured.

But I couldn't. Looking at him would have made me cry even harder.

"Look at me, Bits."

I swallowed hard, pulling my gaze up, and locking eyes with him. His hand was still on my cheek, his eyes swimming with a mix of sincerity and grief. He stroked the apple of my cheek.

"What do you want me to do to make you feel better?" he asked, voice low, deep, and husky. He studied my face, like he really wanted to know what could help.

I couldn't speak as he looked at me. Couldn't breathe. I smashed my lips together, my eyes dropping down to his hands. I knew exactly what I wanted.

I wanted him to kiss me. I wanted him to hold me. I wanted him to keep telling me everything was going to be okay while he stroked my hair and held me close, wrapping me up in his big, strong arms.

But I knew he couldn't do that, so instead I said, "Just...hold me, I guess?"

He didn't hesitate much. He wrapped his arm around me as I hooked one of mine behind his back. He pulled me into him until my cheek was pressed on his chest. It was then that I noticed he wasn't wearing a suit or dressy clothes. He wore a solid gray T-shirt and jeans. It was the most casual thing I'd ever seen him wear.

His chin dropped down on the top of my head, and a hard sigh escaped him. I rested my other arm on top of his lap to get more comfortable, sighing from how calming this actually was. I was wrapped around him, the left half of my face pressed on his chest. He smelled so good. Manly and delicious. I wanted to bury my face into his hard, chiseled body and breathe him in forever.

He lifted his glass and sipped, longer this time.

All I heard was his throat working with each sip he took. The ice clinking around in the glass. I stared at the fireplace to distract myself.

When his glass was empty, he sat forward a bit to place it down on the coffee table, but kept me secure in his arms. When he sat back again, I tilted my head up to look at him.

"Are you scared?" I whispered, catching his eyes.

"Yes."

"You don't seem like the type to get scared."

"When it comes to the people I care about getting hurt, I do."

"Do you care about a lot of people?"

"I can count on one hand how many people I truly care about."

"And who are those people?"

"My mother. Your father, of course. Mindy, your mom. My sister, Loralei..." He paused, eyes sparkling as he looked down at me. "And you."

I was relieved when he didn't say Kelly's name. More than relieved actually. Apparently I was more important to him than she was. Or maybe he didn't love her. Still a good sign to me.

It was then I realized how close our faces were, how hard I was pressed against his solid body. My arm was still on his lap, my hand close to his groin. He looked down at where my hand was, like he'd noticed too, but didn't want to mention it.

I squeezed the hem of his shirt, my head still tilted up. I should have moved away, but I couldn't. That drink was chasing away all of my inhibitions, making me want to attempt something bold.

"I'm glad to know you care about me," I whispered. I leaned in more, until our lips were a hairsbreadth away. His eyes were on my mouth, his grip tightening on my waist, probably without even realizing it. My pulse skittered, but I leaned in more, until his lips created a feathery-light sensation on top of mine.

"Kandy," he warned.

"What?"

"No." A solid command that couldn't be mistaken.

I never liked being told no, though. Maybe he was right about the whole *brat* thing. I could act like a spoiled little girl when I wanted to. I liked things to go my way, and sometimes that made me pesky and infuriating.

I slid my hand down, running it over the bulge in his pants anyway. I moved it over the denim, shifting it back up gradually. I felt him getting harder, his breaths unsteady now, body tensing.

"Kandy," he said, but this time it wasn't a warning. It was a plea.

"Should I stop?" I asked, my voice so low I could hardly hear it myself.

He didn't answer—only stared down at me with intense, hungry, smoky eyes. I kept moving my hand up and down on his groin, pressing in more and more, making sure my breasts were completely pushed against him.

"You know damn well you should stop," he mumbled on my mouth, but I felt his grip get even tighter around me, like he was saying one thing, but thinking the complete opposite.

I pressed my hand down again, getting a better feel of the thick, hard ridge resting on the inside of his thigh.

I couldn't help myself. I couldn't stop. I couldn't believe this was happening, and I refused to pass this chance up.

Quinton Cane was hard for me, and I wanted him. Bad.

10

KANDY

Without giving it much thought, I pressed my lips on his, and climbed on top of his lap, deepening the kiss. His lips were soft and smooth, just like I'd imagined they would be.

His body tensed up again, and a guttural groan filled the back of his throat. He was straining in his jeans, rock solid.

He broke the kiss, pressing a hand against my shoulder to push me back. He frowned at me, eyes hard and intense as he tore himself away. "What the hell is wrong with you?" he snapped through a raspy voice.

"Nothing is wrong with me." I smashed my lips together, focused on his mouth, wanting another illicit taste.

"Fuck," he cursed. He watched me longer. "Why are you doing this to me, Kandy?"

"What am I doing?" I whispered.

"You're making me want you."

"You want me?"

"Yes, I fucking want you, and I hate that I'm even admitting it."

My heart caught speed, and I climbed off his lap to sit beside him again, but fisted his shirt in my hands. "Cane, please. Don't treat me like a kid tonight, okay?"

His head shook, his self-control slowly but surely slipping away. I slid closer to him, running my hand over the hard rock in his pants like I did before. His eyes fell down and locked on my mouth. I kept rubbing him, feeling his cock twitch through the jean and beneath my palm. Our lips moved closer. I wanted him so bad I couldn't think straight.

Grabbing my face between his fingers, he tilted my chin, looking me all over with a searing-hot gaze. He exhaled raggedly, the tip of his nose running down my jawline and then back up, over my cheek and then the arch of my nose. He sighed and groaned, bringing his mouth down, closer to mine.

He paused, hesitated, hardly breathing.

I wasn't breathing either. Not much. How could I? Cane—my Cane—was touching me the way I'd always wanted him to. I didn't want to make any sudden moves, fearing he would stop if I did.

Just when I thought he would pull away, he brought my face closer to his, fulfilling the ache. He crushed my lips with his and pressed his body to mine.

I sighed when his tongue traced the line between my lips, demanding that I give him access. I parted them, and his tongue slid through, dancing and playing with mine.

I could taste the scotch on his breath, and a trace of the cigarette he'd probably smoked before picking me up. His breathing was heavier, more ragged, like he couldn't control himself. Like he wanted to stop, but wasn't strong enough to pull away.

I tore at his belt buckle then, unzipping his pants blindly. I wasn't an amateur at this. I'd made out with a lot of boys at parties I wasn't supposed to attend. I'd lie to my parents and say I was just having a sleepover at Frankie's place, when really I was planning on going to a party with her and then crashing at her place afterwards.

It was in that moment, when his jeans were unzipped and my

moan filled him up, that Cane took full control. He gripped my shoulders and forced my back down on the couch. I shoved his jeans down with my hands and feet, and then pulled his shirt over his head, revealing his upper body.

His body was just as I'd imagined. Strong. Broad. Solid. Tan, smooth, and toned in all the beautiful places. He had even more tattoos, so many different and creative works of art on his body. He was a work of art himself.

He lowered his body, thrusting his groin between my thighs, and kissing my neck as my fingers ran over the dips in his muscular back.

His lips trailed downward until he reached my collarbone. I could feel him grinding between my legs. He was so hard.

"Goddamn it. What the hell is wrong with me?" he rasped, coming back up and sucking on my bottom lip, still grinding between my legs. He sat up a bit, pulling my sweatpants down in a flash and revealing yellow panties. I was glad I had my good panties on, the lace ones I bought at Victoria's Secret with Mom during one of our rare shopping dates. His eyes blazed with hunger and lust, like he loved what he was seeing.

"Look at you," he groaned, his eyes glittering as they scanned my frame. "Fucking *look* at you."

Gripping my hips and hauling me closer, he pressed the hard ridge of his cock on my lace-clad pussy, grinding up and down, making me clench, ache, and sigh.

"Fuck," he cursed, squeezing his eyes shut. "I can't do this with you, Kandy." He groaned when I tried to kiss the hollow of his throat.

"I want it," I said on his chin. "I want you, Cane. Please, don't stop."

He cupped the back of my head, tangling rough fingers in my hair. He tugged on it, just enough to crane my neck and expose it.

"I know you want me," he growled. His tongue swirled on the bend of my neck, and then he sucked, thrusting his cock between my thighs again, the thick weight of it still on my pussy. "You feel how hard I am for you?" he panted. "You make me so fucking hard, and I hate myself for it."

One of his hands slid down, and he shifted his hips sideways to push my panties aside. Oh, God. It was happening. It was really happening.

The tip of his finger dipped inside the slit of my pussy and then glided up to my clit. I gasped and vibrated with pleasure when he slid his finger back down and slowly plunged into me.

"So tight and wet." His voice was heavy with desire. He thrust his finger in and out while his thumb gently rested on my clit.

"Oh, God," I whimpered as he swirled his thumb on the aching bundle of nerves. I had no idea how he was playing with both areas, and I didn't care to question it. He had obviously done this many, many times before, and it felt amazing.

My back arched, and I heard him breathing faster. I could still feel his cock on my thigh, heavy and long in his boxers, straining and dying to be set free.

This was so wrong—doing this with him. My father was in the hospital. He could have been dying for all we knew, yet here we were, being careless fools, doing things we shouldn't have been doing. Doing things that my father would have *killed* him for.

I felt awful, but I couldn't stop. I really wanted to, but his touch was my escape from reality. I didn't want to think or remember or hurt. I just wanted the thrill. The getaway.

For all I knew, this could have been another dream. Well, if so, I needed to relish in it before I was shoved back to reality again.

Cane hovered above me, still making magic happen with his finger. His mouth landed on mine again, and he sucked hard on my bottom lip.

"You're so pretty like this," he groaned on my mouth, breath warm on my skin. "When I play with your pussy."

"Ohh," I moaned, squeezing my eyes tighter as he added another finger.

65

"Come for me, my pretty little Kandy." He kissed his way down my throat again, and in my ear he said, "Fuck my fingers, little one. Make them yours."

So I did. I rotated my hips in full, round circles, wanting him deeper, aching for more. For it all.

He added another finger, and I gasped from the sudden pressure, but found myself ratcheting even higher with the added pressure.

I shifted up, and he curled the tips of his fingers just enough for me to feel them. He kissed me over and over again with warm, damp lips. He was so hard. I could feel him, so big and pulsing, ready to burst.

I wanted his cock, but was lost with his fingers inside me. My body was swirling with desire and that splash of liquor. He kept going, in and out, kiss after kiss, until finally, I let go.

My body locked up, paralyzed for a fleeting moment before crying out in ecstasy. I shattered into a million tiny pieces, holding him tight, slowly but surely being pieced back together again somehow. I sucked in a sharp breath, my entire body feeling weaker than before.

Holy shit.

Holy. Shit.

That was...*amazing*. And to know he did that with only his fingers. I couldn't imagine what he could do with his cock.

When I opened my eyes, his were locked on me. "You happy?" His face was serious, jaw locked. His sudden change of mood confused me. He gripped my face between his fingers, brows stitching. "I was stupid, and I had a weak moment, and I cared enough about you to let that happen, but it can never happen again. Do you understand?"

I swallowed the thick knot that'd formed in my throat. "D-did I do something wrong?"

He released my face and sat up, adjusting himself rapidly. "All of this was fucking wrong." A rough hand ran over his head and then he swiped it across his face. "You—*fuck*. You're too fucking young, Kandy. And I'm older. I should fucking know better! You're too . . . too small. Too close to me. You're *Derek's daughter*, for fuck's sake! I fucked up, I know. It's my fault for giving in. Just know I can never put my hands on you like that again."

I didn't blink as I watched him pick up his shirt and tug it over his head, sliding into it like he was aggravated. I couldn't look away from the thick, large boner in his pants either.

"I wanted it, Cane." My voice was a broken plea.

He looked sideways at me. "I know you did, but you shouldn't want me. I'm the wrong fucking man for you, Kandy. I can't do shit like that with you—doesn't matter if you want it or not." He walked to the dim lamps and shut them off. The hallway light was still on, so I could still make out his silhouette. "Get some rest. I'll call your mother, see what's going on. I'll be around if you need me." I could tell he didn't want to leave me alone right now, but in this moment, I knew he had to. He needed to restrain himself. Cool off.

He didn't meet my eyes anymore. Instead, he walked away, leaving me alone in the dark with only my panties and camisole on. I pulled my pants back on and then rested sideways on the sofa, tears running over the bridge of my nose.

I'd always dreamed of kissing him, making out with him, but never in a million years did I think something like *this* would actually happen. Maybe not all dreams were meant to come true. That was the ultimate dream, but by the end of it, it felt like a nightmare.

I almost regretted it because I knew it would change everything between us, and I wasn't prepared for it at all.

11

CANE

I had to get as far away from Kandy as possible. The only place safe and distant enough was my bedroom.

I don't know what came over me.

Kandy was...she was so fucking young. She was Derek's daughter, and he would have *murdered* my ass if he'd know what I'd just done to his little girl. His life was on the line, for fuck's sake, yet there I was, wondering what it would be like to give that girl what she was really wanting.

I paced my bedroom, my dick hard as hell, jaw flexed as I shoved inked fingers through my hair.

"Fuck," I cursed beneath my breath. "Fuck. Fuck. Fuck." I couldn't manage to get soft, even when I knew I shouldn't have been hard in the first place. I kept thinking about her. How vulnerable and excited she was. How eager she was, and how she fucked and clenched my fingers like she couldn't survive without them inside her.

I kept wondering what it would have been like to replace my fingers with my cock. Would I be too big for her? Would she whimper? Get teary-eyed as I stretched her? I knew she was a virgin. By how tight she was, there was no way in hell she'd been broken in yet, and that thought alone pleased me much more than it should have.

When did she become so goddamn sexy? She was eighteen years old and I knew she was too damn young for me, but I kissed her, touched her, and fingered her tight, slick, virgin pussy anyway. She was so damn wet, and her touch alone set my blood on fire. She'd hardly touched me when it all started, and I was already rock solid.

I couldn't lie and say I didn't find her attractive. She was a beautiful girl, and she was developing in plentiful ways. I noticed so much more after touching her. How her hips had filled out and how perky her tits were. She was gorgeous and any guy her age would have killed to have her.

I knew she had a crush on me. I could always tell. Her teasing, the jokes, and the way she tried to get a reaction out of me by doing and saying any little thing to annoy me, was proof of it. And the way she'd look at me with those big, maple-brown eyes, like the only man she wanted was me—fuck. I knew she wanted me. I knew it, but never thought too much of it. I ignored it because, before tonight, it was irrelevant.

I'd given her what she wanted, but at what cost? This was going to change everything between us. She wasn't going to be a kid to me anymore. She was going to be Kandy Jennings, the virgin who craved my cock.

I had to pull my shit together. I couldn't keep thinking about Derek's daughter like this. I stripped out of my clothes and hopped in the shower. After washing clean (as if getting clean would rid me of the wicked, dirty shit I'd just done to Kandy), I put on a pair of boxers and tried to get some work done at the desk in the corner of my bedroom.

It was damn near impossible.

I couldn't stop thinking about what had just happened.

About *her.*

She was downstairs, most likely thinking about it, too. Knowing she was so close—that I could easily just go down there and bury my head between her legs, just to see if she tasted as sweet as she smelled—left me hard all over again.

I couldn't sit around being this hard, knowing the only result would be a sad case of blue balls. I needed to fuck something...so I went with the only option I had.

My fist.

I picked up the lotion on my dresser and sat in the chair again, rolling my briefs down and then squirting some of it in my hand. Wrapping my lubed palm around my cock, I blew out a hard sigh, tossing my head back and squeezing my eyes shut.

My muscles flexed as I pumped, slowly at first, breathing deep as I remembered her soft moans, the silkiness of her pussy around my fingers. How she told me she wanted me.

Her sweet, warm, wet pussy.

Her slender body bucking, going wild with just my fingers inside it. The way tendrils of hair fell over her face, and her mouth gaped with each gradual thrust I provided.

I couldn't stop staring at her.

Watching her come undone.

Watching her come for *me.* I bet it was her first orgasm. Powerful. Delicious.

My body didn't give me much of a warning. My cock had a mind of its own that night. I pumped faster, feeding the hunger, grunting when I realized how close I was—how fucking hard I was.

"Oh, shit," I grunted, using my other hand to massage my balls. They were tight, my dick so thick and swollen in my hand, ready for release. With only three more smooth, quick pumps, I came.

Most of my muscles locked and before I knew it, my whole hand was soaked with white ropes of cum. I slowly rolled my thumb over the tip and then down to my shaft, relieved...for now.

I opened my eyes and looked down at the mess I'd created. Pearly streaks were all over my lap, a few droplets in the patch of dark hair surrounding my pelvis.

There was so much cum—*too much cum*—and all of it was meant for her. All for little Kandy Jennings.

12

KANDY

I woke up before Cane did the next morning...at least, I think so.

I didn't get much sleep. I tossed and turned and sent text messages to Mom for updates, but she didn't have much information to give. She said he was in critical condition and was still in surgery. The good thing, though, was that he was still breathing. For now, at least.

Around 7:00 a.m., I heard footsteps. I picked my head up and watched as Cane passed by the den. He glanced in my direction, but kept walking, and even with that tiny glance, I spotted his regret as clear as day.

Thirty minutes passed before he showed up again, in fresher clothing and his hair gelled back. He was rolling the sleeves of his gray button-down shirt up to his elbows as he stepped into the den.

"Your mom called, said I could bring you to the hospital with her now." He didn't look at me for long. His eyes shifted over to the window instead as he slid the tips of his fingers into the front pockets of his black slacks. "Do you want me to take you by your house to change clothes?"

I lowered my gaze and studied the sweat pants and pink

camisole I was wearing. These were my pajamas. I couldn't go out like this, and even though I wanted to be as far away from Cane as possible in this moment, I simply nodded and stood up.

"Yeah, that would be great," I murmured.

He nodded once and then turned as he said, "I'll get my keys."

After collecting his keys, he led the way to the door. I noticed that this time he didn't usher me out with a caring hand on the shoulder or arm. No. He didn't touch me at all. Hell, he could hardly even look at me.

I climbed into the passenger seat, my phone clutched in hand, as Cane got behind the wheel and started the ignition. He drove away from his house in complete and utter silence. I was almost tempted to turn the radio on.

Why wasn't he blocking out this godawful silence with some kind of noise? It's like he wanted it to be like this between us—uncomfortable and full of tension.

It didn't take long for Cane to pull up to my house. When he pulled up front, I climbed out with haste, hustling for the front door. Remembering I'd left my things at Frankie's, along with my keys, I picked up the flowerpot beneath the window and grabbed the spare, unlocking the door and walking right in.

The house was so still that it almost felt eerie. Normally, around this time on a Saturday morning, Dad would be in the kitchen helping Mom flip pancakes or humming one of his silly old school tunes. I'd walk down late to breakfast, and he'd tease me, calling me *sleepyhead* or *zombie girl* because I hated being bothered until I had food or coffee.

The rims of my eyes lined with hot tears, but I fought the tidal wave of emotion and trotted up the stairs to my room. I washed up quickly and changed into a purple dress and sandals, tied my hair up into a bun, and I was on my way again—on the way back to an uncomfortable, awkward silence.

I slid into the passenger seat of Cane's car and he backed out of the driveway before I could even buckle my seatbelt.

Seeing as he seemed to be in such a hurry to get me out of the car and away from him, I expected Cane to take me straight to the hospital and deliver me to my mother. Instead, he pulled up at a coffee shop and turned to me, expectantly.

"Want anything?" he asked, and his voice—the offer—made my belly twist. In that moment, I wasn't sure if it had twisted in a positive or negative way.

I shrugged. "I've never been here before. I'm not sure what all they have."

He looked at the vintage brick building very briefly before focusing those tired eyes on me.

His eyes were grayer today, cloudy and unreadable. "Come in and see."

He got out of the car before I could decline. Sighing, I unclipped my seatbelt and stepped out, following Cane to the entrance, but making sure to keep some distance between us. He opened the door for me, and a bell chimed above my head as I entered.

The welcoming aromas of coffee beans and baked goods surrounded me, and for a split second, I wasn't worried about the naughty things that had happened the night before. Instead, I was focused more on the coffee shop, and the industrial structure of it. This place was most likely a warehouse before being renovated with bleached brick walls and a pale green color scheme. The ceiling was very high up, and skylights were built into it, which gave the place a beautiful, natural aura. My love for the coffee shop was instant.

Cane walked past me to get to the counter, and I met up beside him, still making sure not to stand too closely as I scanned the menu. Even though it was nearing nine in the morning, it was warming up outside. I decided to go with an iced caramel coffee.

Cane ordered two more coffees and when they were finished and the cup holder with all three coffees was handed to him, he said, "Other coffee's for your mom. I'm sure she's exhausted."

"Yeah, probably."

Cane got in the car, leveling the cup holder in one hand and shutting the door with the other. I took the cup holder from him and placed it on my lap, grabbing my iced coffee and sipping it. It was amazing. Probably the best iced coffee I'd ever had. I made a mental note to mark Bean & Dreams as my new favorite local coffee shop.

We were off again. It wasn't as awkward now, but only because I could occupy myself with sipping a drink.

We were about five minutes away from the hospital when Cane finally decided to talk—like actually talk.

"Listen, about what happened last night..." He let out a ragged breath, swiping a hand over his face. His other hand gripped the wheel a little tighter, and I saw his jaw pulse twice. While he gathered his words, I studied the letters on his knuckles. It said R-I-S-E, a letter on each knuckle, except his thumb. The tattoo was on his neck too. I wondered what it meant. "I don't want you to think —well, I mean...I just don't want you to expect it to happen again," he went on. I was looking at him, but when he said that, I lowered my gaze, looking at the creamy white lids on the hot coffees instead. "I had a weak moment. We both did. You had that drink, and I was drinking a lot last night. It was late and we were both tired and struck with grief. I probably shouldn't have given the drink to you. I just—we can keep what happened between us, right? If you aren't okay being alone with me anymore, I understand, and you don't have to be after today. I feel terrible about it, Kandy. I never should have put my hands on you that way."

My head shook as he stopped at a stop sign. "You don't have to apologize for something we both wanted."

"Both?" he asked, like he was shocked. "You think I wanted that to happen?"

I smashed my lips together and raised my eyebrows.

"Kandy, I—"

"I wanted it, Cane. I know you regret it because of your friend-

75

ship with my dad and mom, and probably because I'm much younger than you, but...I don't."

"Kandy," he groaned again, and then let out a coarse, dry laugh. "You can't *want* me, you understand? I'm not the guy for you. You're young and have your whole life ahead of you." We were in the parking lot of the hospital a minute later, and just as he parked, he turned to me and said, "Just know it can't happen again, all right? I won't touch you. I won't let you drink around me anymore. When I'm around you, I'll keep my hands to myself completely, if that will help. If you want to tell your parents, you can. I'll accept the consequences." He smiled weakly, like that was the last thing he wanted me to do. "Nothing has to change," he murmured. "I still care about you. I just don't want mistakes like that to ruin the bond I have with you and your family. You understand what I mean?"

"Mistakes?" I repeated, and my throat thickened. I knew it was a mistake, I did, but I didn't expect him to actually say it out loud. How could he pretend he didn't enjoy it? I heard it in his voice—saw the lust written all over his face, the hungry flames in his eyes. "Wow. Um...okay." I jammed my thumb into the seatbelt button and snatched it off. "Sure, Cane. I understand."

I handed him the cup holder of coffees—well, more like shoved it into his hands, leaving him no choice but to take it.

"Kandy, come on," he groaned, but I got out of the car and shut the door behind me before I could hear him say anything else.

Last night really had changed everything. But what he didn't understand was how badly I wanted it. How much I needed it. After nursing a crush so strong for so many years, I finally set it free and gave it something it wanted. It wasn't a dream. It was real and I felt everything.

It was only the tip of the iceberg, but I wanted more. So much more. I was so damn greedy for him that it was hard to think about the consequences that could ensue.

I didn't think about how close he and Dad actually were, or

how Mom would raise hell if she even caught wind of it. It would never work, no matter how much I wanted him.

But still, I let my stubbornness take charge. I didn't walk beside Cane. I led the way, finding the front desk and telling them my dad's name. Once I was given the room number, I made it my mission to get there as quickly as possible.

It was hard to do, but I let my thoughts of Cane and last night go, focusing on the fact that I was finally where I actually needed to be: at the hospital, about to see my mom and dad.

13

KANDY

Once I had the room number, I took off for the elevator, pressing the up arrow when I reached it. I smelled Cane's cologne before I could look over my shoulder and see him meet up behind me.

He wasn't looking at me. He was focused on the digital numbers above the elevator instead.

We boarded in silence.

Being in such a confined, tight space, alone with him, was torture. The scent of him overwhelmed every single one of my senses. He was too close. Too much. I could hear him breathing lightly, but still, I kept my shit together and pretended his presence didn't bother me—that I was on a mission and he was the last thing on my mind

As soon as the doors drew apart, I rushed out, scurrying down the hallway until I found Dad's room number. I opened the door to his room, and as soon as I stepped inside, Mom sprung out of her seat. Her eyes were tired, but when she saw me, they lit up.

"Mom," I breathed, and a rush of relief washed over me as I dashed her way and threw my arms around her neck. I hugged her tight, like this hug would help me forget about what happened only hours ago with Cane—make me forget about the phone call she had to make and the reason we were here. I hugged her like everything would go back to normal.

But it didn't.

Everything was still the same.

I pulled back a fraction to look at my dad.

He was laid on the bed, his head propped up on pillows, wearing a green hospital gown. A bandage was wrapped around his neck and a small amount of blood had leaked through it. I drew in a sharp breath, pulling my eyes away and planting my forehead on Mom's shoulder. I couldn't look at him like this. He wasn't Mr. Strong-O, the man I admired more than anything. He was frail and tired.

"I know, sweetie," Mom cooed, rubbing my back. "I know. But guess what?"

I looked up at her, meeting the brown eyes that were identical to mine. "What?"

"He's going to be okay," she chimed with a soft breath, but I could tell she wanted to scream. I could tell by the smile plastered on her face that, despite his current condition, she was happy. So, so happy.

"He is?" Relief struck me. "Oh, thank God! I was so worried!"

"Me too, honey. But the surgery went well. The bullet that hit his thigh didn't damage too much. He'll still be able to walk but he'll need some physical therapy. And the wound on his neck was just a hard graze. He's going to be a little sore when he wakes up and will probably have to spend a few more days here, but he's going to be okay." She reeled me in for another hug, and I squeezed her tight.

I was crying now, and I shut my eyes, soaking it all in. In that moment, last night didn't matter. Cane didn't matter. My dad was going to live. That was all I could have asked for.

A throat cleared behind me, and Mom pulled away, looking over her shoulder and smiling at Cane.

"Oh, I'm sorry, Cane," she murmured, her voice thick with

emotion. "I didn't even acknowledge you when you came in. Rude of me."

"It's okay. I understand what you're going through." Cane took a step forward. "That's great news about Derek. I'm glad he's going to be okay," Cane murmured, glancing at Dad. "I was really worried about him, too."

"I know you were." Mom took a step away from me to pat Cane on the shoulder. "Thank you for taking Kandy in last night and watching over her."

Cane's eyes slid over to me, and I fidgeted, but didn't look away from him. I saw the guilt flash in his eyes, but he covered it with a soft smile and said, "Of course. Anytime." He changed the subject then, lifting the cup holder and showing off the coffees. "Brought you a pick-me-up. Figured you might need it after pulling an all-nighter."

"Oh, yes please," she laughed. "Thank you. That was really nice of you." Mom accepted the coffee and then came back to me, wrapping her arm around my shoulders. "Do you have to be anywhere?" she asked him. "You can stay a while if you want to. The doctor said he should be waking up soon."

Cane flipped his wrist to check his watch and then looked up. He looked at me first before focusing on Mom. "Don't have to be anywhere important for another three hours. I can hang out here until then."

"Great. I'm sure Derek will be glad to see you when he's up. You're like family to him. To all of us."

Cane nodded, but again, the guilt on his face was crystal clear. He didn't say anything else. Instead, he turned, pulling his coffee out of the cup holder and claiming the vacant recliner in the corner by the door.

As he sipped his coffee, he stared at my dad with wide, distant eyes. He still seemed worried, anxious. Mom grabbed my hand to sit me down with her, and we all looked at Dad, the minutes ticking by ever so slowly, just waiting for him to move or sigh or do anything, but he didn't move. Only breathed.

Eventually Mom couldn't stand the silence anymore, and she grabbed the remote control attached to the hospital bed, turning on the TV and surfing through the channels. She stopped on the cooking channel, sipping at her coffee, letting it be her distraction for now.

I felt eyes on me and knew whom they belonged to, but didn't bother checking to find out.

I couldn't look at Cane. I wanted to, but couldn't.

Every time I looked at him now, I thought about what he did to me only hours ago, how amazing and thrilled I was, and it felt wrong to have those thoughts, like I was betraying Daddy by thinking and worrying about someone else.

Thirty minutes passed, but they were heavy and uncomfortable, filled with small chatter between Cane and Mom. She asked about his job and even Kelly. Hearing about Kelly was something I didn't want to stick around for.

I couldn't sit in there anymore, listening to him go on about how he and Kelly were supposed to be flying to New York together for an art expo. And the way he talked about her, like he was excited to go with and be with her? Ugh. It made me want to vomit.

I needed to get some air, stat.

"Mom, do you think I can borrow some money? I want to go to the cafeteria, see if they have anything quick to eat. Left my wallet at Frankie's," I explained with a shrug.

Mom's eyes swooped up to mine. "Sure, honey. My—Oh, you know what, honey?" She looked around the room until her eyes pinned on the Michael Kors purse on the counter. "I left my wallet in the car, but you can go and get it if you want. My credit card is in there. Get whatever you need." She stood up, about to go for her bag, but Cane cleared his throat, making her stop mid-step.

"No need to do all of that. I have some cash on me if you need it, Kandy." Cane slid to the edge of the recliner and pulled his wallet out of his back pocket. I watched with a suddenly dry mouth as he opened it and pulled out a twenty-dollar bill amongst other twenties and hundreds. His cloudy eyes shifted up to mine as he extended his arm and offered it.

I wanted to decline his offer. I had no problem going out to Mom's car and getting her wallet, but I couldn't act like a stubborn bitch with Cane while Mom was around. I didn't want her asking questions or wondering what was going on between us. I smiled as graciously as I could and accepted the money, tucking it in my bra.

"Thank you, Cane." I noticed him watch me tuck it in. It was a brief glance, but he quickly lifted his gaze to mine again, returning a faint smile as he sat back in the recliner again.

"Of course, Kandy."

I told Mom I wouldn't be long, but I had no plans to rush back to that room. Yes, I wanted to be there when Dad woke up and yes, I should have been behaving and worrying more about Dad and his health rather than Cane and his body, but it was so, so hard.

Every time I moved, I could remember the feeling of Cane's fingers playing with my pussy. It's like they were still there, diving deep, bringing me closer and closer to euphoria. Every time I saw him sip his coffee out of the corner of my eye, I remembered those lips on my lips, neck, and all over my skin.

I didn't go straight to the cafeteria. I went to the bathroom and rushed into one of the stalls. I planted my back against one of the walls and sucked in a deep breath.

"Get it together, Kandy. Seriously." I was here with Mom and Dad. I was happy to see them after an extremely long night. I needed to focus on that.

Forget. Forget. Forget.

After I left the bathroom and grabbed three bacon, egg, and

cheese bacon croissants from the cafeteria, I went back to the room with a new mantra ringing in my head.

Forget. Forget. Forget.

I couldn't get invested in Cane. I couldn't like him. I couldn't need him. I had to be happy with the fact that I was better off without him.

With the mantra ringing in my brain, I was back in the room, handing him a sandwich and his change with a warm smile. His eyebrows dipped, like he was confused by the smile and the offer of the sandwich, but he took it all anyway and thanked me.

He didn't eat his, but Mom and I devoured ours, despite the heavy, gloomy mood weighing over our heads. Who knew distress and anxiety could make a person feel so hungry?

Two hours passed and Dad still wasn't awake. Cane blew a breath when he realized it, and I knew he had to go by the way he slid to the edge of his seat again, looking between the two of us.

"I would stay," he said with a sigh, "but I have a business meeting that includes talk about having another Tempt factory opening in Canada. If I didn't have to be there, I would let my secretary handle it. I'd stay here all night if I could." He flashed his wickedly straight teeth.

Mom stood up. "Oh, Cane, please go. That is your job, and things like that are important. Go," she insisted. "I will let you know when Derek is awake."

Cane stood and looked at Dad, the pain still swirling in his eyes. With a simple nod of his head, he took a step to the left, toward the door. "Please let me know first thing. When he wakes up, tell him I'll be thinking about him until I can see him again."

"I will," Mom assured him.

He exhaled, long and deep, like he didn't want to leave, but he headed for the door anyway. He pulled it open, but before he walked out, his eyes landed on mine. His lips pressed together and as he looked at me, I could have sworn I saw something in his eyes. A small glimpse of sympathy and...longing.

"Take care, Cane," I called after him before he could go.

"You too, Kandy Cane," he teased, but I didn't laugh and neither did he. Mom did, but it was a soft, small chuckle, like things were still the same and he was only joking around. Like that name didn't have a deeper, truer meaning to me. He knew it did—knew all too well how it affected me—and he'd called me it anyway.

Kandy and Cane. His Kandy Cane.

I watched him go, and when he left, the room didn't feel as crowded. My mind didn't reel chaotically with unrequited, forbidden thoughts, and some of the tension in my body had even faded...but not all of it.

Why? Because Dad still wasn't awake. Because I'd done wrong last night, and the bonds that had been created were tainted and murky. The lines had blurred now.

We'd started something—lit an inextinguishable fire in our souls—and that fire was going to burn us inside and out. It was going to consume us whole and probably destroy us.

The fire was going to blaze like a furnace, and neither of us had time to prepare for it.

14

KANDY

It was around midnight when Dad finally woke up. Neither Mom nor I had fallen asleep. We just waited for what felt like centuries, and when we heard him grunt, and then let out a small sigh, we gasped, because the next thing we saw was magnificent: his dark brown eyes.

We rushed for him, both of us hugging him at the same time as he chuckled low and deep.

"Oh, my girls," Dad sighed, voice raspy. "My girls."

We didn't sleep at all that night. We called for the doctor, who came in about an hour after he was awake. He was checked thoroughly, and the doctor was surprised he wasn't in more pain than he let on. Still, she gave him morphine to ease it, assuring him that the pain would kick in soon, once the previous dose had worn off.

"I want you to stick around here for three more days," Dr. Ambrose told Dad. "I just want to make sure you're healing properly and that nothing else has been damaged."

"Okay. Three days I can do," he confirmed.

"I'll call Cane. He said he wanted to know as soon as you were awake," Mom chimed, hopping up and going for her handbag.

Cane's name made my booming heart go a little unsteady, but I kept up a smile for Dad. For now.

"Was he here?" Dad asked after taking a sip of water.

"Yes. He was around earlier, stayed for about two and half hours. We thought you would have been up before he left. He had a meeting to go to."

"Oh. Yeah, bring the phone here. Let me call him," he insisted. Mom handed him her cell, and Dad pressed the call button.

"He kept Kandy overnight, too, when things got a little hectic," Mom added, and I wanted to cup my hand around her mouth and tell her to shush. The reminder was nauseating.

"Did he? That was really nice of him."

"Yeah," I murmured, but I avoided his eyes.

Dad put the phone on speaker and rested it on his lap. Then Cane's voice came through the receiver, and I froze in my seat, staring at the phone.

"Cane!" Dad boomed lightly.

"Hey, if it isn't Mr. Strong-O himself!" Cane boomed back with a light chuckle. "How are you feeling, man? You had me really fucking worried!"

Dad glanced at me when Cane cursed, but I just shrugged. I was eighteen now. Had been since September 23rd. He couldn't protect me from curse words and violence anymore. And Cane was a grown man who could say and do whatever the hell he wanted. Like Dad knew that, he continued the conversation.

"I'm great, man. A little sore here and there, but I'm alive. That's all that matters."

"That's right," Cane agreed.

"Listen, Mindy told me you kept an eye on Kandy the other night…"

Cane hesitated for a brief moment. It wasn't too brief, to the point my parents would wonder why he wasn't responding, but it was enough for me to know that the mere mention of my name was bringing him memories of the night before.

"Yeah, I did," Cane responded.

"I can't thank you enough for that. Watching over my little girl." Dad looked at me, and I forced a smile. "She wasn't too much trouble was she?"

Cane laughed, but it was most definitely forced. "Not at all, man. She wanted to be there, was a little upset when I wouldn't take her to the hospital right away, but she understood."

Yeah, I understood, all right.

"That's good. You know they're going to have me in here for three more days?"

"Three? Seventy-two hours of torture, man," Cane teased.

"Yeah, being in here isn't the best, but they're taking good care of me."

"Well, I'll come see you when I can to make sure you're comfortable and so your ass doesn't get too bored in there."

Dad chuckled. "Bring beer. That'll be all the entertainment I need."

Mom sucked her teeth, playfully smacking Dad on the shoulder. "You know you can't have beer while recovering," she laughed.

I smiled, lowering my gaze.

"I'll see you soon then, and thanks again for taking Kandy in and keeping her in good hands. I know that was a scary night for my girl."

"Of course, Derek. Anytime. You focus on recovering, all right? Maybe you'll get out of there sooner." He was deflecting. He didn't want to talk about taking me anymore. I was kind of glad. I wondered just what he was thinking whenever Dad said my name.

I was certain there was regret.

Dad was his best friend. Probably his only *real* friend. I wondered if he would get so consumed by guilt and remorse that he'd actually end up telling Dad all about it one day.

Would he be that bold?

SHANORA WILLIAMS

Would he put his friendship on the line and risk ruining everything between them over a confession?

I thought about that for the rest of the night and even the next day. But those thoughts vanished as soon as the door to Dad's room opened the next day and Cane strolled in, and following behind him was Kelly, with a bouquet of flowers.

It was clear to me then—with Kelly at his side—that he was never going to tell my dad the truth. He was going to bury it— pretend that what we did had never happened.

I watched him the entire time. He hugged Mom, so of course he had to hug me too, to keep things normal and casual. It's what he always did when he saw us for the first time of any day. He couldn't break the tradition.

When he hugged me, I sucked in a breath. His arms were tight around me, but not as tight as usual. His scent drove me crazy. He always smelled so good.

He pulled away, and I looked up into his eyes as Mom, Dad, and Kelly shared a conversation about the bandaged wound on Dad's neck.

"You brought her here?" I whispered. "During a time like this?"

"Don't start, Kandy," he mumbled, placing his keys down on the counter. "She wanted to give her condolences."

"She could have sent them. She didn't have to come," I whisper-hissed.

"Stop it," he snapped lightly. "Please, Kandy, just stop it, okay? I —*shit*. I can't. I can't do this with you right now and you know it."

Cane looked me hard in the eyes before walking around me and meeting beside Dad. They laughed and their voices boomed as Cane teased him about who the stronger person was now, but I couldn't find it in me to laugh.

I couldn't find it in me to accept what was unfolding right before my very eyes.

Cane came here with Kelly.

Did he spend last night with her?

This morning?

Did they wake up together?

All of it hurt my heart much more than it should have. And hell, I could have been assuming things, but when Kelly placed a hand on Cane's chest and looked into his eyes—an intimate gesture that made my belly clench—I just knew he'd called her over, or he'd told her he was coming to visit.

Perhaps he wasn't satisfied and had to find a reasonable woman to unleash himself on and that woman just so happened to be Kelly.

Did he think about me when he fucked her? Did he remember what he did to me, and pretend she was me?

I think I found that answer when he and Kelly shared a laugh. His eyes shifted over to mine. He scanned me twice. I wore another dress that day. It was white, stitched with cotton, and stopped just above my knees.

Cane's tongue rolled over his bottom lip as he studied me. His eyes were smoldering and hungry. It was a short look. A fleeting glance.

In that moment, I realized that yes, he had most likely imagined sliding between my legs and stealing my innocence.

Yes, Quinton Cane still wanted me, despite the realities laid bare right in front of us.

Despite the friendships and relationships.

Despite the rights and the wrongs.

Despite my age and naivety.

I saw in his eyes the same look I'd seen the night he finger-fucked me, an insatiable hunger and so much lust.

Even though I knew the consequences—feared knowing my father could find out how I felt about Cane and what I wanted him to do to me—I was tempted to make him sin all over again.

15

KANDY

My father's recovery took a little over a month. He hopped around on crutches and attended therapy sessions to strengthen his leg.

Even though he asked me to fetch every little thing for him—and had even made me drive to the store in his truck to get him a *Snickers* bar—I didn't mind doing it. I was thankful he was alive.

During Dad's recovery, Cane only visited twice, and to my complete and utter satisfaction, Kelly wasn't with him during either visit.

The first time he came around, he hung out with Dad in the basement that Dad liked to call his man cave. Little did he know that it wasn't, and that I spent more time down there than he did during the day.

I heard them talking about the nasty gun wound on Dad's thigh (that he so often liked to flash to me and Mom, saying it was a battle scar) and they talked about Cane getting the big opportunity to open a Tempt factory in Canada.

I heard all of this from the kitchen over my lonely dinner at the counter. Mom was working that night—another late shift as divorce attorney Mindy Jennings—and I'd taken Dad's heated-up lasagna down to the basement for him a few minutes prior to Cane's arrival.

I should have been bummed when Dad said he wanted to celebrate Cane's big promotion, but I wasn't. I heard talks about the beach and beer, but I stopped eavesdropping when Kelly's name was mentioned.

I went upstairs before Cane could come back up, and started typing about my day, which somehow led to typing about my relentless infatuation with him, just like a girl with a crush would.

Only this wasn't just a crush anymore. This was my heart. My all. This was my love for him...the love he would never, ever understand.

—

The second time Cane came around, neither of my parents were home. I was on the sofa in the living room watching reruns of *Breaking Bad* when the doorbell rang.

Pushing off the sofa, I slid into my fuzzy pink slippers and shuffled to the door. I expected it to be the delivery guy, seeing as Mom had told me she was expecting a package and wanted me to be on the lookout for it.

I didn't think to check the peephole. I opened the door swiftly and regretted answering it. In pink slippers and sweatpants, I looked like an unprepared idiot while standing in front of the always well-dressed Quinton Cane.

He wore dark gray pants with a creaseless sky-blue button-down shirt, the sleeves rolled up to his elbows. His hair had been trimmed and was gelled in the usual modern-casual style.

His gray-green eyes landed on mine, and as if he wasn't expecting me to answer the door, he blinked rapidly and straightened his back.

"Oh, hey, Kandy," he sighed, and his voice did the same thing it always did: made me weak in the knees.

"Hey, Cane," I breathed, tucking my hair behind my ear. "W-what are you doing here?"

"Uh..." Cane looked back at the driveway, like he was waiting for someone to arrive. "Your dad told me to come by at five to pick him up for the Atlanta Hawks game tonight..."

"Oh." I glanced over my shoulder. "He had therapy today. Mom took him this time since she was free. They're probably just running a little late." I fidgeted on my feet. I knew I was going to have to invite him in, but that meant I would be alone with him...again.

"I'll call Mom and see where they are." I turned, leaving the door open, leaving it up to him to decide whether to come in, go back to his car, take a smoke, or do whatever he needed to do as long as it meant we weren't alone in the same room together again.

Of course, he came in. My heart was delighted, but my brain and body whirled with anxiety. I went to the sofa and picked up my cellphone, sending Mom a quick text. She replied a few seconds later. I sighed while reading the message.

"What's up?" Cane asked, and I put my focus on him. He was already looking at me, but his eyes dropped to my phone.

"Oh, uh...she said they just left the hospital but have to stop by the pharmacy to pick up a prescription."

"Oh, okay." Cane looked around the living room and then focused on the TV. "I guess I'll wait here and watch some TV with you then...if that's okay with you."

"Sure—yeah. Feel free." I stepped back as he smiled at me and took the single recliner behind him. He took the single recliner, so he wouldn't have to sit next to me—at least that's how I saw it.

"Do you want something to drink?" I asked, and he shook his head.

"I'm good, Kandy Cane."

I sat down, slightly rolling my eyes. He knew how I felt about that name, yet he still used it, even after what'd happened.

I tucked my feet under my butt and pretended to watch the show, but it was impossible to focus. Cane was only a few steps away, but it felt like he was right next to me.

I glanced over at him, unable to stop myself, and he was watching the TV in an almost boyish manner. His face was relaxed, eyes wide, like he was amazed by what was going on—like he hadn't watched TV in years.

His legs were spread slightly apart, and my eyes landed on the bulge between them. I could see the print of his manhood—thick and long. From this angle, it looked appealing, the way it rested on the inside of his thigh.

I fidgeted then, finding it completely and utterly impossible to remain still and comfortable in the same room as him by myself. I kept thinking about that night. That godawful, beautiful, terrifying, yet euphoric night. I sucked in a breath.

Cane looked up, as if he felt me looking, and his eyes landed on me. I jerked my head up to look away, but was sure he'd caught me.

I caved and looked back. "Do you plan on going to the beach with us next month?" I asked, looking down at my phone.

"I do, actually. Figured I could use the vacation. Haven't taken one in years."

I frowned. "Years?"

"Yes, Kandy. Years. I've been working so hard to build Tempt that I haven't actually gotten around to scheduling one. But since Derek and Mindy are putting it together and things are going pretty well for the company, I don't see why not."

"Oh. Cool." I swung my eyes over to the television, pretending Jesse calling someone a bitch was more important. "You bringing Kelly?"

I avoided his eyes but felt him staring a hole into the side of my head. "Do you want me to bring her?"

"No!" I blurted, and then immediately clamped my mouth

shut, realizing how pathetic and stupid I sounded. His eyes widened, like he was surprised by my sudden outburst.

"You really don't like her, huh?" He chuckled, and I pulled my legs from beneath me, placing my feet on the floor, and sitting up straight.

"I never said I don't like her." I chewed on my bottom lip, and he watched me do it. "I just...think she's in the way."

"In the way of what?" he asked with a slight frown, like he honestly had no clue. How great of him to play dumb when he *knew* how I felt about him.

"She won't be there. Don't worry," he assured, and I was beyond relieved to hear it.

"I'm glad you're not being too weird," I laughed.

Confused, he asked, "Weird about what?"

"About that night...and what happened, you know?"

"Oh." He looked away with a big shrug. When he did, I couldn't help but watch him. His chiseled jaw ticked again, his nostrils flaring a little, as if the memories of what we did would haunt him in the best and worst ways.

Deep down, I knew that Cane wanted me too, and the fact that he wasn't supposed to want me was making things harder for him. I noticed he didn't show up as much as before, and that could have been due to Dad's recovery and because of Mom's promotion. With her promotion, she had to work more, which meant less scheduled dinners...or it could have been because he was afraid to be around me after what had happened.

I guess I couldn't blame him, but when I said I wanted to make him sin again, I meant it.

I was bad—so damn bad—and blinded by so much lust.

I swallowed hard, placing my phone beside me and standing up. Cane watched me rise, his eyes narrowing.

I knew what I was about to do was going to piss him off. I knew it was going to make him frustrated and annoyed, but what I also knew was that he was going to react to it.

My actions would turn him on.

He would most likely tell me to stop, but his body would be screaming for me to keep going.

I don't know what made me feel so bold and confident around Cane, yet still so small and meaningless. I always felt like I had to prove something to him.

The opportunity to be alone with him didn't come often, and something in the back of my head was telling me to take advantage of it that day...

So I did.

16

KANDY

I wasn't usually this forward with guys. With the boys at school, I let them come to me, but with Cane, I *had* to be the one to make the move.

He was older. Mature. He had more self-control than they did. He had boundaries, but I needed him to know that I liked feeling this way.

I walked to him and sat on his lap. He tensed up, his arms on top of the arms of the recliner, as mine went around the back of his neck. Our faces were close, our mouths less than an inch apart.

"Goddamn it, Kandy. Don't start this shit," he rasped. "What the hell are you doing?"

"I want you to stop treating me like a kid."

"But you *are* a kid," he mumbled, and he lifted a hand to grip my face between his fingers. "You're a fucking kid, and not just any kid, you're *Derek's* kid, so get the hell off my lap."

"No," I snapped, staring him in the eyes. "I know that's not what you want."

"Kandy, your parents will be here any minute."

"Well, I guess I should make it quick then."

He narrowed his eyes. "Make what qui—"

Before he could finish speaking, my lips were on his. I kissed him hard and his hand fell. At first he didn't touch me. He held his hands up, frozen for a moment. I could tell he wanted to push me away—probably shove me onto the floor like I had some kind of disease—but he didn't.

Instead, his hand slid up my spine, and his fingers caressed the back of my neck. They traveled up until they were tangled in the hair at the nape of my neck, and then he clutched a handful of it in his hand, tugging on it and breaking the kiss.

He looked up at me with damp lips, his eyes on fire now, both of us breathing raggedly. He studied my face, my eyes, probably realizing just how desperate I really was for him.

I didn't let him say anything else. I knew he would stop this if I didn't keep going in the heat of the moment, so I pulled his hand away and slid off of his lap, getting down on my knees on the floor and in between his legs.

I couldn't believe I was doing this—right in my parents' living room—but I was drunk on lust. What was it about this man? What made me so crazy and hungry for him? Was it because I wasn't supposed to want him? Was it because he was older? Was it because I knew Kelly was still around, and I was secretly trying to prove that I was better than her? How was that even possible if she was never going to find out about us?

"Kandy," Cane sighed, voice tight. "Please. Not here. Not now."

"Why not?" I asked, unbuckling his belt and then unbuttoning his pants. I tugged on them, but he didn't lift his hips to make it easier for me, which only made me more determined. I tugged harder until I saw his briefs, then I peeled those down just enough to reveal his cock.

He sprung out, hard, long, and dark, with veins running up from his shaft. His tip was round like a bulb, and thick, too. He was so big, and staring at it left me both speechless and curious.

How was I going to fit him in my mouth—let alone anywhere else?

"Kandy," Cane warned, tensing up.

"They're not going to be here for another twenty minutes or so, Cane."

"I don't care. Seriously. We have to stop doing this." He sat up to grip my shoulders. I pressed in more, my tongue sliding over the tip of his cock to lick the pre-cum away. I could have sworn I felt his whole body shudder. "Fuck," he groaned. "Fuck, Kandy. Back off before I hurt your feelings."

"Then hurt them," I mumbled. "It's not like you aren't hurting them every time you come around and act like I hardly exist."

"You made it that way, by doing shit like this."

I pressed a hand on his chest to force him back in the chair. "I want to," I insisted, and then I dropped my head, taking half his cock into my mouth.

"Fuuuccck," he groaned, and the tension only built up within him. His hands turned into fists on the arms of the chair. His head fell backward, face pointed to the ceiling as I took him deeper in my mouth.

I wasn't a pro at this—not by a long shot—but I wasn't a newbie either. I had performed oral before with Carl, though he was very hesitant about it at first.

When we were in his truck after school and even after gradua-tion, I'd attempted it. I would get so angry with Cane for avoiding me that I thought doing something with Carl would be sweet revenge, but it was stupid because Cane didn't even know about it. Carl would drive somewhere private\, one thing would lead to another, and...it just happened.

Turns out, I actually *enjoyed* giving blowjobs.

I enjoyed seeing the guy letting his guard down to the point that the pleasure would consume him. It was empowering for me, watching him become vulnerable.

In this very moment, Cane was very vulnerable for me. He'd let his guard down for now, and I sucked his cock faster, wrapping a hand around the base and pumping it lightly. My tongue swirled around his tip again, and I licked the saltiness away, which caused a deep rumble in his chest.

"Fuck, Kandy," he gritted through his teeth. I looked up, and his head dropped. His eyes were fierce when they latched with mine. He was about to tell me to stop again, but when our eyes found each other's, I was certain his mind had changed.

He watched my head bob, watched as I made his cock wetter with my tongue. He watched me stroke him with one hand, my lips sealed around his thick, beautiful tip.

His teeth caught his bottom lip, and one of his hands came down to the back of my head. He pushed down on it, making me take him deeper. I gagged as he pushed further in, but I didn't stop looking at him.

He liked it—liked the noises I made with him in my throat. My eyes became watery, and I pulled my hand away, letting him take the lead. He could do whatever he wanted to do to me, as long as he didn't stop me. Placing both hands on either side of my head, he tilted his hips up and lightly fucked my mouth.

His cock hit the back of my throat each time, and with each gradually deeper thrust, I choked, but he would ease up, letting me catch my breath before going right back at it.

"You want it? Fine. Keep looking at me," he mumbled. "Keep looking at me while I fuck this pretty little mouth of yours."

His voice made my pussy clench. I kept looking at him, feeling his thighs spread apart to position himself better. He was so hard and big. I almost couldn't breathe, but I knew he was close and I couldn't let up.

Cane wasn't like Carl. Carl just sat there and let me do the work. He would tell me what to do sometimes, but it wasn't much. But Cane? He was different. So different. It seemed Cane was

SHANORA WILLIAMS

testing my limits, seeing just how much of him I could handle. His eyes were on fire—almost taunting. I'd never seen him like this, so vicious and still so wickedly handsome. I loved everything about it.

The way I felt as he stared at me.

How smooth and warm his flesh was in my mouth.

How my pussy throbbed and ached, dying for him to touch me there again.

He released his grip from my head, but continued pumping his hips. I bobbed my head up and down again, creating a mix of shallow and deep swallows.

"Yeah, just like that," Cane groaned, and he gripped the arms of the couch, his nails sinking into the leather. "Shit, Kandy. How the fuck are you so good at this?"

I wanted to smile. His words were like treats to me, and I was the puppy. He was rewarding me with them and didn't even realize it. How was I good? Frankie. She watched porn and surfed Tumblr a lot, often shoving the screen of her phone in my face to show me something she wanted to try. Because of her, I'd made an account and surfed Tumblr too, only to be turned on and helpless. I'd learned a trick or two, though.

Cane was about to erupt. His entire body had become tense, his cock so hard I was sure it could break something. I couldn't believe I was about to do this—make him come under my parents' roof. They could have walked in at any given moment, and that frightening thought still wasn't enough to stop me, but only because I knew they would take a while. The hospital Dad went to was over thirty minutes away.

Pleasing Cane was all I wanted to do. Tasting his cum was my mission in that moment, so I slid a hand up to caress his toned chest.

My eyes shifted up to his face. He was already looking at me, nostrils flared.

"Keep going," he murmured, his voice coarse. "Keep sucking

my cock like that. I'm close." He groaned harder. "Your mouth feels so fucking good."

I palmed his cock, ready to finish him off. My hand wrapped around him, and I pumped up and down, then twisted my wrist, wringing his thickness.

"So good." He shut his eyes, his head falling backward. One of his hands landed on top of my head, and he clutched a handful of my hair, his body stiffening seconds later. Slamming his hips upward, he thrust hard into my mouth one last time.

"Ohh shit," he groaned, and I whimpered around his thickness, not out of pain, but sheer satisfaction. "Oh, Kandy. *Fuck, baby.*" He held my hair tighter, and before I knew it, he was coming down my throat, hard and quick.

I drank him all in, like he was the sweetest juice on earth, and then pulled back up, wrapping my tongue around the head of his cock to lap up every single salty, tangy drop. He shuddered and groaned weakly.

He slouched back when he was sated, his eyes still shut. Looking up at him, I was still kneeling between his legs, giving a faint smile as I watched his chest sink and rise, his body working hard to catch breath.

He finally opened his eyes again to look at me. "How are you so good at that?" he asked, voice deeper, and I saw the dip between his eyebrows form, as if he were truly curious.

"You're not the first person I've done this with," I admitted.

"That guy your mother was telling me about..." He swallowed hard, one of his hands balling into a fist. "Him?"

I nodded. I didn't want to answer with words. I blushed just thinking about it—really about *Cane* thinking about it.

"When?" he asked, voice dry. He seemed agitated now.

"We used to do it after school sometimes."

Cane's frown deepened and then he leaned forward, coming nose-to-nose with me. He gripped my face between his fingers again, and his eyes fell to my mouth. "From now on, those lips will only go around my cock. Do you understand?"

I blinked rapidly, my breaths becoming shallow. Only for him? So that meant that he would want it again? My heart was dancing in my chest, but I pretended that his words didn't excite me.

"You can't tell me what to do, Cane," I muttered.

"I just did." He straightened in the seat. "You want to keep playing dirty, keep trying to get me to unfold for you? Fine. But that's all I will let you do. I'll let you suck my cock as much as you want to suck it. But only on *my* terms."

"Your terms?"

"Only when I say so. No more surprises like what you just did." He swallowed hard then, his throat bobbing. "I know whatever this is you feel for me won't last long, so I'll give you want you want as long as you keep quiet about it and save those lips for me."

He was jealous. That much was clear. Maybe my little back-stabbing trick *did* work.

"Understand?" he whispered on my lips.

I nodded. "I understand."

"Good girl." He stood up, and I slid back, pushing into a stand myself. He adjusted his briefs and then his pants. The whole time he fixed himself up, he was staring me in the face. "When we go to the beach, you won't be able to try what you just did. Your parents will always be around. They might notice, so do me a favor and don't try anything when we're there, okay?"

"Sure," I murmured. And just as I'd said that, I heard the garage door open. Mom and Dad were here. Luckily, Cane was all fixed up. He sat back down on the couch, and I followed his lead, focusing on the TV and pretending nothing had ever happened.

Before my parents walked in, though, Cane said something that I truly wasn't expecting.

"If you're still talking and hanging out with that *boy*, break it off with him." It was a demand, not a request. His face and tone was serious. I didn't say anything, just looked at him.

For one, it was too late to respond because the door was opening, and Mom was singing her "I'm home" song.

And two, because I knew that if I told him no, he wouldn't give me what I wanted, and all I really wanted was Cane, no matter how bad he was for me.

So I smiled and accepted it instead.

17

CANE

The beach trip to Destin was happening in two days, and I was mentally prepared. Physically? Not so much. I'd tried thinking about other things, but it was impossible, and all because I wasn't sure how my body would react with Kandy being around.

She was going to be in the same beach house with me for five whole days. Was I ready for that shit? Could I handle it? Seeing her in bathing suits, shorts that revealed too much leg, and crop tops? Skin, ass, and tits?

After what had happened in Derek and Mindy's living room, I couldn't get her out of my head to save my fucking life. Drinking at night during some of my free time, and even on flights around the country, didn't help. I thought it would help me escape the godawful shit I did, but it only intensified the urges—made the cravings vicious and demanding.

I couldn't get over the way she looked at me, like a good girl begging to be turned bad. She stared up with wide, brown eyes, and when her pouty lips sealed around my cock, I lost it.

I should have stopped her as soon as I saw her walking toward me, but having her on my lap felt good. Having her lips on mine was intoxicating...and extremely fucked up.

I was a complicated man, and she needed to know that. Even if I was several years younger and Kandy wasn't my best friend's daughter, I still wouldn't be the man she needed.

She thought I was a good person, but she had no idea who I really was. She only saw what was on the surface—Mr. Cane, her dad's friend. Anyone who was a friend of Derek's was supposed to be good because he was a good man, but I was nothing like him.

I'd done things—been through so much shit—that Derek would have arrested me for himself if he'd been around. He never would have let me set foot around his daughter. Though she knew what she wanted, she was still innocent—too innocent for me.

I'd had time to think about what I said to her that day in the living room, and I don't know what the hell came over me. Why did I tell her to only use her lips on me? I was being stupid, trapped in a thick, impenetrable moment—a moment that I was never going to forget.

"Mr. Cane," my secretary's voice cut through the speaker, interrupting my toxic thoughts.

I fixed my tie as if she were in the same room and could hear everything I was thinking. I cleared my throat before pressing the intercom button. "Yes, Cora?"

"Ms. Hugo is in the lobby with dinner. Would you like security to send her up?"

My throat worked hard at the mention of Kelly. Kelly Hugo. My...whatever she is to me. The woman I *should have* been thinking about, instead of an eighteen-year-old girl. Everyone considered Kelly my girlfriend, but I wasn't so sure I could call her that. We met up a maximum of two times per week. She liked me, and I fancied her but had never called her my girlfriend. She was more of a friend with benefits, if you will, and I suspected that she wanted more. I never knew how to respond to the "more" option, so instead I did what kept her content.

I pressed the speaker button. "Sure. Send her up." I pushed out of my chair, sliding my hands into my pockets as I walked toward the wide window.

It didn't take long for me to hear Kelly's voice. "How are you, Cora?" she greeted.

"I'm great, Ms. Hugo. I hope you are doing well. He's inside."

The door lightly creaked on its hinges when it opened, and I peered over my shoulder as Kelly came into the room. She was stunning. No, really. Absolutely fucking gorgeous.

Her skin was tan and flawless, her legs as smooth as silk. She had her hair tied up in a tight bun and was wearing a sky-blue dress that made her skin appear a little darker. She'd always bragged about how she didn't need to tan much—that she had a natural glow, thanks to her mother falling in love with her Latino father.

She had a Bobby's Steakhouse paper bag in her hands, the dinner tucked away inside it. I could smell it from where I stood. Her eyes lit up when she spotted me. As soon as she placed the bag on top of my desk, she rushed my way. I turned and she walked right into my arms before I could fully open them, kissing me softly on the lips.

"So nice to finally see you," she sighed.

"I could say the same." I smiled down at her. Though she didn't have to while wearing heels, she pushed up on her toes anyway, and gave me another peck on the lips.

I didn't give much effort—couldn't, really. My mind was somewhere else, thinking about some fucked-up shit. As if she noticed, her brows drew together, and she gripped my shoulders, putting a little distance between us.

"What's wrong?" she asked, squeezing my shoulders. "You feel tense, Quinton."

"Just…work stress. The usual."

I pulled back, capping her shoulder once before heading for the desk. "What'd you decide to get?"

She turned and smiled, as if she'd just remembered the food.

She picked the bag up from the desk and took it to the two-top table in the corner of the room.

Getting the table was her idea. She'd claimed that she didn't get to see me enough, and since we only really met up for rare lunches and dinners outside of work, she got the table so I couldn't make excuses about eating on my $5,000 desk. Since I couldn't always come to her, she decided to come to me.

"I got the T-bone steak you love," she announced, "along with the sweet potato casserole, steamed broccoli, and asparagus for sides." She wasted no time taking the food out of the bags. Normally, seeing Kelly dressed like this—in short dresses and high heels that showed off her legs—made me want to stop her from doing whatever she was doing, bend her over the table, and fuck her.

But not tonight.

Tonight I wasn't in my element. To be honest, I hadn't really thought much about touching Kelly since the shit that happened with Kandy in the living room.

I couldn't bear touching her because I knew as soon as I was inside her, I would imagine Kandy. I would probably say her name by accident. With that girl on my mind and around me, my self-control always seemed to vanish, and trust me, that was really fucking rare.

Kandy. Kandy. Kandy. Fucking Kandy.

She was driving me crazy and wasn't even around me. I was always calm and collected—it was the reason I was in that expensive building I owned, with over five hundred employees. Being in control was what I knew best. Perhaps that was the reason Kandy intrigued me so much.

I'd been reckless before. I'd done a lot of crazy shit without thinking twice about it. I thought I had grown out of that habit, but apparently I still wanted a taste of the risk. Living on edge. Stepping out of line and breaking the rules had always given me an undeniable rush.

Kandy tested my control and broke the rules with me constantly. She knew how to push my buttons and get under my skin. She was probably the only person that could see right through my calm and collected bullshit and see me for who I really was.

"Quinton?" Kelly called. I looked up, and she was frowning. She walked my way. "What is going on inside that head of yours?" She tried to sound playful, sweet, but I could hear the concern deep in her voice.

I forced a smile and shook my head. "It's nothing. I'm fine." Even with Kelly, I pretended to be a good man. To everyone, I was a good man, but if they knew about the turmoil inside me—the chaos and darkness that was a constant threat—they would have thought otherwise.

"Come on," Kelly said, grabbing my hand and leading me to the table. "You just need some good food and great wine to pull you out of that funk." She pulled out a bottle of Tempt's finest wine, and I smiled as she did.

Kelly was a good woman.

A great woman, actually.

She deserved better than me too. Truthfully, I had no idea how we were still seeing each other. I didn't give her my all. There were days when I would get so caught up with work that I'd forget to text or call her, but she never complained.

Perhaps she understood. She grew up with wealthy parents. She never had to worry about a thing as a child, but she did tell me often how she wished her parents had spent more time with her.

Our childhoods were completely different. I didn't talk about mine much with her, or anyone for that matter. The only person who knew much about my family was Derek, and that's only because he was there the night he saved my mother and had caught a glimpse of the hell I'd been through. After seeing that, I really didn't have much of a choice but to tell him a few things about myself.

I was too dark for a person like Kelly—a person who always seemed to exude a bright, warm aura. Kandy may have been right when she said Kelly and I didn't make a good match, but Kelly was a ray of light in my darkness, and maybe it was that light that made me want to hold onto her.

Any light I could find, I held onto it. Derek and his family were a light. My sister was a light, but lately I hadn't had much of her glow. I needed light so I wouldn't lose my mind. I was trapped in darkness for a long time—surrounded by it. Suffocated by it.

I knew by this time that I was stringing Kelly along. Sometimes I felt like she knew it too and was just waiting for me to break it off or talk about it. Sometimes my stress would be so high that I wouldn't want to be bothered. She'd show up at the wrong time, and I'd tell her to leave—and not gently—yet she still stuck around, waiting for me. *Wanting me.*

I admit I was an asshole.

I wasn't fair, but Kelly didn't care that I was an asshole.

Kandy didn't care.

And my best friend? Derek? He definitely didn't care either. He kept me in his life anyway, loved me anyway, and I had betrayed him.

"So, you're gonna spend five days away from me, huh?" I picked my head up as Kelly bit into a piece of asparagus. I didn't even realize she'd topped our plates with food.

"Just a small vacation with Derek. We haven't hung out in a while. Visiting his place doesn't really count, so I figured it'd be fun to get away."

"You know, I could always come and spend a little more time with Mindy. She's a great person and spending five days with her could really help me get to know her."

Here we go. She was doing this again—tossing hints at me, trying to get me to invite her to go on vacation with me.

At first I thought it would be a good idea. Kelly would be my distraction and one hell of a reason to stay away from Kandy, since Kelly loved to be all over me. But then I thought about Kandy and how pissed she would be if Kelly tagged along. I'd told her she wouldn't be there, and Kandy always held me to my word.

Mindy had asked about me bringing Kelly, but I wasn't up for it. Kelly and I were just a *thing*. It started as a fling and grew into… something else. I couldn't quite explain it. We connected about something deep and it took off from there. We were on the border of a relationship, but not quite there yet, even after several months.

We'd spend the night at each other's houses every so often, catch some food when I had free space in my schedule, but vacationing was different. I hadn't been on a vacation with a woman outside of family before, and I wasn't planning on starting now. I kind of wished I hadn't brought her to meet D and the family. Things were moving too quickly with her and I blame myself for it. She begged to know what I did outside of work and whom I hung out with, so I brought her with me to meet them. I should have waited a bit longer.

"I take that as a no," she murmured through a tight smile. She sipped her wine to ease the pain.

"No, Kelly, it's not that. It's just…I can't explain it. Derek and his family hold a special place in my heart. You know that I'm very private with them. They asked me to go, and I'd hate to step on their toes by bringing someone along. They had plans—bought a certain amount of tickets for events happening there. Kind of like a family thing, you know?"

"I see." She was not pleased with my answer.

I bit off a piece of asparagus. "I'll take you to dinner when I get back," I promised.

"We always have dinner, Quinton. Always. It's starting to become tiresome. I feel like we should be moving forward. I'm sure Derek and Mindy will understand, and I don't mind skipping out on the events you guys attend and staying at the beach house until you get back."

"Kelly," I warned.

"No. Don't *Kelly* me, Quinton. I'm serious." Her face revealed that. She reached across the table to place her hand on top of mine and softened her features. "I know you have a hard time opening up. I get that, I really do. You like to spend most of your time alone because being alone and doing things by yourself is all you've ever known, but I'm here for you, Quinton. I want to do things with you. I want to get to know you better. Work always gets in the way, but this vacation would be the perfect opportunity for us to be together for as long as we want without being interrupted by phone calls and emails and everything else. We could really get to know each other there—see if we should take this up a level or if we should keep it where it is."

I swallowed hard.

Fuck. She had me by the balls.

All I could think about in that moment was how pissed Kandy would be once she saw Kelly tagging along with me. I wished it hadn't come to this—to the point where I'd offend Kandy by bringing Kelly around at all. At first it was harmless—just a simple crush, and I knew that—but then it became bigger. That crush led to ogling and deep stares. Then deep stares to heavy breathing. Then heavy breathing to kissing, sucking, and heavy finger-fucking. It was too much for even myself to handle, and I'd dealt with a lot of shit.

But this was different.

I wasn't supposed to want Kandy. I wasn't supposed to touch her or tell her to only use her lips on me, no matter how tempting they were and no matter how angry it made me that she'd used them on someone else. I wanted to rip a motherfucker in half when I found out she'd been touched and used, but how could I? She wasn't mine—could never be mine—and I knew that.

The woman I was supposed to be with was sitting right across from me, begging me to give her this one thing. After treating her like shit, forgetting dates and always cancelling on her at the last minute, this was the least I could do. Seriously, it was. I owed Kelly more than she received. A part of me wanted to please her, even if I didn't take whatever this was too seriously. She was good to me.

Mindy was dying to have Kelly go.

My friends mattered to me.

Kandy mattered to me too, but her crush, I hoped, would pass one day soon. I hoped she would forget about what had happened in my den and in her parents' living room.

I was going to have to make it clear that I was a fucking fool, and that I was never going to let it happen again. She was a young girl. She had plenty of time to find someone else and get over me.

I needed a companion, someone who understood me, no matter how much I knew I didn't deserve her. I knew who that companion was, so I grabbed Kelly's hand and said, "I'll consider it."

18

KANDY

When Dad told me we were taking a private jet to Florida, I thought I was going to die of excitement. He'd said the jet was Cane's, and that Cane was more than happy to give us a ride down there with him instead of letting us drive for five and a half long hours.

Dad put up a small fuss, saying he didn't want us to get in the way of his flight, but both Mom and I told him to shut it and be grateful. His best friend was rich enough to give us a ride on a private, fully accommodated jet. Who in their right mind would turn that down? Dad would, because he hated feeling like he was in the way or being a bother.

Since Clay had summer camp for his college, and Frankie wouldn't be going to UNC for another two months, she'd decided to tag along with me for the trip.

Mom and Dad were fine with her joining us. They didn't want me to be bored, being the only teenager in the house and all. They kept saying I'd be surrounded by adults and "adult talk," like I was still a child or something.

In my opinion, eighteen was old enough to be taken seriously enough for most people, but apparently not my parents. They were afraid to even argue around me, and don't get me started on the swearing.

Dad treated me like a delicate little flower that always needed to be showered with love and affection, and Mom was close to being the same way, though she knew when to give me space.

I had been waiting for this trip to Destin for quite some time now. I knew my parents would spend a lot of time together and even go out, and Cane would be at the beach house by himself. It was the perfect opportunity to get to know him a little better.

We pulled up to the private runway in Dad's truck, Frankie bouncing beside me and trying to hold back a squeal.

"I can't believe this!" She slid closer to the window, staring ahead as we got closer to the jet. It was white, and on the side of it, printed in red, was the word Tempt. Yep, that was definitely Cane's.

I looked around for him but didn't see any cars. Just a man with a pilot's hat and suit on, and another wearing an orange vest with a gas pump in his hand.

"You guys are lucky to have a friend so rich. Seriously. Who can say their best friend has given them a ride on a private jet to go on vacation? The best thing my best friend ever did was give me a big pink teddy bear named Pinx."

I gave Frankie a nudge to the rib with my elbow as Mom and Dad laughed up front. "You are such a dork," I laughed.

Frankie smirked. "But you love me."

Dad parked the car not too far away from the jet and let out a hard sigh. "Well, we're here."

I grabbed the door handle. "Come on, let me out. I want to see that thing up close."

"Okay, but don't get too close. Looks like they're still handling some important stuff." Dad hit the button to unlock the doors and both Frankie and I burst out like prisoners who'd been freed from prison, rushing around the SUV to get a better look.

The jet had already been started, and the engine was loud.

Actually, the entire strip was loud. There were several other jets in various colors on the runway, parked beneath the bold Georgia sun. Some were even flying in.

The sound of tires rolling across gravel caught my ears, and I turned my head to look back, spotting a white Mercedes pulling up close to us. I couldn't see who was driving. Through the window I could tell he was sporting a black hat. He stepped out of the car wearing a black suit and tie, bobbed his head at us, and then went for the back door.

"Who is that?" Frankie asked. As she did, Dad was getting out of the car, grunting a bit when he had to put a little weight on his bad leg.

The driver pulled the back door open, and Cane stepped out. His presence gave me chills, despite the blazing temperature. My core tightened, and my lips pressed flat as I took him all in.

He wore aviator sunglasses over his eyes, a button-down shirt rolled up to his elbows, and khaki slacks. The ink on his arms seemed to stand out even more, a stark contrast against the whitest shirt I'd ever laid eyes on. His hair had been trimmed neatly, the soft fade on the edges leading up to hair that'd been fingered into waves with gel.

"Holy shit," Frankie whispered under her breath.

Holy shit was right. Cane looked fucking amazing. Even going on vacation, he was hot. He exuded confidence, the sex appeal gushing right out of his pores.

I realized I was staring at him like an idiot as he came closer, so I dropped my head, but of course Frankie kept gawking. She'd only seen him in person once, but not this close up.

"Cane," Dad greeted with a hearty chuckle. They did their silly, manly handshake and then gave each other a brotherly hug before pulling away.

"How are you feeling, D?" Cane asked, and Dad let off a simple shrug.

"I'm about to get on a private jet to go on a very relaxing vacation with my family. Can't get any better than that, man."

Cane chuckled. "I hear that."

Mom walked around the front of the truck and gave Cane a hug around the shoulders. "You look great, as always, Cane."

"Thank you, Mindy. And you look very relaxed," Cane noted. "The linen pants suit you well."

Mom smiled, the same smile she always wore when she knew she'd chosen well. "Thank you. Figured I'd break them in for the upcoming week."

The driver walked to the other side of the car and opened the other back door. I assumed he was getting Cane's luggage and some other things, but a sandal appeared, and then a head with brown hair popped up.

Her body lifted in one smooth motion as she accepted the driver's hand and thanked him for his assistance, and when the door was closed, my fluttering heart came to a standstill.

My breathing faltered.

"Who is she?" Frankie asked, looking Kelly up and down.

Kelly? But he said he wasn't bringing her...

At first I assumed she was just seeing him off, but when the driver headed for the trunk and took out suitcases, some of them pink, some of them Tiffany blue—only colors Kelly would pick—the truth hit me.

Kelly was coming on vacation with us.

With Cane.

Sharing a room with him.

I blinked hard before finally putting my eyes on Cane. Mom and Dad were talking, and his eyes shifted over to me. It was a very, very brief look, but I saw the apology in his eyes. He didn't even have to say anything. It was abundantly clear.

I could practically hear him thinking it: *This wasn't my plan. It just happened. I'm sorry.*

"Oh, Kelly!" Mom squealed, as if she'd just realized Kelly was around.

"Mindy! Oh, look at you! You look great!"

They squealed like middle school girls, and I wanted to fucking vomit. Not only had Kelly wedged her way between Cane and me, but now she was winning Mom over. Before I knew it, they were going to be best fucking friends, and she'd be in my face all the time.

Dad went for the trunk and started to unload. I decided to help him. I couldn't look at Kelly or Cane for too much longer.

"Who is that chick?" Frankie asked over my shoulder, following after me.

"Nobody," I muttered.

"She's clearly somebody," she guffawed.

I grabbed the handle of my suitcase and turned rapidly, bumping right into someone's chest.

Cane's chest.

A soft gasp tumbled out of me, and even though I was livid—broiling inside with frustration and an edge of fury—I couldn't deny my body's reaction to him. My nipples stiffened, almost to the point of being uncomfortable. My eyelashes fluttered, and my mouth went bone-dry as I found his eyes.

"Kandy," Cane murmured. "Let me take that for you."

"No," I said tightly. "I've got it. How about you help your *girlfriend* instead."

I pushed past him with my shoulder, not giving a damn if Mom or Dad saw. They could assume I was being rude for all I cared. Mom would apologize for me like she always did, and Dad would just laugh about it and call it hormones.

I didn't care. I wasn't in the mood for his bullshit. He lied to me. He told me she wasn't coming. In that moment, I was being a spoiled brat and I knew it, but I couldn't shake the feelings inside me. In my head, Cane was mine. Not Kelly's. Mine. How could he not see how much this was killing me inside?

I leaned against the truck, my suitcase on one side of me and Frankie on the other, as we watched Cane talk to the pilot and a woman who I assumed was a flight attendant. They bobbed their heads as he spoke, paying very close attention to whatever he was saying.

"We can start boarding now," Cane announced when he came back our way. Mom and Kelly had been mindlessly chatting about things to do in Destin, and where to catch drinks, and how they heard the water is *so beautiful*. Frankie was quiet next to me, like she'd sensed my sudden change of mood and didn't want to bother me.

The only thing was...I didn't know if I wanted to open up about it. I hadn't told Frankie—or anyone—what Cane and I had done. Frankie knew I liked him, but that was it. We had two hookups, and I had to pretend they'd never happened for the sake of his friendship with my dad and for myself, period.

Frankie...well, in a way, she looked up to me. She would never admit it, but she always came to me for guidance and advice and always wished that her mom was into her as much as mine was into me. I didn't want that to be ruined because of my drug of choice, Mr. Cane. I was very, *very* addicted to that man.

As we got on board and picked our seats, Kelly said, "Kandy, I love your dress! You look very pretty."

I tried so hard not to roll my eyes. I hated when she talked to me like I was ten. I didn't need her to tell me I was pretty. By eighteen, I knew how I looked. I had my insecurities, like every other girl, as well as my flaws, but I wholeheartedly knew I wasn't ugly.

I'd purposely worn my favorite peach dress that hugged my waist and stopped really high on my thighs. Dad hated this dress, but since it was our vacation, he was giving me a pass. While on vacation it was okay to show a little skin, but wearing it out—say to school, a party, or to a boy's house—would have given him a serious heart attack.

"Thanks," I mumbled.

I took the seats that were diagonally across from Mom and Dad. Kelly took the seats across from theirs. There was a lot of open space between the rows, so we had plenty of leg room, and also enough space between us where Frankie and I could chat without really being heard.

Dad was pleased about all the space. He sighed loudly, stretched his legs as far as they could go, and said, "Oh, yeah. That's what I'm talking about."

"We all set?" Cane asked when he boarded the jet. He looked at Mom and Dad. He was avoiding eye contact with me, that much was clear.

"All set, man. Ready when you are," said Dad.

"Want some water or anything before we take off?" Cane offered.

"Nah. I'll save my drinking for the beach. Destin isn't ready for this liver." Dad beat his chest lightly, like an arrogant college frat boy would after chugging beer from a keg.

Mom gave him a look out the corner of her eye and then shook her head with a smile at Cane, who returned a shrug and a half smile. Frankie laughed and pulled a magazine from her bag.

I took out the romance book from my tote bag and started reading, but I didn't miss Cane take the seat beside Kelly. *Of course he'd sit there, because where else would he sit?*

Kelly smiled at him, rubbed his arm, and murmured something in his ear that made him smirk.

I rolled my eyes. I wasn't sure if was going to be able to deal with that for five whole days. Seeing Cane and Kelly all over each other was going to make my stomach hurt.

During the flight, I became more and more confused. Why would he tell me to save my lips for him if all he was going to do was shove Kelly in my face every chance he got?

I didn't get it. I wanted him to be straight-up, honest, and blunt like he normally was, but right now he was being a very selfish and confusing asshole.

19

KANDY

"I just don't understand why he brought her with him." I yanked on the zipper of my suitcase with a huff.

We'd landed in Destin over an hour ago. Cane had a Mercedes van waiting for us when we arrived.

We made a trip to the property management office to collect the keys for the property, stopped by a popular smoothie shop (where Cane paid for everyone's drinks), and were now at the beach house.

I was sharing a room with Frankie in the loft. The loft was located on the top floor of the three-story beach house. It was pretty much like having our own apartment. There was even a kitchenette if we wanted to make something quick. Other than the pool and the beach, there was really no need for us to even go downstairs.

Cane and Kelly were on the second floor, and I silently prayed Kelly would be modest enough to sleep in her own bedroom and not share one with him, but I knew that wasn't going to happen. I could hear Kelly giggling and fawning over the view from their room when Cane brought their luggage in.

Mom and Dad were on the first floor in the master bedroom,

and Mom was very pleased that their balcony led straight out to a private deck that gave an amazing view of the beach.

"What's the big deal?" Frankie sat on the queen bed across from mine, studying her cuticles. "She's his girlfriend, Kandy. You can like him, but he still has a life outside of your crush."

Frankie, Frankie, Frankie. She just didn't get it, and she never would, because only I knew the truth.

"Yeah, but he knows about my crush. It's like he doesn't even give a shit how I feel." I sighed, agitated. "It's just…this is a family thing, you know? She's not family." I took out a folded skirt and placed it on the bed.

"Well, neither am I." Frankie cocked a brow and crossed her arms, challenging me, probably expecting me to make up for that statement.

"Frankie, you've been my best friend since I was five years old. You've practically spent half of your life in my house. Some of your bras are in my panty drawer. Trust me, you're family."

"Eh, I guess that's true, but come on, K.J.! Get real! You can't expect someone like him to stay single forever!"

"I know, Frank! I know!" I gave up on unpacking, plopping down on my bed instead and crossing my legs. "Am I being imma-ture about it?"

"You really are," she laughed. "Just think about it. We're in fucking Destin. I saw, like, five hot guys jogging at the beach just now and don't even get me started on the college boys that were at that smoothie shop." She stood up and started walking my way. "There are plenty of fish in the sea. Mr. Cane is hot as hell and all, but there's plenty more out there to look at and even do things with. Guys who are closer to our age and easier to bag." Grabbing my hands, she forced me to stand and then capped my shoulders. "Get over your crush with him. He's a grown man with a life and lots of fucking money. His girlfriend is here, but so what? Doesn't mean we can't still watch him swim shirtless."

I laughed at that. "I'm pretty sure Cane won't be swimming."

"Whatever. If he's on vacation and doesn't take his shirt off at least once, he's better off being coddled by that Goody-Two-shoes Kelly."

Frankie and I spent the rest of our day sunbathing on the beach. It was the perfect day, breezy and blue. The sky was clear of clouds, the sun shining from the perfect angle. The heat of it was gentle enough on our skin for us to soak up the rays for over two hours.

By the time we'd finished tanning and taking thousands of pictures in our bikinis to upload to Facebook and Instagram, the sun was starting to set. I grabbed my towel and the beach bag and followed Frankie to the exit.

We took a short, private trail that led to our beach house and made a pit stop at the outside showers. Frankie finished rinsing before I did, and after announcing that she was making use of the hot water first, she dashed for the house, leaving her towel behind.

My hair was kinkier than Frankie's, so it took me a while to get most of the sand out of it.

As the water streamed over me, I got the oddest sensation of being watched. I turned away from the showerhead and looked toward the house. I scanned the pool area and then the balconies. I didn't see anyone at first, but then I saw a bright orange flicker.

Fire.

I watched the flicker dissolve into a glowing orange light. Smoke fizzled up behind the cigarette, and behind the stick was Cane.

He inhaled twice, his eyes trained on me. I had the urge to turn away from him, focus on getting the sand out of my hair and from under my breasts, but instead I took the liberty of washing off in front of him.

His eyes sparked from the illuminated end of his cigarette and the pool lights. He took several drags from it, like his life depended on it, as I ran my hands over my breasts and then under the hem of my bikini top to wash the sand away.

My nipples stiffened beneath my top, my stomach contracting as I stifled a few breaths. The water was getting colder, but it didn't matter. I felt like a fool doing it, but something told me by the blazing hot look in his eyes that I looked good to him. Very good.

My hand skimmed over my belly and then my pelvis. Cane took another drag from his cigarette before putting it out. I watched him as he watched me. Tendrils of smoke drifted out of his nostrils, wisps of it running through his supple lips.

Then I remembered something.

I was supposed to be upset with him. Despite being upset, I still wanted to please him. Turn him on. See if I could get a rise out of him. Knowing I could still do all those things, even with Kelly around, made me stop before dipping my fingers beneath my bottoms to touch myself.

Cane jerked his head away too and looked over his shoulder. As he did, I noticed Kelly stepping outside to meet up with him. She was dressed in a black, one-piece bathing suit, her hair damp like she'd taken a swim a short while ago. I wondered right away if Cane had watched her swim. If he noticed the water trickling between her breasts, which were bigger than mine, and over her lips as she surfaced.

My heart pounded a little harder. I shut off the shower and picked up my bag, hurrying for the door. I could still feel him watching me.

I had to go through the kitchen and living room to reach the stairs. I wanted to run straight up to our floor without bumping into anyone, but I didn't make it far. Mom was sitting in the recliner, and she took a peek over the lid of her laptop when I crossed the room.

"Oh, there you are." She smiled and lowered the screen of her laptop, like she was glad to see me. "How was the beach, sweetie? I see you got a tan."

I nodded, looking myself over. I saw a bit of un-tanned skin was revealed at my waist, where I'd almost lowered my bottoms for Cane. The rest of my skin was golden brown, bronze almost. "Yeah, I did. It was nice. Me and Frank took a lot of pictures."

"That's good. I already told Frankie, but Cane is being nice enough to treat us to dinner tonight. We're eating out and should be ready to go in an hour or so. Dress nice, but don't overdo it." She looked at me over her thin-framed glasses, and for a moment I panicked. I felt exposed, like she knew all of my deepest darkest secrets—my fantasies and lust with Cane. Did she know? Had she found my journals and read them? Did she snoop on my laptop? No, she couldn't have. She wasn't *that* kind of mom. She believed in privacy and confidentiality. "You know what I mean by that, right?" she asked as I met up to the staircase with a rapid heartbeat.

"What *do* you mean?" I asked, trying to keep my voice steady.

"Don't give your dad a heart attack by wearing anything too revealing," she answered with spunk in her voice, like I should have known the answer all along. Duh, I should have known that. She said it to me all the time.

"Oh, yeah! Right!" I looked around with a tight smile. "Where is Dad anyway?"

"He went out for beer." She rolled her eyes, and I knew that eye roll. They'd probably talked about the beer, like how it could wait until after we went out, or how he didn't need to drink too much on the first night. Something along those lines. "He'll be back soon so hurry and get dressed."

I nodded, taking the stairs by twos after that. When I reached the second floor, I couldn't help looking to the right. Cane's bedroom door was open, and only a few steps away. I wanted to walk by and see what was going on, but I wasn't strong enough. For all I knew, they could have been making out on the bed. Or worse, he could have been finger-fucking her until she came, just like he did to me. He obviously had some practice at it.

I made it up to my room, showered, did my makeup, and got dressed quickly. After helping Frankie with the zipper of her floral dress, we were headed down the two flights of stairs to join everyone.

When we made it to the living room, I spotted Cane standing by the front door with his phone in hand, and Kelly sitting on the loveseat next to Mom, who'd finally gotten rid of her laptop and had changed into a royal blue jumpsuit.

"Oh, girls. Good. You're ready." Mom shot to a stand and Kelly gracefully unfolded, smiling at us. "We should get going. Your dad's waiting outside, and we don't want to be late for our reservation."

"Reservation? Sounds fancy already," Frankie said with a small shimmy of her shoulders.

I reached the door where Cane was still standing. He looked great in his sky-blue button-down shirt and black dress pants. His hair was styled just the same, and even passing by, I could smell his cologne.

He slid his phone into his back pocket, locking eyes with me for a fleeting moment before bouncing them over me.

I didn't have to look to know he'd given his attention to Kelly.

20

CANE

As long as I don't look at her, I'll be fine.

That's what I kept telling myself, but it was a fucking lie. Why couldn't I get over this girl? Kelly was on a trip with me, looking beautiful as hell. For dinner, she wore a tight red dress and tall red heels, her hair styled in an elegant updo. She looked amazing, yet I was focused more on the eighteen-year-old wearing the little black dress and sandals instead.

They were polar opposites—Kandy and Kelly. Kelly was sophisticated and neat and classy. Kandy had her classy, neat moments, but she was far from sophisticated. She was reckless, wild. She was everything I shouldn't have wanted, yet I craved every single inch of her anyway. She didn't mold her way into society. She was her own person. That reckless spirit of hers was trouble, but it was so familiar to me. She reminded me of myself when I was her age.

Seeing her out by the showers rinsing the sand away surprised the hell out of me. She put on a show—she knew I was watching and that I wouldn't look away—*couldn't* look away. She had me under her spell, and I was certain that if Kelly hadn't been on that trip with me, she'd have snuck to my room just to suck my cock again right after. I had no doubt whatsoever, and that thought alone made my cock throb and ache.

Dinner was held at a beachfront restaurant. The girls loved it, raving over the view. The sky had transitioned and was tinted with pinks, blues, oranges, and splashes of purple. It was like nothing any of them had ever seen before, so of course, like girls their age do, they took a thousand pictures on their phones until they got the right one. I'd always loved the sunsets in Florida. They always relaxed me.

I did my best to occupy myself with sports talk with Derek, talking about anything and everything in hopes of avoiding a conversation that included Kandy or even Kelly. I got the sense that Kelly knew something was wrong with me. She rubbed my arm or leg too many times and asked if I was okay way too many times to count.

She wanted to get to know me so badly, but if she knew what I was really thinking about, she would have been running the other direction.

"You're really chugging those beers down, honey," Mindy said to Derek as he took a hard swig from his fourth beer.

"It's a good thing I'm not driving then," Derek laughed, and Mindy looked a little on edge. Her eyes flashed over to meet mine, and I knew that look. Knew it all too well.

See, I wasn't the only person at that table with secrets. Derek had a lot of them too, and normally he did his best to hide them, but for some reason, he wasn't that day.

I took Mindy's looks as my signal to set him straight. "D, how about we go for a little walk, man?" I asked, pushing back in my chair. I focused on Mindy. "If you've got room, feel free to order some dessert for yourself and the girls."

"Oh, Cane. Seriously. You're being too good to us. Dinner was enough. Thank you, though."

"Uh—what?" Kandy's friend exclaimed. I think her name was Frankie. Well, I assumed she was, seeing as Kandy had told me before that she had a best friend. Kandy didn't exactly introduce us when we showed up at the runway—not that I expected her to. The death stare she gave me was more than enough for me to understand she didn't want to be fucked with at the moment. "I'm sorry, Mrs. Jennings, but I never, *ever* deny dessert!"

Kandy giggled.

Mindy laughed. "Well, what would you like, Frankie?"

"The chocolate-caramel cheesecake will do." Frankie looked at me, batted her eyelashes, and put on a bright, wide smile. "I'll eat every bite, Mr. Cane. I promise."

I bobbed my head with a smirk and followed Derek to the gate that was only a few steps away. He was quiet for a few seconds. He knew what this was about. All three of us knew—Derek, myself, and Mindy.

"She's overreacting," he said before we could make it down the second set of stairs.

"After seeing you have four beers in less than an hour, I wouldn't call that overreacting. I'd call that being careful."

"Nah." Derek sighed and stopped, focused on the ocean. I looked with him, watching the tide come in, the waves crashing to shore. The water was darker beneath the multi-colored sky. Perfection. "I'm years past what I was, Cane. You know I am."

"You are, but as your best friend, I have to be honest with you." I put my focus on him again, taking a step back. "Ever since the shooting, you've been drinking more. Mindy has mentioned it to me a few times because she's worried. At first she was understanding. She felt you needed a drink or two after you recovered, just to feel like yourself again, but you went from buying a pack of beer once or twice a month, to buying one every other day, D. You're spiraling. You need to talk to someone."

"What?" he snapped. "I'm talking to you, ain't I?" He gave me a serious glare, his throat bobbing. He was revealing his defensive side. I knew all about that side, too. It was rooted deep—the part of him that wasn't proper or well-spoken. His Georgia accent only showed when he was angry, agitated, or fed up. "I don't need a fucking shrink, man. I'm good."

"You're not good. You're drinking to escape. Plus there's nothing wrong with seeing a shrink." I peered over my shoulder. Kelly had taken Mindy to the bar for drinks. Kandy and Frankie were showing each other their phones, most likely gossiping. "Look at your girls, D. They count on you. This vacation isn't just about you. It's your chance to heal and bond—to forget about that shit and live a little with your family, you know?"

Derek scoffed. "I don't expect you to understand, Cane. You're the fucking CEO of a million-dollar company—"

"A company I built from the ground up," I added, cocking a brow. "A company that I sacrificed everything for."

"I know. Shit, I know. I didn't mean it like that. It's just...being a cop is rough," he continued. "I love my job, I truly do. Since I was a boy, I always knew I wanted to be a good guy. The kind that helped people and saved them, you know? I mean, we're supposed to be the good guys—the ones the world is supposed to trust. But most of us get such a bad rep now because of a few fuck-ups who are way too trigger-happy." He stopped talking for a moment, giving me a sideways glance. "Fuck, I can't believe I'm about to tell you this. I haven't even told Mindy about it," he mumbled.

"Told her what?"

"Why that guy really shot me that night."

"Why did he?"

"Because I was black." Derek scratched at the scar on his neck, as if he could still feel the pain, remember the burn of its graze as it passed by. "The guy was high as hell. I don't know what he was on—probably meth or some shit. His daughter was on the front lawn when I arrived, and she had bruises all over her body and blood was between her legs. She wasn't breathing, so I tried to help her—give her CPR or something. Her dad was yelling at me the whole time and kept telling me to back off, that he didn't want me on his property. Calling me a boy, shit like that. I couldn't keep an eye on the girl and him, and that's probably where I fucked up. I should have been watching him. Before I knew it, he'd pulled a gun on me. Told me he'd be damned if he let a *nigger* put his mouth on his daughter—that he'd rather her die than be tainted by someone like me."

"Damn, D. *Shit*—I'm so sorry, man." I didn't even know what to say to that. Fuck, what could I possibly say?

"I ran toward the car, but he got my neck. My thigh. But the bullet wounds aren't what hurt the most. It was his words. They brought back memories, for sure," he said through a painful laugh. "Really bad ones." He scratched his head.

I knew all about the memories. Derek was abused as a child. His mom married a man who was, inexplicably, a bigot. Derek's birth father was black and had died when he was two. I'd seen pictures of his mom, and she was a beautiful biracial woman, but her skin was fair and many shades lighter than Derek's.

His stepfather was white, and didn't bother hiding his distaste for his *black* stepson. That word he'd just used? His stepfather would call him that repeatedly. He would tell him he *owned* him, and that he would never amount to anything in his life.

His mother knew nothing of it. She loved the man, and Derek wanted her to be happy. Unfortunately, she died when he was sixteen. She was a pretty wealthy woman, a jewelry store owner, but nothing was left for Derek when she passed away. His stepfather took everything and didn't look back, which put Derek in an orphanage for four months until he got in touch with his father's brother and moved in with him. Derek hadn't heard from his stepdad since.

"Fuck, I'm sorry about that. I really am. Like you said, the man was high. And luckily back-up came, right?" I asked. "He's locked up. He can't spread that hate around and poison the good people."

"His daughter died, Cane. If I'd been on my toes and reacted the right way, she'd probably still be alive, you know? It would have been wrong cause he hadn't touched me yet, but I could have arrested him or something while I helped her. I could have done anything, man."

"You can't blame yourself for that, D. You were shot, man. You said yourself that you should have been watching him. You can't carry that guilt around. It'll eat you alive." I blew a breath. After hearing that, I needed a fucking cigarette. Hell, even a hard drink. I grabbed his shoulder. "Look, when we get back to the house, I'll pour you a shot of my favorite bourbon. Just one, though."

He laughed, but it was painful and forced, and his eyes were still sad and distant. "Two, and I'll call it a night."

"All right, two. But promise you won't go crazy with the drinking. We're on vacation, so I get it. But Mindy's worried about you. You'll have to tell her what's going on with you eventually, D. She's your wife. She deserves to know what's going on inside your head more than anyone."

"You're right," he sighed. "You're right. I'll tell her eventually. I just don't want her overreacting or pushing for the guy to get brought up on hate crime charges in addition to everything else. It makes me look weak."

I laughed, and then clapped his shoulder, catching his eyes. "You're good, though, right?"

"Yeah," he said, shrugging lightly. "I'm good." He put his focus on the ocean again. "This was what I needed. To get away from it all. To not have to be *Officer Jennings*, but just a husband, a father, and a friend. Not only that, but I'm a lucky man. I can still work. I recovered well and wasn't trapped behind a desk or on disability."

"That's right." I dropped my hand and watched the rippling water with him. I couldn't ignore the twitch of pain in my chest, though. My best friend was going through something, and I had been too worried about having his daughter wrapped up around me to notice.

What the fuck was wrong with me? It was clear he needed me. I had to be there for him, like he was there for me all those years ago.

I glanced over my shoulder and found Kandy's eyes. She was standing now. She'd just finished taking a picture with Frankie in front of the sunset. She turned to look at us, and her smile fizzled, but still lingered at the corners of her mouth when her eyes swung over to lock with mine.

It killed me to do it, but I pulled away, and made a promise to myself to pull my shit together. Not just for Derek's sake, but for Kandy's, too.

21

CANE

"What was the whole walk with Derek about?" Kelly was lying flat on her back on the bed, staring up at the ceiling fan.

She'd had a few martinis with Mindy at the restaurant and planned on drinking a little more with her by the pool after they changed clothes and got comfortable. I could tell she was wiped out and was only doing it to get closer to Mindy. Kelly always tried too hard to please everyone, even if it meant stepping out of her comfort zone.

I unfastened my cufflinks, and then unbuttoned the first two buttons of my shirt. "Nothing important," I mumbled.

"Really? Nothing important? 'Cause it seems to me that Derek has a little trouble with alcohol. Mindy said he's hard to handle when he drinks, which leads me to believe either he can't handle his liquor or he's got a drinking problem."

"Kelly, I'm not in a position to talk about it, so I suggest you let it go."

She released a light scoff. Through the mirror, I saw her sit up, stand, and walk to the closet. She pulled down a cotton dress and made a noise, like she had more to say. "You know, the whole point of me joining you for this vacation was so we could get to know each other better. Talk to each other a little more," she noted.

"I remember."

"So...why can't you talk to me about what happens in your life?" she asked with a slight dig to her voice. "I never knew Derek had a drinking problem and never would have guessed it, either."

"Because it's not your business, Kelly, and that's not *my* life, it's his." I put my focus on her, and by her shocked expression, it was clear I'd hurt her feelings. She dropped her eyes to avoid mine, and I sighed, taking a step toward her. "He's my best friend," I said, a little softer. I sometimes forgot how sensitive she was. "I'm just —I'm not sure what all you expect me to say about it. It's not really a problem, it's just...he's aggressive when he drinks. He's not an alcoholic or anything. He knows when to stop, he just doesn't do well after a few hard ones, is all."

"I understand," she murmured, but she truly didn't, and she probably never would. Her thick eyelashes fluttered as she put her focus on me again. She closed the gap between us by taking three simple steps, and then her sun-kissed arms were wrapped around my neck, her lips on my jawline. "Why do I get the feeling that's the reason you didn't want me to come? Because you didn't want your perfect friend Derek to rear his ugly head."

That wasn't why, but she could believe whatever she wanted for now. "I never said I didn't want you to come. I just wasn't sure how they'd feel about you coming without asking first, but they're fine. They always get through it." I sighed. "Everyone seems to be warming up to you."

"Yeah..." Her smile disappeared, her eyes a little more serious. "Everyone but Kandy." She huffed and pulled back.

I kept my expression casual as I asked, "What do you mean by that?

"She's so...*cold* to me. She gives me this grim look sometimes like she wishes I wasn't around. And I don't know if it's just me, but I'm pretty sure she likes you, Quinton—and I get it. I've had a lot of crushes on guys who were older than me. Some of my dad's friends were really hot, and it didn't help that they visited our house so often. It's just a girl thing, I guess. I just…I mean it's been that way since I first met her. I always get this distant, icy vibe from her. I'm trying to get her to warm up to me as much as I can, but she is *not* having it."

I turned so I wouldn't have to look at her and was glad she didn't notice.

"I thought she'd be way past that now, but hopefully she gets over the crush she has on you soon. Mindy said she's noticed a little distance happening with her too—that Kandy used to tell her everything, but now she's kind of keeping to herself, or locking herself away in her room. Or hanging out at Frankie's more. She also said Kandy called it quits with some football player she was talking to? I'm wondering if maybe that's why she's been acting like that."

Shit. She really did it. No wonder she was pissed. I'd told her to end it with him, got her hopes up, only to crush them by bringing Kelly along with me.

"She'll get over it—the distance, I mean," I said. "She's still young and has a lot to learn." I turned and grabbed Kelly by the waist, reeling her in and kissing her lips. I wanted her to stop talking about Kandy. The mere mention of her name made my cock ache.

"I just want her to like me, you know?" She whined. She was doing it again. The whiny thing she did when she wanted something to go her way. It was a terrible mindset to want everyone to like you. It just wasn't realistic. "I'm going to be around for a long time, don't you think?"

I pressed my lips. "Yeah. I hope so."

"We'll be like family soon. She's a good girl—I see it. She kind of reminds me of a little sister. Maybe right now we're just feuding like sisters do." She gave me a peck on the lips. "Maybe I can warm her up by taking her and Frankie shopping in the morning. Buy her whatever she wants. Derek is so strict with her about what she wears. As a young woman, she deserves to explore her options. Mindy said she had to sneak Kandy to a lingerie store for one of her birthdays because she was begging to go for their annual sale. Can you believe that? She shouldn't have to beg or sneak to a store created for women. There's nothing wrong with expressing interest in those things."

I sighed. I knew Kandy was going to hate the idea of shopping with Kelly, but I had to pretend Kandy was just my best friend's daughter. In Kelly's mind, I was like an uncle to Kandy, which meant she wanted to be like the aunt. "I think they'll enjoy that," I told her. "Just...don't push too hard, okay? Kandy has a mouth on her, and she isn't afraid to use it when she's fed up."

Kelly smiled, patting my chest. "I think I can handle it. I'm glad you support the idea." She kissed me on the cheek and then walked around me to undress. She put on the orange cotton dress that stopped just above her knees and then slid into a pair of sandals. "Going to have a drink or two with Mindy. Maybe she'll want to go shopping tomorrow, too."

I nodded and watched her go. When I heard her going down the stairs, I made my way out of the door and walked to the balcony, pulling the pack of cigarettes from my shirt pocket. After that conversation, I needed a buzz.

Before I lit it up, someone said, "If you want to live to see sixty, you should probably quit soon."

I turned to my right, spotting Kandy sitting in one of the white rocking chairs. She had on a pair of black lounge shorts and a crop top. The diamonds in her ears that Derek bought for her seventeenth birthday shimmered beneath the moonlight. I remember them because he'd sent me a text message asking if I thought she would like them. I knew she would.

The waning moon was bold and bright, lighting up the whole sky and everything beneath it, including Kandy. I could see every inch of her, from the curly, dark brown hair that was pulled up into a messy bun, down to the silky, beige legs that were folded in the chair.

"Haven't I told you before to mind your own business?" I said with the cigarette clamped between my teeth. "I think you were about nine when I told you that."

Despite what I said, I didn't want to pass my bad habits onto Kandy, so I pulled the cigarette from my lips and dropped it in the pocket of my shirt.

"Maybe I should. Maybe I shouldn't." She looked away. "How am I supposed to know what to do when it comes to you?"

"What's that supposed to mean?"

"It means you're an asshole," she replied quickly, with no hesitation whatsoever, like that word had been bottled up inside her, waiting for the perfect moment to be used.

"Me? An asshole? Damn. And all this time I thought I was the nice guy."

She fought a smile, still focused on the ocean.

"Where's your friend?" I asked.

"She's on the phone with her boyfriend. I didn't want to hear her whining about how much she missed him, so I came out here."

"On the second floor balcony?"

"Ours doesn't have rocking chairs. Just cheap, plastic chairs that are too uncomfortable to sit in."

"Mm-hmm."

We were quiet for a moment.

Kandy dropped her feet and exhaled. I could tell something was on her mind. I didn't have to ask to know what was bothering her.

"Why did you bring her, Cane?" she questioned. "I'm honestly just curious. I've been racking my brain trying to figure it out, but I just don't get it. Do you love her?"

"Kandy—"

"Because if you do, then it all makes sense. But what you told me that day in my parents' living room doesn't…"

I breathed hard through my nostrils. From where I stood, I could see Mindy sitting on a lounge chair with a wine glass in her hand. She was giggly and bubbly. Tipsy for sure. I could hear Kelly talking, but couldn't see her.

"I care about her," I said, and it was the truth.

"But you're not in love with her."

I shook my head. It felt wrong to try and say it out loud.

"Is she your girlfriend?"

I sighed. "I don't know what she is, Kandy. She's just a woman I'm dating."

"For a whole year? She must be desperate." She laughed, but her laughter contained no joy.

"You know she's trying to get to know you better."

"Yeah. She's trying *too* hard. I don't want her to get to know me."

"She knows you have a crush on me, too."

Her eyes widened at that. "*What?* How?"

"She just…sees it, I guess."

"It's not just a crush anymore. You know that right?"

"You need to let this go, Kandy." My voice was stern, my smile fading.

"I can't help who I want, Cane." She let out an unstable breath. "I can't help *what* I want or *how* I want it, either."

I breathed evenly through my nostrils, doing my best to ignore the sultriness that took over her voice.

She stood up then, and I watched her rest her elbows on the guardrail. She stared out at the ocean, then up at the moon and stars. "I wish I could erase it all—the way I feel about you, you know? I wish that I looked at you as more of a brother or an uncle or something, rather than…whatever this is I feel for you."

I sniffed, but nothing more.

"I know I'm not allowed to touch you right now, and that's killing me. Having to hold back and keep to myself is harder than I thought," she continued. "I also know it will hurt my parents, especially my dad, if he finds out that we ever touched each other in that way. I don't want to ruin what you guys have. They're happier when you're around. *I'm* happier too…but only when it's just you and you alone."

"What are you saying?"

She shrugged and waved it off. "It's not like you'll do anything about it anyway."

"You did something I told you to do."

She frowned a little. "What are you talking about?"

"You got rid of that guy, like I told you to." I rested my elbows on the guardrail.

"I didn't do that for you."

"Bullshit," I laughed. "Lying straight through your fucking teeth, Bits."

"I didn't!" she exclaimed, but her words ended with a small giggle.

"So why end it with him? Right after what I told you?"

"I just wanted to." She shrugged again. "Stop acting like you have this great big power over me because you don't." She stepped back and was about to make her way to the door, but I caught her hand before she could go.

I don't know what came over me—or what it was that hit me in that moment. Maybe it was her words, and how easily she defied me. Maybe it was because she looked so pure and sweet beneath the moonlight, and all I wanted to do was dirty her up. Her eyes. Those lips. Everything on her was ready for me to devour.

You're a fucking fool, Cane, my conscience screamed.

A subtle gasp fell through her parted lips when my hand wrapped around hers, and then her eyes swooped up to meet mine.

"I know exactly what kind of power I have over you, Kandy," I rasped, looking her over.

"You don't have any," she challenged. "Not with *her* around."

"Really? If I told you to drop to your knees right now, you would do it with no questions asked, wouldn't you?" Her eyes shimmered, betraying the tough persona she was trying to keep on display. Her throat bobbed, and she caged her bottom lip between her teeth.

"Maybe if I was yours, I would, but I'm not yours."

She tried pulling away, but I didn't let her. I reeled her in closer, my heart drumming in my chest. My cock twitched from being so close to her. "Doesn't matter what kind of shit we go through, you'll always be *mine*, Kandy. Doesn't matter how fucked up the situation is, or how wrong it fucking feels...*you are mine.*" I let my lips touch the shell of her ear. "Don't you ever forget that, you understand?"

I felt her shiver when my chest pressed on her shoulder. Goose bumps trickled up her arms and she looked up into my eyes, studying them. Studying me.

It was like she could read every single thought running through my head in that moment.

Fuck, I want you.

I want to feel your virgin pussy wrapped around my cock. Hear you moan. Sigh. Gasp. Make you beg me to fuck you.

But there's Derek...

Mindy...

Kelly...

You...

But she ignored all of that. "I want you, Cane," she whispered feebly. Her hand skimmed over my cock, and I twitched hard in my pants. "It's killing me that I can't touch you—that I can't be with you." It was killing me, too, but I couldn't admit that to her. I started to pull away, but before I could, she cupped me in her hand. My cock sprung to life when our eyes locked again. "I can get on my knees for you...if you want me to..."

"No. Don't." My voice was thick. Coarse. If she was to kneel, I would have lost it—fucked her right on that balcony and destroyed every good thing in my life in a single act. "Go back to your room."

But of course she didn't fucking listen. She never fucking listened. She was so damn hardheaded and persistent, which only increased my need to fuck some respect and discipline into her.

Like an innocent pet, begging for guidance and affection, she dropped to her knees and stared up at me with wide brown eyes.

"Do you like seeing me like this?" she whispered. "Below you? Ready to worship you?"

I sucked in a sharp breath through my teeth, shaking my head swiftly as I shut my eyes. "Kandy…"

She started running a fingertip along my belt, and the urge to pull her up was high and demanding, but so was my desire to watch her pretty, glossed lips wrap around my cock again.

"Has she pleased you?" she asked softly, tugging the tab of my zipper. "Since we got here?"

"That's none of your business," I grumbled.

"Does she kneel for you?"

A noise filled my throat. Kelly didn't like to get on her knees. She felt it was degrading to women and would have rather sat on the bed while I stood in front of her, or get between my legs while I lay on my back.

"No," I said, and it was a little harder to get that one word out. I was trying to hold on to control. It was damn near impossible. I swore I wouldn't touch her anymore. I promised myself not even an hour ago, but *fuck*…

I couldn't stop looking at her. My cock was so hard. *So fucking hard.* I was straining now, dying to unleash myself—thrust my dick through her pouty lips until I felt the back of her throat.

"Let me please you, Cane. The way you really want to be pleased. I'll do whatever you want me to do."

My head swayed side to side, and I finally squeezed my eyes shut. I grabbed her arm blindly and hauled her up, jerking her against me, her nipples hard and digging into my chest. "You really want to please me?" My voice was gruff.

"Yes," she pleaded.

"Then be a good girl, listen to me, and go to your room. We can't do this here."

She dropped her eyes to my lips again. She wanted to kiss me so badly.

"What is it that you want, Bits?" I asked as she breathed raggedly.

"You, Cane. All of you."

"My lips?"

"Yes," she sighed.

"One kiss," I told her, and she didn't hesitate. She clasped my face in her hands and forced her mouth on mine.

I gripped her face between my fingers, forcing her back. She whimpered, and that whimper alone made me want to tear her clothes off and bend her over the guardrail. If only we were alone.

"Don't be greedy," I crooned. "Savor it. Enjoy it. *Feel* me."

She sighed and nodded, and I took the lead this time. I held her face in my hands, bringing my lips down and kissing her slowly at first.

I deepened the kiss, and she moaned like I was making love to her. I pulled back, staring down at her lust-filled eyes. "Quiet," I instructed, and she bobbed her head rapidly, leaning in for more. Our lips connected and then her tongue tried to find mine. I allowed it to come through. Our tongues clashed and danced, pirouetted and coiled, and it was me who had to fight a moan next.

She wrapped a hand around the back of my neck, being greedy again. This time, I didn't mind. She was young and still learning. I wanted to teach her everything about her body—that patience and control was a virtue that could be practiced, even during kisses and sex.

I kept hold of her face, breaking the kiss again. She had her eyes halfway open, searching for my lips, desperate for them. Dropping my head, I thrust my tongue through her full lips again and groaned as quietly as possible. Her fingers curled in my shirt, her breaths ragged and rushed as her other hand tightened around the back of my neck.

I was a goddamn fool. Reckless and stupid all over again. Only she could do this to me. Little Kandy Jennings. I don't know how she always pushed me to break my own rules. Kissing her felt like I was both drowning and breathing at the same time. How was that even possible? How could she give me life and damn near kill me at the same time? It didn't make any fucking sense, but it didn't have to. All I knew was that I was hard as fucking rock, throbbing like a motherfucker, and dying to be buried in her virgin pussy.

"Hey, yo, Cane!" Derek yelled from a distance.

I snatched myself away from her with haste. "Shit!" I hissed.

Kandy stumbled backwards, still in a daze. When she heard her dad's voice again, she pulled herself together and scurried back over to the rocking chair, staring down at her lap and acting like nothing happened.

"Yeah, out here!" I called. I took the single step it took to get to the door, expecting to see Derek, but it wasn't him standing there, looking through the door with wide eyes and a chin on the floor.

It was Frankie.

22

KANDY

"Ah…*shit*…" Cane looked at me, and I stared at him, unsure of what to do. Had Dad seen us? *Were we caught?* My rapid heart boomed harder and faster, my pulse heavy in my ears. I pushed out of the chair again.

"What?" I asked.

But he didn't get the chance to answer because Frankie walked outside with her phone in hand. She looked from Cane to me, and I started to panic, but then I remembered this was Frankie.

Frankie, my best friend. Frankie kept all my secrets.

"Frankie? What are you doing?" I whisper-hissed.

"What am I doing? What are *you* doing! The two of you—"

"Shh!" I looked over her shoulder, but Cane was already gone. I stepped in front of the doorway and spotted Dad and Cane talking by the top of the staircase. Dad turned to make his way back down, and Cane was about to follow him.

He looked back at me once, his glare serious. A glare that shouted, *Tell her to keep her mouth shut or I will.*

"Kandy!" Frankie hissed, her eyes the widest I'd ever seen them. "What in the hell was that? He was—he was *kissing* you!

144

Touching you! What the fuck!" She was doing a whisper-yell now. Her *loud* whisper-yell.

"Frankie, please. Be quiet." I looked over the guardrail and saw Mom still out by the pool, waving around a glass of wine. I clutched Frankie's hand and rushed through the door and up the stairs with her.

When we'd made it safely to our room, she exclaimed, "Why didn't you tell me, Kandy! I thought it was just a crush!"

"It *was* just a crush, Frank! I swear it was but—*shit*." I shoved my fingers through my hair. I was panicking all over again. What if Dad had been there instead of her? What if he'd caught us instead? I had no doubt he would have thrown Cane over the guardrail if it came down to it. My dad was that crazy.

"Hey—listen to me!" Frankie grabbed my arm and forced me to sit on the bed. She took the spot beside me and looked me straight in the eyes. "Don't freak out! You know me, K.J.! You know I won't tell a fucking soul. Cross my heart." She crossed her heart rapidly, her brown eyes still serious and also desperate for answers. "Now, with that being said, you have to tell me what the hell just happened. You're lucky it was me who witnessed that and not your dad!"

I dropped my gaze, staring at my legs. I still had goosebumps from that kiss—that passionate, toe-curling, delicious kiss. My heart was still racing. Fuck, my emotions were all over the place.

"Remember that night when my dad got shot?" I asked.

She nodded. "Yeah, Cane came to pick you up."

"Yeah, well, that same night, he didn't take me to the hospital because my mom didn't want him to bring me there, so I ended up staying with him, just in case anything happened. Anyway, we were talking that night, and I was crying and just so sad about Dad. He was drinking, and I asked him if I could have some of what he was having. He was hesitant at first, but he didn't know how else to make me feel better so he let me have a little. Only I kind of drank the whole thing. It was scotch. It was really fucking strong."

"Yeah, that shit is strong," Frank half-laughed, then waved her hand like that part didn't matter right now.

"So I drank that, and then he started talking about how he and Dad met. How my dad saved his mom's life, and how he felt like he owed him for life—a lot of stuff that I didn't know. And then I cried again because I was scared about Dad, and that story really touched my heart. I asked Cane to hold me and then...I don't know what came over me. I mean, my hand was on his lap, and my face was so close to his, and he smelled so good, Frank. *So good.* He didn't want it to happen, but I'm fucking stubborn—you know me—so I got on his lap and kissed him anyway. He stopped me at first, but then I asked him if he wanted me. He told me yes he wanted me and that he hated admitting it."

"Holy fucking shit," Frankie whispered. "Then what happened?"

"He kissed me, and then we started kind of dry humping, you know? And then he...*finger-fucked* me..." I cupped my mouth and stared at my best friend, waiting for her to blast me with judgment.

Only she didn't.

She let out one loud laugh and then cupped her mouth too, like she couldn't believe it'd happened either.

"Your dad's best friend?" she gasped.

"I know!" I wailed. "That's what makes it so bad. He felt horrible about it the next morning. He couldn't even look at me, Frank. On the way to the hospital, he called it a mistake and...it kind of hurt my feelings, but deep down I knew it was true. It was a mistake on both our parts, but here's the kicker." I held up a hand, like I was holding the power of the universe in my palm. "That's not the only thing that's happened between us."

Her eyes stretched wider. "Wait—there's *more?*"

I nodded. "There was one day when my parents were at my

dad's rehab. Cane showed up because he was supposed to be taking my dad to a basketball game." She nodded, impatiently waiting for the details. "He was sitting in Dad's recliner, and I went to him and sat on his lap. He was a little more hesitant this time and told me he didn't want to hurt my feelings again, but I didn't care. I wanted him so bad that day. I don't know why. I always get crazy around him, or I act like nothing else matters if we're alone. So…I pulled his pants down and…gave him a blowjob in the living room."

"Holy shit, K.J! You are a fucking vixen!" Frankie stood up and held her hands out beside her head, like her mind was blown. Actually, I think she was *proud* of me for what I'd done. Her smile was bigger and her eyes were wider.

"You aren't mad that I didn't tell you?" I asked, standing with her.

"What? No! Fuck no! I'm just glad to know I'm not the only one with a naughty side. You play the good girl role well, my friend." She grabbed my upper arms. "Seriously, though, you didn't have to hide shit like that from me. I'm your best friend, K.J. You're my only *real* friend. I would never betray you by telling anyone about that."

"I know…but Cane didn't want anyone to know, so I kept it to myself. I didn't want him to lose trust in me."

"I understand, but from now on, I'm the exception." She shook her head and stepped back. "Wow. Now I see why you're so pissed about Kelly being here. I would be too, if I knew he wanted me."

"Yeah," I laughed.

"I mean…shit! It's just crazy! He was kissing you like he…like he fucking *owned* you, K.J. He was all over you. He can try and deny whatever he wants, but from what I saw, he wants you just as badly as you want him."

"I don't know." I shrugged and sat down on the bed again. "I can't tell. I mean, he told me he wouldn't bring Kelly, and he brought her anyway. He told me to break it off with Carl, so I did.

He told me to use my lips only for him, so I am, but then he brings her? I don't get it. He's so fucking confusing sometimes. The only time he's not is when it's just the two of us."

"Hmm…well, maybe he brought her because he didn't want what just happened on the balcony to keep happening. And because there would be a huge possibility of the two of you getting caught without someone being in the way. Fuck, if your dad even catches wind of this, he'll fucking kill him. You do realize that, right?"

"I know, I know! Trust me, I feel bad about it. My parents adore Cane, and if they find out what we did, they'll flip out. I think that's why Cane brought her, too. I think he's trying to escape me, you know? Like he's trying to have a reason *not* to be around me. He knows how I feel about her. He's not an idiot. The sad thing is Kelly is so nice! She's super sweet, but she has Cane and can do whatever she wants with him publicly or privately, and it makes me hate her."

"Dude…this is some crazy shit," she laughed, flopping backwards on the bed. I fell back with her, and we stared up at the vaulted ceiling. "If I were in your shoes, I don't think I'd be able to hold back either. You see how hot he is? I'd prefer someone as experienced as him to take my V-card. It would make the experience better, unlike my first time." She looked at me. "Wait…is that what you want?"

I nodded and felt heat rise to my cheeks. "I wouldn't mind it, but I know he won't do it."

"You never know. Maybe there will be another time where you two are alone. You took what you wanted twice before. Why not do it again? From what you've told me, he doesn't seem to be able to resist you." She sat up, smiling hard. "Isn't that fucking bizarre to you? That a thirty-five year old CEO of a million-dollar company can't resist *you*, an eighteen year old? I would walk around like my shit doesn't stink every fucking day. Hell, I'd make him my sugar daddy for life. Make him pay for my tuition, my car —every-fucking-thing!"

I busted out laughing, playfully pushing her away and going for my suitcase. "He's just Cane to me. Not a millionaire CEO." I shrugged. "Gah, I'm so rattled. I think I need to hit the pool. You joining?"

"You know I'm down. And hey!" Frankie rushed to the area where the kitchenette was. She opened the mini fridge and took out something and then came back. "Look what I took out of my mom's liquor cabinet." She held up a glass bottle of clear liquid with a blue label on it.

"Tequila?" I gasped. "Frankie, that shit is going to fuck us up!"

"That's the point," she laughed. "We'll sneak a shot or two and take a swim. It'll be fun!"

I laughed and shook my head. After that kiss, I needed something to take the edge off. We got dressed in a flash. Afterward, we found plastic cups near the small kitchen area and took two shots of the tequila.

By the time we made it down to the pool, I could feel the alcohol kicking in, swimming through my veins and giving me a slight buzz. Mom and Kelly were sitting in lounge chairs by the gate. Dad and Cane were sitting at the outside bar, watching a soccer game on the TV.

"Taking a swim? That's fun!" Kelly yelled our way. After what had happened, I decided not to be so much of a bitch to her. I mean, it was clear Cane still wanted me. She may have been in the way, but I had a feeling I was more important to Cane than she was.

"Yeah, it should be!" I smiled at her, and she immediately looked over at Mom with wide eyes, like she couldn't believe I'd given her such a chipper response. Mom returned the same shocked expression, and they both watched Frankie and me swim for a few seconds before chatting amongst themselves again.

Before I knew it, Kelly and Mom were walking to the pool

with their wine glasses in hand. They sat and dropped their feet in the water.

"Girls, what do you think about going on a shopping spree in the morning?" Kelly asked with a bright smile. "On me."

"Really?" Frankie exclaimed. "On you? Like you'll be buying whatever we pick out?"

"Mm-hmm." Kelly pressed her lips around the rim of her glass and sipped it.

"Sure, that sounds fun," I said, dropping lower so the water could wrap around my shoulders.

"I'm always down for shopping," Frankie announced, and Mom and Kelly smiled. They sat there for a while, talking and sipping, and then Mom got up, going for their table where the empty wine bottle was.

"Should I grab another?" Mom asked, waving the bottle.

Kelly looked over her shoulder and gave a swift nod. "Yeah. I think I can squeeze in one more." Kelly got out of the pool and followed Mom to the door. They went inside, and through the window of the kitchen, I could see Mom opening the wide fridge while Kelly rested her elbows on the island counter, like she couldn't handle another sip. She probably couldn't, but was trying to wing it to get closer to Mom. Mom was a wine connoisseur through and through.

Frankie swam to the deep end of the pool, and I followed her, plunging beneath the cool water and letting it run through my hair. It felt good on my hot skin. I resurfaced and gripped the cement edge. When I looked toward the bar, I spotted Cane.

Dad was into the game, hardly paying attention to us. Cane had turned halfway, so that he could see both the pool and the game with just a simple turn of the head. He locked eyes with me, his face mellow. I couldn't read his expression, but I did take note of the way his eyes lowered to my breasts.

I was wearing my favorite black two-piece bikini. It was the bikini Dad hated. It made my C-cup boobs look bigger, and the bottoms were cinched in the middle so it made my butt look more like a peach.

Water dripped from my hair and landed on my shoulders and lips. Cane watched my mouth again, eyes focused, hungry. He licked his lips once, and when Dad said something, he tore his gaze away, turned around, and focused on the game again.

He took a swift sip from his short glass, probably hoping it would erase the taste of me from his lips.

For me, the taste of his mouth would never be erased. Everything about him was engraved in me, seared deep, and soaked in my blood cells—his touch, his smell, even the taste of his cum.

Everything he'd given me was going to be cherished. I just wished he could say the same.

23

KANDY

Kelly couldn't help but to try and please everyone.

I realized that as we shopped. It was in her nature, probably twisted into her DNA. She constantly asked if we were okay, if any of us were thirsty or hungry. She'd even asked Frankie if she needed her to come into the fitting room to see if the dresses fit okay, to which Frankie declined while fighting a laugh.

After spending three full hours around Kelly, I felt bad for being such a bitch to her. She only wanted to fit in and be liked. She was trying to understand me, but I hadn't given her the chance. All because of a man.

I was truly in over my head. It wasn't like that same man was ever going to call me his girlfriend or make me his wife someday, like he could with Kelly. It wasn't like Cane had the option to put me on display and show me off to the world. I mean, he did, but neither of us were brave enough to do that. Plus, I loved my parents dearly. The last thing I wanted to do was break their hearts and ruin our bond, as well as their friendship with Cane. Our lives were much more fun with him in it than without.

After our three-hour shopping spree, we were sitting in the food court with bags of various colors surrounding us. When we first arrived, Kelly told us her credit card was loaded and of course Frankie went berserk. I didn't blame her. Her mom wasn't exactly the kind of woman to go on a shopping spree. Frankie's Mom hated malls, and instead would give her money to go alone. Frankie usually ended up going school shopping with Mom and me.

In the food court, Kelly sat across from me, Mom beside me, and Frankie to the left of Kelly. I'd just finished eating a chicken sandwich and cinnamon pretzel. I felt like a pig for being the only one to buy something sweet, but then my best friend spared me my shameful, fat-girl thoughts by saying, "I think I want some ice cream." She pulled out her wallet and stood. "Anyone else?"

"Oh!" Mom sipped her tea and then nodded, standing with her. "I was eyeing the ice cream, too. I'll come with you. Kandy, Kelly? You guys want anything?"

"No, I'm okay," I said.

"I'll take mint chocolate please." Kelly started to hand Mom her credit card, but Mom rapidly shook her head and forced her hand back.

"You've spent enough today. The least I can do is get you something sweet." She smiled at Kelly and then took off with Frank.

Then we were alone.

We glanced at each other, giving awkward, lopsided smiles.

"I just wanted to tell you," Kelly started with laughter in her voice, breaking the ice. "Make sure you tuck the lingerie deep in your suitcase and unpack it as soon as you get home so your dad doesn't see it."

I laughed. "Yeah, I will." Silence surrounded us again. I ran the pad of my finger over a heap of the cinnamon on my tray.

"Did you get all you wanted? We can always do a little more shopping if you want to grab some more—"

"No, Kelly. Seriously. It's okay." I gave her a smile. A genuine one. "I have more than enough stuff." I glanced at the four bags full of clothes by my feet. "Thank you for this. Frankie really appreciates it too."

She smiled, like her heart was melting in the best way possible from the compliment. "Anytime, Kandy. And hey—" she stretched her arm across the table and placed it on top of mine, "anytime you need a girl to go shopping with, I'm here. I love to shop. It's all I do. Did Quinton ever tell you that I design houses and offices?"

I shook my head and straightened my back a little more at the mention of his name. "No, he never told me, but I can see you doing something like that."

"Yep. I'm an interior designer. I've designed for all people, but my favorite person that I got to design for is someone you'll never be able to guess..." She gave a smug smile, waiting for me to guess.

"Who?"

"Adele." She beamed, and I gasped.

"No way! You know Adele?"

"Yes! I worked on an office for her mother in London for two weeks. She loved it. Couldn't stop gushing about it. And she was such a lovely woman."

"Wow—" I had no words. Kelly had met Adele. One of my favorite singers ever. Suddenly I wanted to become her best friend. "That's so awesome."

"Yeah. Maybe I'll have another big job like that, and I'll be able to send you pictures." Kelly leaned forward, her hazel eyes a little more serious now. "I really would like us to become friends, Kandy. I don't want to force it—trust me, I remember what's it's like to want my own space as an eighteen-year-old woman—but if you ever need anything, just let me know. Don't be afraid to ask me."

I smiled. "Thanks, Kelly. I'll keep that in mind."

She returned a soft smile, sitting back and sipping her tea. "Quinton will be happy to know we got along."

"Quinton." I laughed.

"What?" she tittered, eyes sparkling.

"You're the only person I know who calls him that. It's funny to hear his real name sometimes."

"Oh!" She laughed, placing her cup down. "Trust me, he hates it, but when I met him, it's how he introduced himself. Quinton before Cane, so I guess it just kind of stuck with me." She shrugged and looked sideways, like she was thinking about the first time they met.

Now was my chance to ask. Cane couldn't stand talking about Kelly with me. The only way I was going to get answers was through the primary source: her.

"How did you guys meet, anyway?" I asked, running my finger over the cinnamon and pretending it was a casual question.

"Oh, gosh." She sighed and laughed, as if the memory of meeting him would never fade. "Well, I was actually attending a bachelorette party for one of my friends in Charlotte. We went out one night to this club and had a section reserved for us. I had volunteered to get drinks for everyone, so I went to the bar and ordered way too many to carry—but I tried! I probably shouldn't have, though, because as soon as I turned, I forgot there was a step I had to take down and ended up tripping and dropping every single drink."

"Oh my gosh," I gasped, fighting a laugh.

"Yeah! Everyone was just laughing and all the girls came down in their gorgeous bridesmaid outfits, trying to help me clean it up. I mean, there was glass everywhere—all over my shoes, my skirt, my shirt. My shirt was literally soaked by the way, and it was light pink, so my bra was pretty clear for everyone to see. Then, out of nowhere, this guy came up and asked me if I was okay. He was so concerned, and didn't drop his eyes to my chest like I expected a man to do. He took me to a back office, and at first I freaked out, thinking this guy was trying to do something or come onto me, you know?" Laughing, she says, "I told him that if he was expecting something freaky, he had the wrong fucking idea."

"Yeah? To Cane?" I giggled.

"Yes, and he immediately told me to relax—that it was his office, and he had an extra shirt hanging up that I could wear. It was a white button-down shirt. He gave it to me and then stepped out of the office to let me change. When I was done, I met him outside the door, and he took me to the bar and ordered all the drinks I had requested before, but this time he had someone bring them up to us. I felt horrible about what I'd said to him. He was only trying to help me, you know?

"So I finally chugged down a few drinks because at that point, I needed them, but the whole night, I felt someone watching me, and I just knew it was him. Every time I looked up, I would spot him watching. He played it cool in his own way. He would keep his head bowed, but those eyes would be right on me."

I tried not to sigh. I knew all about the eyes. That searing hot, hungry glare he gave when he wanted something and was trying to figure out how to get it. He was like a beast trying to catch its prey. Watching. Circling. Waiting for the perfect moment to strike. When the beast finally got its prey, there was no running, no hiding, no denying what would happen. You either craved every single inch of him, down to the cell, or you died trying to pretend you didn't want anything from him at all.

Cane had that kind of power over women, and he knew it. He knew when to use it and when not to. He'd used it on me many times.

"So by the end of the night, the girls are demanding that I go talk to him and get his number. The bride-to-be was more determined to hook me up than she was about celebrating her upcoming wedding. It was a fun, hilarious, insanely embarrassing night, but if it hadn't happened, I never would have caught his attention and never would have spoken to him."

"Wow. That's nice." I lowered my gaze. The next question slipped out before I could think to stop it. "Do you love him—I mean, are you in love with him?"

She gave me a puzzled looked, as if she weren't sure how to

answer it. "I...do love him, yes. And I think I'm starting to fall in love with him." She sighed, and her bangs swayed. "I just...don't think he feels the same."

"So why stay with him? Why stay with someone who doesn't love you back?"

She thought on it for a moment, her eyes a little wider. "Because Quinton is a complex man. He comes with many layers. What he shows you is just one of the layers—the person he wants the whole world to see, which is his good side. But after spending several months with him in a bed, listening to the things he says in his sleep, and even watching him wake up out of nowhere, gasping like his life depends on it...well, it's understandable." She paused for a moment, studying the table. "I'm a patient woman, I suppose. And I know it will take time for him take the next step and love someone that way because—," she smiled, as if it pained her, "if you don't love everything about yourself, how can you possibly take on the task of loving everything about someone else?"

24

CANE

The last thing I expected to see was Kandy walking into the house, laughing, with Kelly trailing closely behind her. I had to blink hard twice, just to make sure my eyes hadn't deceived me.

"Did you see that guy?" Kandy laughed. "He was staring so hard at Frankie's butt! Freakin' perv!"

"I saw! I can't believe it! He had to be my dad's age!" Kelly chimed.

They both laughed again and as they passed by the living room, Kelly looked my way, winking with a smug grin. Wow. When she said she could handle it, I didn't think she'd actually be able to pull it off.

I put my attention on Kandy, but she didn't even look my way. It was like I wasn't even there to her. "I'm going to put my bags in the room," she announced, switching glances between Kelly and her mother. "You guys want to come lay out with Frankie and me at the beach?"

"Sure, sweetie." Kelly smiled graciously, like she was happy about the offer. "I'd really love that."

"Cool. Meet you down here in twenty." She and Frankie

hustled up the stairs, squealing and laughing about God knew what.

Kelly met up to me, sitting on the arm of the sofa as Mindy went to her bedroom. Derek was already in there, taking a shower.

I closed my laptop when she eyed it. "You aren't supposed to be working on vacation, Mr. Cane," she said playfully.

"I wasn't. Just checking a few emails." I sat up in my seat. "What was all that about?"

"All of what?"

"The laughing. The invitation to hang out at the beach…"

"Oh, with Kandy?" Kelly waved a hand, like it was a simple work of nature. But I knew Kandy. She wasn't simple. She was complicated as fuck. "We had a really good time at the mall. I got her to open up a lot with me. I'm telling you, a shopping spree will win over any girl's heart." She winked and stood up. "Remember that."

"You really going to the beach with them?" I asked when she started to walk away.

She shrugged and pressed her lips. "Sure. Why not?"

Don't be too obvious, I reminded myself. "Just asking."

She turned and faced me. "Don't worry, Quinton. I've got this. We're bonding, and I like it. I won't push too much. I promise."

I nodded and forced a smile, but that wasn't what I was worried about. Someone with a personality like Kandy's would befriend a woman I talked to, just to get under my skin. She tested my patience and my boundaries constantly. I should have known it would come to this. Kandy wasn't a dumb girl. She knew how to play her cards right, and knew exactly how to get to me.

Not even twenty minutes later, Kandy came back downstairs with Frankie behind her. She had on a sheer white cover-up over a pink bikini. The cover-up was pointless. I could see every fucking thing and seeing it made me want to tell her to go back upstairs and put something less revealing on.

Boys would look.

Men would look.

I didn't want anyone looking at what was mine.

In that moment, though, I grasped the full concept. If I hadn't known Kandy, I would have assumed she was a little older than eighteen. My guess would have been twenty-one or twenty-two. With tits that voluptuous, thighs that thick, and an ass that round, it occurred to me that maybe I'd missed what she'd been trying to show me all along. Her full figure had been hidden beneath her clothes, but without them...I could really see her.

She was a woman now.

Young. Ripe. Ready.

And though she had a free spirit and a wild heart, she knew exactly what she wanted...

Me.

25

KANDY

I'd spent two hours on the beach with Frankie, Mom, and Kelly. Surprisingly, it wasn't so bad. Mom didn't nag me about my bathing suit. In fact, she said she loved it, even though it was a little more risqué, hence the reason I wore the cover-up on the way out of the house. I didn't need Dad catching sight and demanding that I change.

After shutting off the shower, I turned and looked toward the balcony where Cane's room was. I could feel him watching me again as I showered off.

There was no sign of Kelly. Only him. His eyes weren't hot and hungry this time, though. They were narrowed and curious.

I tried to ignore the way my belly fluttered as I grabbed my things and went inside, heading straight to my floor where I saw Frankie crossing the room with damp hair. She'd gone in about twenty minutes before all of us. Her period started. Fucking sucked.

After I hit the real shower, I got dressed. Apparently we were going out for dinner on Cane again. I put on a white jumpsuit, paired with rose gold bangles and my favorite rose gold necklace with a white feather at the end of it. Frankie was still getting ready, so I decided to go downstairs for something to drink, and that's when I spotted Cane at the counter.

He had one elbow resting on the marble countertop, his phone in hand as he scrolled through it. I looked around for Kelly but didn't see a sign of her. For some reason, after Kelly's story at the mall, I felt bad for going after him so much. I know that made me wishy-washy, but it was true. The guilt always got me. I was an over-thinker. I assumed the worst about everything.

She loved him. I could tell. She loved him so much it hurt, just like me, and she knew he didn't feel the same. That was already heartbreaking enough. I was certain the last thing she wanted to see was Cane all over an eighteen-year-old girl. In a way, we were kind of in the same boat.

I stepped past him and opened the fridge, pulling out a bottle of water. I cracked it open and took a few gulps, avoiding his eyes. I was about to make my way to the living room, but his voice stopped me mid-step.

"So now that you've become best friends with Kelly, I don't exist to you anymore?" His voice was low, but clear enough for me to hear.

I turned to face him, tilting my head. "What makes you say that?" I played dumb.

"You just walked right past me. You did it earlier, too, when you got back from the mall." He rested his lower back on the edge of the counter, folding his arms across his broad chest.

I'd been so busy avoiding him that I didn't even realize he was wearing jeans. Cane in jeans. Such a rare sight, yet I think I loved it just a little bit more than his suits. Dark blue jeans hung low on his hips, and the black T-shirt he wore revealed most of the ink on his arms and throat. It instantly reminded me of the night Dad was shot—the night when he kissed me. Touched me. Shared forbidden words with me.

When I took in the sight of him, my plan to keep him at a distance somewhat backfired. I could smell his expensive cologne and even spotted the defined print of his manhood in his pants. His shirt fit him snugly, molding to his abs. I had no idea how a busy man like him even had the time to develop abs.

I blinked rapidly, pulling myself out of my lust-filled haze. "I got to know her a little better," I said, taking a step toward him. "She's a good person."

"I know she is. You knew that too." His eyes were cloudier as they studied me.

I dropped my head. "She was telling me how you guys met... and that she loves you but knows you don't feel the same. I instantly felt bad for her...and for all the things I did behind her back with you."

"The things you did," he repeated with a soft growl to his voice. "You mean the things that made your pussy *wet* while you did them?"

I picked my head up, focusing on him. He'd pushed off the counter and was looking me up and down like he was ready to eat me alive.

"If you don't love her, why stay with her?" I asked quietly. "Stop wasting her time."

He narrowed his eyes, and as if my statement had punched him in the gut, he looked to the right, away from me. He was quiet for a beat, so quiet I could hear Mom and Dad's shower running.

"Come with me," he ordered lightly. He walked past me, going for the door that led out to the pool. He made his way out, and I blew a breath, looking over my shoulder before following behind him.

It was still warm outside, and also a little humid. I thought about my hair, and how frizzy it would get if I stayed out here for too long.

"Cane, what are we doing out here?"

He kept walking, going past the sitting area made of wicker and plush white cotton, until he reached a door. He opened it, turned on a light switch, and stepped inside. My eyes stretched wider when I realized where we were.

"Holy shit." We were in a home theater. There was a large projection screen plastered to the north wall and a projector in the aisle between the reclining leather seats.

A popcorn maker was pushed up against the back wall, as well as a counter that was topped with a bowl of various candies and goodies. Beneath the counter was a stack of movies. I had a feeling I was going to make good use of this place with Frankie during the rest of our stay.

Cane took a step aside, closing the door quietly as I scanned the room again. "You have to pay extra to have access to this room," he said. "Derek wasn't up for paying for it, but I knew you would like it, so I gave him the money to get it."

"Wow. Thanks, Cane, but you didn't have to do that." I turned to face him but he was already looking at me. "What?" I asked, tucking my hair behind my ear. I was nervous now. He was looking at me like I had two heads. Did I look bad? Did I not put on enough makeup? Had my hair become a ball of frizz from that short walk here? "What? Stop looking at me like that and say what's on your mind already."

His stare switched then, to that same searing hot gaze he always used—the gaze that awakened my soul and made me feel my pulse in every sensitive part of my body.

I realized what this was right away.

He wanted to show me this room himself. He wanted me to know he'd gotten it just for me, but he also wanted something else. *Needed* something else.

Before I could completely process this moment, Cane took a step toward me, grabbed me by the waist, picked me up like I was the weight of a feather, and pressed my back to the wall. His chest warmed mine, his groin sinking between my legs. Without warning, his mouth swept over my neck, nipping, sucking, and biting.

I didn't know where this was coming from, but I refused to stop him. No matter how much the guilt swallowed me up, or how badly I knew we needed to quit this before I ended up hurting my parents or even Kelly, I didn't stop. He'd gotten me when my walls had crumbled, and he didn't give a damn about stepping over the bricks in order to catch me.

I sighed and twisted my fingers in his hair, the heel of my sandals digging into his lower back. He groaned, bringing his mouth up to my ear.

"Why the fuck can't I stay away from you?" he growled. "Why? I don't fucking get it."

"I don't know," I breathed. I really didn't know why Cane couldn't resist me. Kelly was much more mature, and she was very pretty. She was any man's dream girl. She kept in great shape, ate well, and knew how to cook, too...but he seemed to want me more.

Was it because he knew he couldn't have me? Did the forbidden thrill him just as much as it thrilled me? Or did he just like that I was untouched and uneducated about sex, and wanted to teach me all the dirty things?

"All I want to do is touch you. Taste you. I've never been this fucking weak for a girl in all my life." He sucked on the lobe of my ear and I shivered. He took a step back, placing me on my feet. "Get on your knees," he ordered, breathing quickly.

I frowned a little. "W-what?"

"Get on your knees, Kandy."

My brows stitched but I didn't hesitate. It was a dream of mine to please him—to give him whatever he wanted, no matter how bad he was for me.

I lowered to my knees, and on the way down I noticed how hard he was. His cock was pushing on the fabric, trying to break through the jeans.

"Unzip my pants."

I unzipped them, and he pushed them down just enough to reveal his hard, angry, beautiful cock. Veins ran along the length of him, straight down to the round, thick tip that was glistening with pre-cum. Kelly hadn't pleased him since we arrived in Destin. I could tell. He was way too hard, like he hadn't fucked in weeks.

I would never forget how big he was. So big that it frightened and thrilled me all the same. He didn't have the size or girth of a beginner. He was fully developed and intimidating as hell. I was sure I would cry tears of joy when he entered me for the first time, and then cry out in pure bliss when I adjusted around his size and came all over him.

"What now?" I whispered, looking up.

"I'm sure you know what to do."

My tongue ran over my lips, and I leaned forward, kissing the tip of his cock. He shuddered and groaned, closing his eyes like he couldn't handle my teasing—like he would explode if I didn't hurry up.

I started to lift a hand to hold his waist, but he shook his head, lightly pushing my hand away. "No hands. I only want your mouth."

I focused on him, enjoying the instruction. I spread my lips apart and wrapped them around his tip. He let out a hard, heavy sigh, glaring down at me.

"Suck," he rasped. "But be quick. They'll be looking for us soon."

I nodded and brought him deeper into my mouth, making his cock slick. I leaned back and then mounted forward again, hungry for another taste. He tasted clean and fresh, like he'd showered not too long ago, and his flesh ran smoothly through my lips.

He sighed heavily, over and over again, his breaths becoming more and more shallow with every mouthful. I lowered myself to suck his balls too and he hissed through clamped teeth.

"Shit, Kandy," he groaned. "Do that again."

I did it again, and he groaned even louder, his body tensing up.

It was hard not being able to use my hands, but I did it, and I felt like a professional. Like I was a master at giving blowjobs. I felt confident, eager, and ready for my grand prize. The prize was to have every illicit drop of his cum.

With that in mind, I didn't stop. It only fueled me.

So I sucked faster. Head bobbing, throat constricting as I gagged. He loved when I gagged. Every time I did, he'd thrust forward, trying to see how long I could last without breathing.

I don't know how I ended up with my back against the wall, or how Cane ended up with his palm pressed to it. He had his other hand on top of my head and was thrusting forward and backward into my mouth now.

"Oh yeah, baby. Stay just like that. Let me fuck this gorgeous face."

I stayed still, mouth wide open for him. Faint tears crept to the corners of my eyes, but this wasn't torture to me at all. No, this was the satisfaction of submission. This was exactly what he wanted—what *I* wanted. I knew it. He knew it. All I wanted to do was give myself to him. Please him. Do everything to, for, and with him.

"Don't close your eyes," he said when I was about to shut them. "Look at me while I feed you my cum." His voice was a near growl, raspy and thick. It was foreign to me. I'd never heard him this way, so feral. A true savage.

His nostrils flared, and the hand he had on my head was bringing it forward until my lips were pressed to his pelvis and his cock was touching the back of my throat. I heaved hard.

Heaved again.

I was about to lift my hands and plead for a little breath, but he said, "I'm close, Kandy. Don't. Fucking. Move." By his tense tone, I could hear how close he was—could *feel* it by how hard and thick he'd become in my mouth. I toughed it out.

He jerked back, giving me a few seconds to reclaim oxygen, and then he thrust himself back into my mouth again. "Breathe through your nose," he ordered, voice tight. And I did. It helped. I could breathe. Could focus. "Fuck, your throat feels so good," he groaned.

I could feel his eruption starting, moving from the base, and building up, pulsing between my lips. He came in a matter of seconds. It was an intense orgasm, so intense that he was cursing repeatedly beneath his breath and had even squeezed his eyes shut.

"Fuck," he cursed one more time. A taste of him landed on my tongue when he jerked back a bit. I swallowed as quickly as I could, moaning while remembering to breathe through my nose.

Finally releasing his grip on my head, he groaned, pressing his forehead to the wall. I pulled back just a little, sucking him clean, making his entire body shiver with satisfaction.

"You're too good," he said through a low chuckle, revealing two straight rows of white teeth. "Too fucking good, Bits."

I stared at him. He was so beautiful from this angle. The chiseled jaw, slight stubble, and pink lips. "You have a nice smile," I told him. "Maybe you should show it more often."

He pushed off the wall and grabbed my hand, helping me stand. "Not a chance." He stared at me as he fixed his jeans. I tried to fix my hair, my jumpsuit—anything that would help me avoid the awkwardness of the aftermath.

"What are we doing?" I finally asked, taking a step back.

He blinked and dropped his head, looking toward the popcorn stand. "I have no fucking clue, Kandy Cane."

I smiled. I couldn't help myself. I loved that name so much. "I'll be in college soon, you know."

"Yeah, I know. Indiana is far as hell from here."

"Yeah. This will probably end by then...whatever *this* is."

He sighed and shrugged. "Maybe it will be for the best. Maybe you'll meet some college guy who will distract you enough to make you forget about me."

I thought on that for a moment, and found myself shaking my head. "I doubt it. I've tried getting over you before. It didn't work. We're always led here, doing things like what we just did and...I like it, Cane. I like when you teach me and tell me what to do. I don't think some college boy is going to do it for me."

His glassy eyes turned a shade darker, his lips pinching together like my words had taken him to a darker place.

"But it's complicated," I continued. "You were right. We can't keep doing this while my parents are around. It's too risky."

"Yeah, it is," he agreed. He studied me briefly before taking a step back. He swept his eyes over me, fixing his shirt. "You'd let me teach you? Dominate you?" he asked.

"*Dominate* me? Like BDSM stuff?"

He narrowed his eyes, smirking. "What do you know about BDSM?"

"I read. I know there are, like, whips and chains and gags and stuff..." I could feel the heat rising in my cheeks as I fought a smile. "I don't think I'd be able to go that far..."

He stepped forward, holding my waist. "You wouldn't have to, because BDSM isn't my thing."

"Well, what is your thing?"

"I like to be in control of situations. I like giving orders. Pushing and testing limits. I love the mixture of pain and pleasure, and because I do, some women think I'm cruel. You wouldn't be able to handle what I really put out, Kandy."

I put a hand on my hip. "What makes you think so?"

"Because you're still a fucking virgin," he rasped on my lips, and chills ran down my spine, trickling down like tiny flakes of snow. "I'd have to break you in several times before we even reached that point."

"The dominance?" I asked.

"Yeah," he mumbled.

"I want it," I challenged. "So break me in. I want you to."

"I can't."

"Yes, you can. It's what I want. Take my virginity."

"I can't. You may know what you want now, but you're so young, Kandy. You have time ahead of you. Trust me, I'd love to give you what you want, but it would be hard for me to go through with."

I started to speak, but he caught my chin and stopped me. "I want to be selfish with you and if D wasn't my friend, maybe I would, but you and I both know we can't go that far. It would ruin everything, and the last thing I want to do is ruin you."

I was about to speak, but the doorknob jiggled and Cane snatched his hand away, practically taking a leap back and turning toward the popcorn and candy.

"Hey!" Mom exclaimed with a small smile as she entered. "What are you guys doing? We're all waiting for you."

Cane turned casually, as if he wasn't at all bothered by the situation. "Kandy said she was getting bored of waiting so I thought I would show her the theater room, give her something to look forward to when she got back." He smiled. Only a little.

"Oh, Cane." Mom continued to smile, and I was glad she hadn't suspected a thing. I was also glad she couldn't hear my heart pounding in my chest. "You spoil her, you know that? We could have done without the theater." Mom focused on me. "Did you tell him thank you, Kandy? He got this room for you."

"Mom. Yes." I tried hard not to roll my eyes.

Mom looked to Cane for reassurance.

"She did," Cane confirmed, and he put on a charismatic smile. A smile that would have made any woman, even my mom, blush.

And sure enough, she did. "Well, come on!" she insisted. "We have twenty minutes to get there, and I'm starving." I walked her way and she ushered me out. Cane followed behind.

On the way back, Mom was a few steps ahead of me so I glanced back at Cane.

I could tell he was having thoughts similar to mine.

We'd almost gotten caught again, and it hadn't even been twenty-four hours. This was a dangerous game. We couldn't keep playing with fire like this—the only result would be getting burned.

Though I hated the thought of it, I knew we were going to have to put an end to this soon, no matter how hard it would be.

26

KANDY

Three days passed, and Cane and I could hardly even look at each other. Well, okay...I'm lying. We looked, but we didn't say much to each other or linger around one another for long periods of time. I guess after almost getting caught again, it put a scare into both of us.

Not only that, but Kelly and I had bonded a lot more. I never thought I'd catch myself thinking this, but aside from being Cane's girlfriend—or whatever—she was actually pretty cool.

She'd come up to our floor and help us pick out which bikini to wear to the beach. She helped make blueberry pancakes with Mom and me, and she'd even snuck Frankie and me a glass of her wine.

She was cool...but she still wasn't a good match for Cane. To be honest, she may have deserved *better* than him.

I wondered day and night why she stuck around with him after so long. She explained it before, but it still didn't make sense to me to be with someone who didn't want to love you—or be in love with anyone for that matter—but they still got drunk together, and she still hugged on him and kissed him.

I couldn't even be pissed about it. She was trying...and failing.

Before I knew it, it was our last day. We'd packed up and cleaned most of what we could in the beach house, and were eventually on Cane's jet again, flying back to Georgia.

Something had changed, though. On our way to Destin, Cane had no problem sitting beside Kelly, but during our flight to Georgia, he was sitting in the row behind her, working on his laptop. She was reading and sipping on sparkling water. I had a book glued to my face, but I wasn't really reading it. I was too busy passing glances between the two of them. Not once had she looked at him, and not once had he looked at her. Now that I thought about it, I realized they'd hardly said two words to each other that whole day.

We got home when the sun was setting, and Mom ordered Italian for everyone, but mostly to thank Cane for all he'd done for us.

I sat on a stool at the island counter with Frankie beside me, munching on garlic breadsticks. The beach scene was over, and I was glad to finally be able to devour some bread again and not have to worry about my belly pooch sticking out. Frankie and I had worked hard for our summer bodies, doing strenuous work-outs in her backyard, and I was happy it had paid off. Not to mention that my softball conditioning and workouts helped me for the most part.

"I should probably get going," Kelly announced as she picked up her handbag from the counter. "I have a lot of work to catch up on, and I promised to meet a client first thing tomorrow morning." She sighed while walking to Frankie and me. She dropped a kiss on the side of our heads and then went to Mom to give her a tight hug. "Thank you guys *so much* for letting me join you for the trip. It was just what I needed to be inspired again."

"I'll walk you out," Cane offered, pushing off the counter. Kelly pressed her lips with a simple nod. She still wasn't talking to him.

She said goodbye one more time and then they were walking out the kitchen and going through the front door.

"You staying the night, Frank?" I asked, hopping off my stool and taking my plate to the sink.

"Yeah. I don't feel like calling for anyone to pick me up right now." She sighed. "The beach was so amazing, Mr. and Mrs. Jennings. Thank you for letting me annoy you for five days straight. I hope I wasn't too much of a bother."

Mom chimed with laughter as Dad let out a hearty chuckle.

"Trust me," Dad started, placing his plate on the countertop, "no one can annoy or bother me as much as my own daughter."

I sucked my teeth and gave him a soft punch on the shoulder. "Whatever, dude." I walked to the exit of the kitchen. "I'll set up the pull-out for you, Frank."

"Okay." She turned and continued talking to my parents about a boat ride she saw advertised at the beach.

I walked through the foyer to get to the linen closet. On my way, I caught sight of Kelly standing in front of an Audi.

She and Cane were standing by the back doors, and someone was waiting behind the wheel. I think it was an Uber driver. Kelly's face was stern while Cane was going on about something and waving his hands, as if the conversation being held was pointless.

Kelly stepped closer to him and said something...or maybe she'd asked him something.

Cane gave her a blank stare and no response, to which she dropped her gaze. She stepped away from him, shook and bowed her head, and pulled the door open to get in the backseat.

Cane stood there, shoving his inked fingers through his hair as the driver pulled off. Before I could blink again, the car was nowhere in sight.

Cane stood there for about twenty-seconds, and I watched him. Watched as he dropped his hand to his hip, tipped his head so his face was pointed to the sky, shut his eyes, and inhaled for three long seconds.

One.

Two.

Three.

Then he exhaled. He started for our house again, and I turned away, grabbing some fresh sheets out of the closet, shutting the door, and hurrying up the stairs before he could come inside and spot me.

Whatever they were arguing about seemed bad. I was curious and had hoped he would stick around long enough to tell Dad about it so I could eavesdrop, like I always happened to do. Unfortunately, he didn't.

Cane was gone by the time I returned to the kitchen.

27

CANE

It'd been a week since we arrived back in Georgia. I hadn't heard from Kelly since the night we got back. I knew why she was avoiding me, but I wasn't up for talking about it.

I hadn't seen Derek or the family that whole week either. The day after our arrival, I had to catch a flight to Boston to work out a deal. I stayed in Boston for two days before flying to Washington to meet with a potential investor. I spent the rest of the week there and had flown back in Monday morning.

It was hot that day. I was catching up on paperwork at the office when Derek had sent me a text message asking if I wanted to meet up for lunch.

I was now sitting in a booth made of fake red leather at a small breakfast diner, waiting for him to arrive. The place was packed with patrons, the salty scent of bacon floating around, mingling with the sweet, sticky scent of syrup and the thick aroma of coffee.

It was comforting, to be honest. It reminded me of the days before Tempt, when my sister and I would walk a few blocks together to catch a meal. I'd worked at a fast food restaurant after school and would spend all of my money on her and Mom. I always bought groceries with my money, or new clothes and shoes if they were needed. It didn't matter if I was broke by the end of the day. They were my family, I loved them more than anything on earth, and I wanted to be a *real* man who provided for the people he loved, unlike my father.

I'd ordered coffee, and as I poured my cream and sugar into a mug, the bell above the door chimed and I watched Derek walk in.

Derek had the kind of build that could intimidate the average man. With his police uniform on and the belt strapped around his waist with weapons clipped to it, I figured only an idiot would challenge him.

The night he saved my mother, I heard he had to take my father down. My father wasn't a small man. As a child and even a teenager, I always remembered being daunted by the height and size he had on me, so to know Derek had taken him down—tackled him to the ground and even got around to arresting him while hardly putting up a fight—made me automatically respect him.

My father was a shitty human being, but he was blessed with muscles, height, and brawn. I was lucky to have gotten the same genetics.

Derek scanned the restaurant until he found me. He put on a lazy smile and came my way quickly, taking the seat across from me.

"What's up, man?" He sighed, immediately grabbing the carafe of coffee and pouring himself a mug.

"Everything all right?" I asked. Though he'd smiled when he arrived, I noticed the lines around his eyes and the tension in his shoulders.

"Yeah, yeah. I'm good. Just a long fucking morning. Nothing a little coffee and greasy lunch won't cure." If I thought my job was stressful, I was certain it had nothing on being a cop. He loved his job, but it wore him out daily. That much was clear.

I sensed that wasn't the only thing bothering him. I knew not to budge, though. He'd cave eventually.

"How was your flight back?" he asked, stirring a spoon in his mug.

"It was decent. I'll have to fly again this weekend."

"All that flying," he huffed a laugh. "I bet you're sick of it."

"Not when it happens to be on a jet." I smirked. "No one to bother me. Quick trips. No phone calls or messages."

"Oh, yeah. Not even from Kelly?" He picked his head up and cocked a brow, giving me a stern look like he knew something I didn't.

"She's been busy."

"I call bullshit." He sipped from his mug. "Mindy told me a few days ago that she called Kelly. Said they met up for brunch." He placed his mug down. "She said she invited Kelly over for dinner, but Kelly declined because she didn't think you would want her coming around when you two aren't together anymore."

I tipped my chin, locking my jaw. "I see."

Derek's eyes widened, and for a moment they reminded me of Kandy's, when she was curious but also demanded answers.

I exhaled. "It's...a long story."

"I've got nothing but time, brother." He sat back, still looking at me. "I thought she was a pretty cool girl. She was patient with you. Seemed like you guys had fun at the beach. What happened between then and now?"

I shrugged. "Apparently spending five days with me made her realize that we may not be a good fit for each other. She said I'm *too distant* because I don't want to open up to her about my past." I swallowed before speaking again. "She also thinks I'm hiding something from her...but I can't let her know too much about my past, D. There's—there's too much. You know all about the shit I went through. I just don't like reliving it. I feel like she knows enough."

"Well, if you love her, you'll have to tell her one day. Just like you told me to tell Mindy about my situation with the shooting, you have to tell Kelly yours, no matter how hard it might be to relive. You can't keep that shit from her forever."

I shook my head. "That's the thing. I don't really love her. Like? Yeah. But I don't love her. Not like that. I wasn't head over heels for Kelly like she was for me, and she sensed that, but she stuck around anyway."

"Well, if you feel that way, why string her along? Why bring her to the beach and share a room with her for almost a week?"

"She begged to go, Derek. It's not like I asked her to. She insisted—said it would be good for us, and a way for us to really get to know each other. Well, she got to know me, and I guess she didn't like what she got."

He sighed with a smile. "You're a complicated man, Cane. Even I know that. You're already difficult as a friend. I can't imagine having to be in her shoes and trying to understand you as a lover."

I shrugged. I wasn't about to tell him the real reason why she didn't want to deal with me anymore. What I told him was only part of it.

Our server arrived, and we both ordered hot turkey sandwiches and french fries. Derek's phone chimed and he pulled it out to check. When he did, he sighed agitatedly.

"What's up?"

He tucked his phone into his back pocket. "Mindy," he mumbled. "Wants me to pick up dinner tonight since she'll be working late."

"Oh."

"She's been working late all week, trying to catch up after our vacation. Get this, I went to visit her at the office to bring her some coffee and donuts yesterday, and I saw this guy in her fucking office."

I narrowed my brows. "Who was he?"

"Her fucking boss. He's laughing with her and shit, giving her compliments about her work and leaning all over her fucking desk. It annoyed the hell out of me, so when she got home, I told her I didn't like the way her boss was all in her face. She insisted that it was harmless, but fuck that. I know men, and I also know Mindy. She's too damn nice sometimes and always wants everyone to be satisfied, especially about her work."

I laughed. "I highly doubt she wants anything from him, man. Maybe another promotion, but you know her. She loves you too much."

"I know, I know. I just didn't like the way he was acting around her. Something about him irked me. And then he sized me up when I kissed her, like I couldn't see him through the corner of my eye. He wants her, but if he lays a finger on her, I'll arrest his ass for assault and break his arm while doing it." He rubbed his forehead. "We got into a heated debate about it last night. She went to work upset this morning. I'll have to make up for it somehow."

I chuckled. "Picking dinner up will be a start."

"Yeah, I guess. Kinda glad we'll have some time alone soon. We haven't had time to ourselves in months. Our anniversary is coming up in a few weeks. Going to Paris for the first time."

"That's good for you guys and a great getaway. You'll love it there, D. There's a completely different vibe in that city. And it's so diverse. That's what I love most about it."

"Yeah. I hear a lot of great things about it." He finished off his sandwich and then took a few gulps of coffee. As he chewed and swallowed, the walkie-talkie on his shoulder crackled and a voice came through. It was low enough for only the two of us to hear.

He grabbed the walkie and pressed a button, responding to the call, then said, "Ahh, I gotta go. Some break-in downtown." He slid out of the booth and dusted himself off before standing up straight. "Oh, uh, before I take off, I wanted to ask if Kandy could use your pool this summer? She's been dying to take a swim since we got back from the beach. Claims she misses the pool and has been nagging that we need to have one built. She talks about it every damn day, and it's driving me crazy. That girl is not going to be happy until my pockets are inside out , I swear." I laughed when he did, but the mere mention of her name stirred my stomach, making it feel too small for the sandwich I'd just eaten.

I played it cool. "You know you guys are always welcome, D. Tell her she can drop by anytime and to grab a key from security at the gate. I'll add her to the entry list today."

"Cool, cool." He looked me over twice, and for a moment I wondered if he could sense that I was hiding something. "You're a great friend, man. You know that?" *Relief.* "Ever since I met you, we instantly connected. You remember that? The click was impossible to miss. Not sure what the hell I would do without you, Cane."

He clapped my shoulder, and I gave him a slight smile before he took off. Though I was glad he hadn't sensed my deception and lies, his words still slayed me.

Derek trusted me. Deep down to his core, I knew if anything were to ever happen to him, he would want me to take on the role of being Kandy's father figure. He'd said it once, a long, long time ago.

Taking on that role could never happen now. He'd have to find another candidate—a man who didn't want to bend his daughter over and fuck her senseless.

28

KANDY

"I'm so glad Mr. Cane is letting us use his pool!" Frankie was excited, but I think I beat that excitement by a million.

I had begged Dad over and over again to get in touch with Cane to see if he'd let us swim in his pool. I mean, Cane had bragged about it over dinners at the beach so much that I wanted to experience myself. He wasn't lying about the built in waterfall. It was beautiful.

I knew if I had asked, Cane would have made an excuse, just so he wouldn't have to be around me without them, but if Dad asked, he wouldn't say no. Sure enough, it worked.

Frankie picked me up from my house the morning after Dad told me, and drove us to his place first thing.

"I'm glad too. You still volunteering at the camp this weekend?" I asked, rubbing sunscreen on my thighs.

"Yeah. It's like a big brother thing. The kids are all in foster care, and I kind of know how it is to feel abandoned, you know? It'll be great to connect with them and let them know there's hope."

"Aw, Frank. I think that's the sweetest thing you've ever said!"

"Yeah, maybe it is. But if you ever tell anyone about it I'll cut you in half."

I laughed, placing the bottle of sunscreen down and turning over to lay on my belly. I placed one hand on top of the other, then rested my chin on top of my hands.

"Are you and Mr. Cane still messing around?"

"Meh. Not really. Not since the beach. He also hasn't really been coming around much. Haven't heard much of Kelly either. I saw them arguing the night we got back from Destin. I think she was mad at him about something."

"They probably broke up. Don't get me wrong—Kelly is so pretty, but she is not a good match for him."

"That's what I said!"

"She's way too nice for him, and it's pretty obvious that he's not that interested in her. Maybe he was in the beginning, but now it kind of seems like he's just with her so other people won't assume he's gay."

"Oh my gosh, Frank. Shut up," I laughed. "Trust me, he's far from gay."

"After the way I saw his tongue going down your throat, yeah, I'd bet a million bucks that he isn't."

My friend was a straight-up goof.

We sunbathed and swam for about two hours before leaving. There was no sign of Cane.

The next day, after doing some dorm room shopping with Mom, I figured another swim wouldn't hurt, so I had her drop me off after we unloaded the car. She didn't think anything of it. She also had to go into work for a meeting and was running late, so I told her I'd be okay waiting until she could pick me up again.

I loved his pool. It was never too cold or too warm. The temperature was soothing, and I spent the day floating in the water, basking in the sun. The sun had drained me by the time I was ready to get out, so I started to collect my things, but when I stood up, someone was standing in front of the glass door.

Cane.

He stood there with his hands in his pockets, and it seemed he'd been standing there for a quite some time.

I waved, and he took a hand out of his pocket to wave back. I slid my bag over my shoulder and walked to the door. He opened it for me, and ushered me inside the cool house.

"Had a good swim?"

"Yeah." I nodded. "It was just what I needed."

"Didn't get enough in Destin, huh?"

"Not by a long shot. If I could live there, I would. I loved that beach."

He smirked and took a step back. "Well, if you want to shower, I have a guest bathroom with everything in it. I'm assuming you're hungry after being out there all day?"

"Ugh. Yeah, I'm starving."

"Good. I ordered some Chinese." He shrugged. "I feel like being a pig tonight. Go shower. Food should be here by the time you're done."

I nodded, walking past him to get to the stairs. I looked over my shoulder, but he wasn't watching like I'd expected him to be. Instead, he had turned and was making his way to the kitchen.

I don't know why I was expecting dinner to be at his fancy dinner table in the dining room. Instead, Cane had taken out two folding trays, placed them in front of the couch in one of the dens, and then set his plate down on top of one of the trays, along with a glass of what I assumed was scotch.

He was acting weird today, but I said nothing of it. Instead, I topped my plate with *lo mein* and chicken fried rice, grabbed two fortune cookies, and joined him in the den.

He had the TV on and was watching a sports channel. This was definitely unlike him. The only time I saw Cane watch TV was if he was visiting my dad, who loved TV. He'd even told me once that he was too busy to sit around and watch a lot of shows, though he did try to catch a few games here and there if my dad told him it was a big one.

"Is everything okay?" I asked. I couldn't help remembering this was the den where everything between us started. Maybe he was thinking about that.

"Yeah. I'm good." He took a bite of his food.

"What makes you want to watch TV?"

He shrugged and placed his fork down, replacing it with his water. "I don't know. Had a shitty day. One of my deals didn't go through, and I can only blame myself. My head wasn't in the game." He huffed. "I just wanted to come home and forget about work for a while. Feel a little more human, and not so driven. You know?"

I bobbed my head. "I get it." I was quiet for a second, using the prongs of my fork to shift my food around. "Why wasn't your head in the game?"

"Just a lot of shit with my mom. Some stuff about Kelly, too." He said his last sentence softer than the first. But to me, it rang the loudest.

"What happened with Kelly? I haven't seen her in a while."

He looked at me through the corner of his eye before focusing on the TV again. "We aren't talking anymore."

"Why not?"

He shrugged for, like, the tenth time that night. Cane really sucked at pretending to be careless. "She got to know the *real* me in Destin, I guess."

"What is that supposed to mean?" I asked through a small laugh.

He took a brief pause, squeezing the bridge of his nose and shutting his eyes. He swallowed hard after several seconds and then continued. "It started when we were at the beach. I'd had a little too much to drink and so did she." He sighed. "We were in our room there. You guys were downstairs with music on, playing UNO. She was kissing me, trying to get me in the mood, but I was so damn drunk—" He stopped talking abruptly, staring me in the eyes. "I called her by your name, Kandy."

When he said that, my heart sped up a notch. I wasn't expecting that at all. "W-What?"

"Yeah." A small smirk swept over his sculpted lips as he focused on the amber liquid in his glass. His eyes then flashed up to mine, and he took a long swallow before pulling his gaze away. "That's how I know you're fucking with my head, Bits."

What was I supposed to say to that? *Oh, I apologize that the woman who was in the way of us, left you?* If that was the case, I wasn't sorry. Though I liked Kelly now, I was glad she was out of the picture—happier than I should have been about it, honestly. I was selfish with Cane. So very, very selfish, and he knew that. We both did.

"She was drunk enough that she didn't remember the name I'd called her the next day. I think all she remembers is that it was another woman's…which is a good thing."

"A very good thing." If Kelly would have heard him say my name, I was certain she would have gotten suspicious and figured things out. She had developed a bond with my mom, so I knew she would tell her first thing.

Kelly was a Goody-Two-shoes kind of woman. Mom was all about justice. They liked honesty, which made them the perfect duo. Two good, honest, kind-hearted women.

"Well, if I can be honest for a second, I'm glad you two split up."

His smile was faint. "Of course you are, Bits." He drew in a breath. "Shit like this usually doesn't bother me, but I guess since she'd been around for so long that it feels weird when she doesn't call, text, or visit."

"Yeah, I guess I can understand that." It sucked to hear, but I was glad he was telling me.

He placed a hand on my knee. "But I have you. I'll always have you, right?"

"Aren't you usually trying to get rid of me?" I laughed.

He ignored my joke. "I mean it, Bits. If all else fails, I know you'll be there. It feels good to know there are people out here who care about me." He held my gaze, and I felt a swirl in the pit of my belly. A clench between my thighs. He had no idea how badly I wanted to climb on top of him and kiss him, show him how much I *really* cared about him.

I more than cared about Cane. I was in fucking love with the crazy man, and he was too blinded by lust and confusion to realize it.

A knock sounded at the door, and I gasped while Cane jerked back. I had been leaning into him, ready to press my lips to his. I believe he was about to give in and let me. He stood from the sofa and glanced back at me once before stepping around the corner and going for the door.

"Hi, Cane! I didn't realize you'd be home so early!" It was Mom.

I straightened up and busied myself with my food.

They stepped around the corner and into the den. Mom smiled at me. "Did you get enough sun? You're going to be burnt to a crisp if you keep it up," she joked.

Cane chuckled.

I forced a laugh to keep the mood light.

"Yeah, we can go. Let me just take my plate to the kitchen."

"Oh, Kandy. Don't worry about that. I got it." Cane took a step forward and grabbed my plate. "I'm sure your mother is tired. Maybe you should drive her home."

"Yeah, maybe you should," she agreed. "I'm tired of being your chauffeur."

"Then get me a car." I stuck my tongue out at her.

She laughed, but nothing more. I was still waiting on the day they'd give me a car. Mom and Dad had well-paying jobs, Mom in particular, but I was still carless at eighteen. It didn't make any sense to me why they weren't spoiling me with a Maserati or a Tesla. Okay...that was a bit much, but still.

I grabbed my bag and met up with Mom, who wrapped her arm around my shoulders and walked with me to the door. Cane followed us out, and when we got into the car, he told us goodnight.

His eyes lingered on mine more than they should have. He backed away and stood on the cement walkway that led to his front door, while I pulled out of the driveway and away from the house. I glanced at him one more time before pulling off.

"Cane is so good to us," Mom exhaled. "Letting you use his pool *and* feeding you. He's a busy man, and I'm sure he just wants to come to a quiet home and escape the madness. Have you thanked him for letting you use the pool and for being in his home while he's away?"

No, in fact, I hadn't thanked him. But I would eventually. I lied anyway, just so she wouldn't scold me. "Of course I thanked him. He is a nice person."

"Yes, he is. You know, your dad has had a lot of weird, dumb, selfish friends, but Cane is none of those things. He's probably the only friend of your dad's that I actually approve of and like being around. He's very supportive and uplifting of everyone and always gives me a good vibe when he's around. There's never any negativity from Cane. He's also great with your Dad when it comes to that crazy temper of his."

Great, Mom. Just great. Keep making me feel like shit for wanting him.

She sighed. "To be honest, I still wonder why he sticks around so much. We don't have much to offer him, other than our friendship. During the times he visits for dinners, he could be eating in a fancy restaurant or going on a date. I don't know." She shrugged and let out a short breath. "I guess it's just nice to know his time spent with us is real and genuine. You know?"

"Okay, Mom. You should probably stop. You're being super sentimental right now."

Her laughter was a soft chime, filling the car. "God, I know, baby. I know. It's just…me and your dad's anniversary is coming up, and you'll be in college soon. It's all happening so fast, you know?"

I reached over to rub her shoulder. "It's okay, Mom. Seriously, I'll visit all the time…especially if you give me a car."

In that moment, it seemed an imaginary sponge had soaked up all her tears. She gave me a dull look with a slight smile and said, "Nice try, little girl, but I'm a lawyer. I see right through that little sympathy card you just tried to pull on me."

"You can't say it wasn't a good one, though!"

She stared at me, trying to fight a grin.

It was useless.

We both broke into laughter, the sounds nearly identical.

29

KANDY

Something unexpected happened three and a half weeks before I was supposed to be going to college: Dad asked me to go out on a father-daughter date with him.

How was this unexpected? Well, it had caught me off guard because Dad and I never really spent time together outside of the house. Yes, we had the vacation, and yes, he'd come home every day, happy to see his family, but outside of home, we never really hung out one-on-one.

If I could recall the last time we did go on one of our father-daughter dates, I was sixteen, and the only reason we hung out that day was because I needed a new dress for the homecoming dance. Mom couldn't take me, so I had to drag Dad along with me. We bought a dress, and then he teased me about how he was going to feed me so much ice cream that I would feel sick and couldn't go to the dance to be ogled by teenage boys. He was a goof that way.

There was a knock on my door, and I instantly knew it was him by the knock. He double-tapped three times. I was in the middle of reading a magazine article about a new matte nail polish.

"Come in," I called.

Dad opened the door with a small smile. I expected to see him in his uniform, but he was dressed in casual clothing. He ran a hand over the top of his dark, wavy head of hair, stepping inside and looking around, like he hadn't seen my room in a while.

Now that I thought about it, maybe it had been a while since he last stepped foot in here. Dad was very much like Mom in the sense that they didn't like to invade my privacy. They felt everyone deserved their own place of solitude. Outside of my room, though, there was no such thing as privacy. I'd lost count of how many times Dad asked me teasingly who I was texting whenever we were around each other.

"What's up, kid?" he asked. I gave him a suspicious look.

"Um...nothing." I closed my magazine, sitting up higher in my recliner. "Why are you being weird?" I laughed.

"I'm being weird? Really?" His eyes stretched wide, and then he shook his head. "I just wanted to pop in. Say hello. It's also my day off. Wasn't sure if you had any plans with Frankie or anything..."

"I don't. She volunteers at a summer camp on the weekends," I told him.

"Oh, okay." His eyes lit up then, like he'd had an idea but wasn't sure it would work out. "Well, since we're both free, I thought we could have one of our father-daughter dates again. You know, like how we used to have, with a movie, some popcorn, and those peanut M&M's you like? You still like those, right?"

I laughed. "Yeah, Dad. I still like them."

"Well, good. Let's catch a movie then. Figured we should try and hang out since me and your mom will be going to Paris soon. What do you say?"

"That sounds great, actually." I climbed off the bed. "I'll meet you downstairs in ten."

"Cool, cool." He stepped back and grabbed the doorknob. He was about to turn back and say something, but he stopped himself, deciding to close the door behind him instead.

If there was one thing I knew about my dad, it's that he was never really sure how to handle my teenage self. When I was younger, he said I couldn't get enough of being around him, but as I developed, he realized that I wanted to be alone more. I became closed-off, feisty, and talked less.

Dad said he didn't have any siblings and also that his parents weren't very good role models, so he was still learning. For that, I cut him some slack. He wasn't doing a terrible job. Not by a long shot.

***

Dad drove us to the same movie theater we always went to when I was a little girl. It was the one that had the pink riding dragon in the lobby, where I used to punch in a quarter and ride the thing for two exciting minutes. Sometimes more than once.

We ordered a large popcorn with extra butter and a king-sized pack of peanut M&M's. We were seeing some action movie that had Michael B. Jordan in it. While we did, I realized that I missed these moments—hanging out with my dad one-on-one, cracking jokes on him and letting him do the same to me.

He always teased me about my hair, saying I most likely got it from him because when it frizzed up, I looked like I had an afro. He could be such an ass. It was no wonder he and Cane got along so well.

Thinking of Cane instantly brought my mood down. His best friend was all I could think about, and he didn't even know it. My dad had his issues, yes, but overall he was a great person and didn't deserve betrayal or secrets.

After the movie, we went to grab some frozen yogurt. I got the cheesecake flavor and topped mine with gummy bears and chocolate chips. When I sat down, Dad looked at my sweet concoction and scrunched his nose.

"What?" I laughed, digging right in. "Don't hate. You're just jealous that mine has more flavor than yours. Who comes to a place like this and only gets vanilla yogurt? So lame," I joked.

"Yeah, yeah, whatever." His laugh rumbled deep. That one really tickled him. "Won't be surprised if you start complaining about how much your stomach hurts later." His eyes widened. "Oh, man. That reminds me. I remember when you were seven, and we went out to a self-serve ice cream parlor for your birthday. I let you get whatever you wanted on it. Girl, you piled it high with everything. Gummy worms, chocolate fudge, cookie crumbles, caramel, more chocolate fudge—everything! Your mom flipped out!"

I busted out laughing. "Oh—now that you say it, think I remember that!"

"Yep. But I told your mom it was okay, that it was your birthday, and you could have whatever you wanted."

I bobbed my head. "Mm-hmm."

"Turns out you weren't okay. You got home, jumped all over the place because you were pumped with sugar, and then you threw up all over your bed. It was a mess."

"Oh, God," I groaned, wincing.

"Your mom told me off. You know how she is," he chuckled after taking a bite. "But it was cool. I told her I had it handled, so I tossed your sheets in the washer, helped you get in the shower, and then took you down to the man cave so we could watch your favorite princess movies."

"Really?" I smiled, dropping my gaze.

"Yep. I remember that day so well because it was the first time you asked *me* to take care of you. Before that, you would always ask your mom to help you with stuff like that, but when you asked me, it made me proud, you know? I felt like a real dad in that moment. And holding you in my arms as we watched those cheesy, girly movies was the icing on top. Wouldn't trade that moment for the world."

"Wow, Dad." I was in awe. "That's so sweet."

His smiled lingered as he finished off his yogurt. I saw a sad shadow run over him, and my chest tightened. When he was done, he set his empty cup down and watched me for a moment. "Look, Kandy...I know I'm not the greatest dad sometimes. I suck at expressing myself. I guess because I wasn't really raised in a home that encouraged that." He scratched at his neck, where the scar was. "I can do crazy things and can get really out of hand, but none of that changes my love for you, you know? I love you so damn much, and I would do anything for you. Even though you've grown up and don't want to spend as much time with your old man, it doesn't change anything. I will always see you as my little girl. My baby. You hear me?" He grabbed my earlobe and tugged on it, like he used to do when I was little.

I smiled and bit back tears. "I know, Dad. And stop lying to yourself. You're a *great* father. You're busy, just like Mom, but that doesn't make her less of a mother or a bad mom at all. I get it."

"I'm never too busy for you. I know that shooting kind of messed things up, and I can't do as many of the activities I used to, but I'm here. Anytime you want to catch a movie or grab some lunch and dessert, I'm down, you know? Unless you don't want to be seen in public with this guy?"

"I mean...you *are* kind of lame," I teased, laughing with him.

"Lame? Could a lame man pull a woman as beautiful as your mother?"

I giggled. "You always use that as your defense!"

"Well, hey, it's true. When I met your mom, there was a *line* of guys after her. I went to a college party, and she was known as the pretty, smart girl who was working toward being a lawyer. She was also a party-girl. How she kept on top of her grades and did all the drinking she did, I have no clue. But she did it." He winked. "And somehow, out of all the guys there, she noticed me, and I didn't even go to that school. It's obvious I have swag."

"Oh my gosh, Dad. Did you really just say *swag*?" I busted out laughing. "Please do yourself a favor and never say that again."

He flashed a wide smile as I continued laughing. I loved seeing Dad like this. Smiling. Happy. Playful. These carefree moments made my heart beat with glee.

He reached across the table and rubbed the top of my forearm. "Just know I'm always here for you. Doesn't matter if you're right upstairs or thousands of miles away. If you ever need anything, I'm here for you, you understand?"

I nodded.

"I would kill for you, Kandy, and I mean that. You're my baby girl, and nobody messes with my girl. Nobody." He winked and flashed a dimple. I smiled, but couldn't help the pounding of my heart. It was as if the guilt had snuck its way out of the darkest corners of my body and was streaming through my blood like poison, paralyzing my heart.

I looked into my father's adoring eyes and hated myself. How could I do this to him? How could I do this to Cane? I loved Cane, yes, but I loved my father so much more. So why was it so damn hard to let go?

"Hey, what's wrong?" he asked, his eyes serious now. "I didn't say any of that to make you feel bad. I just want you to know I love you, and I'm always here for you."

"I know, Dad. Trust me, I'll never forget it." I dropped my hands and twisted my fingers in my lap, blinking back the tears.

"Good." He ruffled my hair then knuckled my cheek. "Come on, let's get out of here."

During the ride, the anxiety coursed through me. It was powerful. I felt awful, and, honestly, sick to my stomach. I wished in that moment I was still the innocent the seven-year-old girl with the weak stomach. I wished I could erase the memories I had with Cane. I wished that he really was nothing more to me than my dad's friend.

Why did I have to want him so badly? Why did he have to want me just as much? Why was all of this so fucking complicated? I hadn't even gone to college yet, but it felt like life had already set me up to fail.

I couldn't handle the guilt. It was literally eating me alive, to the point that my stomach truly began to ache. I told Dad I didn't feel well when we got home, and he left me to rest, but resting didn't happen.

Hot tears ran over the bridge of my nose instead. My eyes were tight and raw.

The guilt was undeniable, painful, and the saddest part? I wasn't going to stop wanting Cane, despite knowing the guilt and lies could destroy me.

30

KANDY

The day before my parents left for their anniversary, I was surprised with a white 2-door Honda Civic. My first car and I loved everything about it.

"Oh my God! Seriously!" I squealed. "I love you guys so much!" I squeezed them both around the neck. "Thank you! I knew you weren't going to let me be eighteen and carless!"

They both broke into fits of laughter.

"You better take good care of this, you hear me?" Dad scolded lightly. "No reckless driving, no texting, and definitely no driving drunk."

"That's right," Mom agreed.

"Yes, yes! I promise!" I shouted. They could have told me I had to wash dishes every night for the rest of the summer, and I would have agreed.

"And it better stay clean!" Dad demanded.

I nodded way too eagerly, squeezing my hands together, desperate for the keys.

Mom insisted on taking a hundred pictures of me with Bubby —the name of my car. As soon as Dad handed me the keys, I took it for a spin by going to Frankie's house, where she took a hundred more pictures of me with my new car.

The next day my parents left for Paris. I was sad to see them go, but was happy that they'd been together for over twenty years and were able to do something special together.

I drove them to the airport. Dad cupped the back of my head and gave me a rough kiss on the forehead after shutting the trunk of my car. He could be rough that way—*tough love* is what he called it.

"We'll see you in a week, sweet cheeks." He gave me another rough kiss before Mom stepped up and gave me a tight hug and kiss on the cheek.

"See you when we get back, okay? Be good." She kissed me once more.

"I'm going to have the whole house scanned for prints when I get back, so don't even try it with the house parties!" Dad shouted from behind her.

I laughed as Mom shook her head and narrowed her eyes at him, giving that adorable, loving expression she always gave when she thought he was the *hottest goof on earth*. Those words exactly, because she said them often when describing him to me.

To be honest, my parents were adorable as hell. I loved their relationship, and was glad they weren't another statistic—you know, where there are two busy, working parents with a child or children and they lose their love for each other? Sure, they'd had their ups and downs, but they got through all of it together and let love win. They raised me together, and I think I turned out pretty okay.

I smiled as they walked off, both of them waving as I got into the car. I rolled the window down and Mom blew a kiss at me, and I returned the gesture. I watched them until I could no longer see them, then I drove back to a quiet home.

It was roughly nine in the morning, and I was kind of hungry, so I made a bowl of cereal while scrolling through my phone at the counter.

I cleaned my room next, hung up a few of the shirts Mom had washed for me before she left, and then I went down to Dad's man cave to watch Netflix.

During all of it, I tried ignoring the nagging in the back of my head, the dark thoughts, the ones behind the locked door in my mind.

Eventually, they broke out and left me pacing the house, trying to find any little thing to do to occupy myself.

Cane came to mind. My Cane. My parents were going to be gone for an entire week. Cane said he would be working in town for a few days and told them he'd keep an eye on me. I'd overheard his phone conversation with Dad.

He was in the city.

I was home alone.

This is perfect, the thoughts whispered.

I stared at the dark screen of the phone sitting on the cushion beside me. The better thing to do would have been to ignore the whispers and let a movie consume me, or even use the money Mom gave me to take my new car out and go shopping for a new dress or blouse.

None of that happened. My fingers tingled, and my heart began to whisper too, begging me to pick up the phone and get in touch with him. *Just see what he's doing,* my heart whispered. *Check in with him. Let him know you're thinking about him. See if he's thinking about you, too.*

My heart knew no boundaries. She didn't care that she wasn't supposed to want him. And at the end of the day, willpower was not my specialty. I could never deny myself what I wanted, whether it was cake or Cane.

And here's the thing: School was going to be starting in two weeks for me. That meant I only had two more weeks to see as much of Cane as I possibly could. Of course, I listened to my heart, because after those two weeks, I wouldn't see him again for months. I couldn't bear the thought of that.

My summer was quickly coming to an end, and there was something I needed more than anything.

I was sick of the foreplay and sneaking around. Yes, I knew it was wrong to want this so badly, and yes, the guilt trips still killed me, but there was something about Cane that kept me coming back for more. His presence never went unnoticed while he was around, and no matter how hard I tried, I couldn't deny the way my body reacted, even when I was just thinking about him.

I tried to stop it, I really did, but it was so hard.

He'd stopped touching me since we'd left the beach. He hardly even looked at me. I assumed his break-up with Kelly was really bothering him. I hadn't seen her in weeks, and during dinner it was all Mom could talk about. She really liked Kelly and while she thought she was a good fit for Cane, I silently disagreed.

I'd continued to use Cane's pool, but he'd come around less and less. I was sure it was on purpose. His guilt was fierce, too. The only way he could resist was if he wasn't around me at all.

I was desperate. Truly, unbelievably desperate, so I did the only thing a girl my age would have done: I sent him a text.

I told him something that would grab his attention right away —something he wouldn't ignore, no matter how busy he was.

> **Me: Remember when you said you'd give me anything I wanted? I know what I want as my going-away gift.**
> **I want you to take my virginity.**

That was the message, and after hitting the send button, I felt like a damn fool. My throat went dry, and I dropped my phone like it was on fire.

"Oh my God," I gasped. I couldn't believe I'd actually sent that. It didn't help that four agonizing hours passed, and I still hadn't gotten a response. I had popped a bowl of popcorn and went down to Dad's man cave again to watch movies, in attempt to forget I sent it, but it didn't work. Every ten-seconds I would glance at my phone, waiting for it to chime.

Around 10:00 p.m. that night, eight hours later, his name finally popped up on the screen. I immediately pulled my attention away from the movie and snatched up my phone. My heart was racing as I went to my text messages.

His response:

Cane: Kandy, you can't send me stuff like this. Choose something else. Something realistic.

I replied instantly.

Cane, please. It's the only thing I want. It will be the last thing I ever ask for, I swear.

He responded:

No.

I was beyond frustrated, but I was also Kandy Jennings, and I wasn't a quitter. I had fourteen whole days to convince him. I could do it.

The next day, I packed my pool bag and jumped in my car, making my way to Cane's house. I hoped he would be there, but of course he wasn't. I entered an empty house, poured myself a cup of lemonade, and went out to the deck to sunbathe. I believe an hour passed before I heard voices bouncing around inside.

I lowered my sunglasses and saw someone pass by the windows. It was Cane, with his phone to his ear. The thrill sent my heart into overdrive; I could hear the beat of it in my eardrums.

Pushing out of my chair, I walked to the door, drawing it open and stepping onto the cool marble. I heard him in the kitchen and went there, but was surprised to see he wasn't the only person around.

Cane looked my way, as well as a tall man with a blue polo and khaki pants. He had a bag of tools strapped around him, and was saying something about lights before he caught sight of me through the corner of his eye and stopped.

They both stared at me, and I took a slight step back. I was only in my bathing suit—a sky-blue one that made my boobs extra perky. I thought it would only be Cane around. Damn, this was embarrassing.

"Kandy?" Cane cleared his throat and moved around the man. "I didn't know you'd be stopping by today."

"Uh, yeah. I thought I'd make use of the pool today since I don't have much else happening right now."

Cane nodded, and then looked at the man. That's when I realized he was ogling me—literally staring at me like a dog would stare at a piece of meat.

My face heated up, and I took another step back. "We can catch up later," I murmured.

Cane was still staring at the man. I turned and walked away, but heard Cane say, "Stop fucking staring at her," when I was halfway down the hallway.

"You date her?" the man asked.

"She's my friend's daughter," he snapped. "How much are you gonna run me? I need the light fixed by this weekend."

I didn't hear much after that.

I took a quick swim and felt eyes on me again about ten minutes later. Cane was standing on the deck with his arms folded, aviator sunglasses covering his eyes, and his brows dipped.

"What is he fixing?" I asked.

"The chandelier in my living room." His forehead creased even more. "Why are you here, Kandy?" He took a step forward and I swam to his end of the pool.

"I'm swimming, Cane. You said I could use the pool whenever I wanted."

He pressed his lips and shook his head.

I went for the stairs and walked up, going for my towel on the wicker chair. I could feel him watching me the whole time. "Can I use your shower?" I asked.

He bobbed his head. "You already know you can. Just do me a favor this time and don't walk around half naked."

"Possessive much?" I grabbed my bag and walked past him to get to the door. "It would be better if you joined me."

"Go shower," he snapped, and I turned, fighting a smile as I made my way to the staircase. I went to the guest bathroom and took a hot shower, then brushed my hair into a low ponytail. When I was downstairs again, the man who was working on the chandelier was nowhere to be found. Cane was sitting in front of the desk in his office on the first floor, typing away.

"Emails?"

"Yes," he answered absently.

I placed my bag beside the recliner and walked to the stool that was beside the desk, taking the seat. I knew I was distracting him. I didn't care. All I kept thinking about was the time he called me a brat, yet he fed into my spoiled ways constantly. God, I needed to get over myself, but I couldn't help it around Cane. He made me feel innocent and irresistible at the same time.

"Why can't you give me what I want?" I asked, and he immediately stopped typing, swinging his eyes over to mine.

"I'm not in the mood for this right now."

"Well, I need an honest answer. Right now is the perfect time, Cane. My parents are going to be gone for eight days. I'll be nineteen in September, and in two weeks I'll be in college. I'm an adult, and they won't have a clue what I'm up to."

He didn't say anything. The clicking of the keyboard filled the void.

I huffed hard then looked past him, out of the window where men were cutting grass and trimming hedges on his front lawn.

"You asked me what I wanted for a going-away gift. You said it didn't matter what I asked for, you would give it to me." That caught his attention, and he stopped typing, but kept his eyes on the screen. I leaned forward. "I want this, Cane. I don't want anyone else to have it but you. Shouldn't that make you happy? Shouldn't that *please* you?"

He made a noise, but it got stuck in his throat.

"I will never ask for anything again, I swear. We can do it once, and that's it. I'll never beg you like this ever again, Cane." He finally met my eyes, and to my surprise, his were sympathetic.

He was quiet for several seconds, pulling his hands away from the laptop. "Godammit." With a sigh, he sat back in his chair, shutting his eyes and squeezing the bridge of his nose. "Fine, Kandy." He dropped his hand and said, "Okay. I'll give you what you want."

"Really?" My heart sped up several notches. I couldn't fight my smile.

"I'll be at my lake house this weekend for a short getaway to catch up on some work. I'm leaving Friday. You can come with me."

"Oh my God! Seriously?" I hopped off the stool and dropped on his lap, which caused him to grunt lightly. I kissed him everywhere—his forehead, cheeks, nose, and chin. "Thank you!"

He had no idea how ecstatic I was. Friday was three days away. This would be happening soon. *Holy shit.*

"A lake house?" I asked.

"In North Carolina," he answered, and I noticed a hint of a smile on his lips. Was it because I kissed him? Did kissing him all over make him feel good?

A lake house meant we'd have a water view. It sounded romantic already.

"I'll give you what you want, but I want you to realize something," he started.

"What?"

"After we do this, that's it. It's over. I can't keep doing this behind Derek's back, and I don't want to ruin you."

"Okay, I understand not doing it behind my dad's back. I get it, that's why I said I'll never ask for this again. But how could you possibly *ruin* me, Cane?"

He shook his head, jaw tensing. "Trust me, it's possible." He dragged a hand over his face. His shoulders became tense, his jaw ticking. "Can't believe I'm really agreeing to this shit."

"Cane." I grabbed his hand. I understood his turmoil, and I felt bad for it. He loved Dad. He loved Mom, too. They were like family to him, and the more he wanted me, the more he was risking his bond with them and the loss of their trust. "I know it's messed up. I already told you I wish things were different but... there's no one else I want to take this from me. I want it to be special, and for it to be with someone who knows what they're doing. Someone I trust." I chewed on my bottom lip. "After this, I won't ask for anything else, I swear it. I won't lead you on. I won't tempt you or come onto you. We can stop and really try to be friends. I don't want my family to lose you. *I* don't want to lose you." But that didn't mean I wasn't being selfish. I was being extremely selfish by doing this. I knew it, but I couldn't stop myself.

"All right." He glanced at his computer. "I have some work to finish right now. You can stick around if you want to, but it might take me a while."

I shrugged. "No, it's okay. I'm going to grab something to eat and then head home to watch movies."

"You sure you're okay being there alone?" he asked, squeezing my waist before I could push to a stand.

"I'm okay. I promise. I actually enjoy the quiet of the house. Helps me think."

"Think about what? Ways to get me to *fuck* you?"

I giggled, and my belly fluttered from the growl in his voice. "Maybe."

When I stood, he let out a throaty laugh. "Drive safe, Kandy."

I grabbed my bag and headed for the door, but when I looked up, the man who was fixing the chandelier was standing there. His eyes were wide, his jaw slack, and what he said next made me stifle a laugh..

"I thought she was just your friend's daughter?"

"She is!" Cane snapped. "Go fix my damn light before I hire someone else, Larry!"

I laughed and walked past Larry, whom I felt watching me go.

"If you don't get your eyes off of her, I'll poke them out," Cane grumbled.

"Shit...I can't help it. Look at her! I'm your cousin, Q. You're supposed to tell me everything, right?"

Cane said something, but I couldn't hear. It was a good thing Larry was his cousin. And by the way he and Larry spoke, I assumed Cane trusted him enough not to say anything, or maybe he just didn't care if Larry had something to say. Either way, it was nice to know his family actually existed.

31

KANDY

Today was the day. Friday.

I had my bags packed with my favorite dresses, skirts, and even some lingerie. I was ready.

I checked my phone for the time. He told me he would pick me up at 11:00 a.m. It was 10:50 a.m. I stood by the door and waited way too anxiously. I couldn't find it in me to do anything else to occupy my time. I hadn't seen him since Tuesday, when we made the agreement.

At 10:58 a.m, I heard a car door close. I pushed the curtain aside and spotted Cane walking toward the house. He knocked, and I waited a few seconds before answering, as to not seem too desperate.

"Hey," I breathed when I caught his eyes.

"Morning," he murmured. He dropped his eyes to my bags. "You ready?"

"Yep. All set." I started to pick up my suitcase, but he beat me to it with a smile. He turned, and I followed him out the door, locking it behind me, and then meeting up to his car. He shut the trunk and rounded the car to get to the driver's side. We both got in at the same time, and when the doors shut, my heart galloped in my chest.

"I thought you were going to be a no-show," I said, clearing the thick silence.

"When have I ever stood you up?" He push-started the car.

I thought on it for a moment, and realized Quinton Cane had never stood me up. Wow. As busy as he was, he always showed. For my graduation, my softball games, dinners—everything. "Exactly," he said with a smug grin, and then he pulled out of the driveway. "It takes about four hours to get there, by the way, so get comfortable."

"Okay."

He drove away from my house, and for some reason I looked back. I don't know why, but a sudden realization hit me. I would return to that house without my virginity. I would come back a new woman. An *experienced* woman. All because of Cane.

"You hungry?" Cane asked.

"No. Now can you please cut the small talk? And all this time I thought I was the nervous one."

He flashed a crooked smile. "I'm just…" He inhaled deeply before letting it go. "I don't know. I just thought you'd be over me by this point of your life. College is a blink away. You're young and attractive and can have any guy you want, but you still want me. I guess I'm just shocked…and worried."

My eyebrows drew together. "Worried?"

"Yes, worried. You're my best friend's daughter. You can rat on me at any time if I do something wrong."

"I would never do that, Cane."

"I know, Kandy." He ran a hand over the top of mine. "I know. I'm just rambling now. Ignore me."

"It's okay," I assured him. I understood where he was coming from. He was worried something bad would happen between us. He knew I would never tell my parents a thing about us, but he also knew that if anything went haywire, I'd never look at him the same again.

I don't know when I'd fallen asleep.

I was so excited that I didn't think I would be able to settle down enough to rest, but after having a burger and a milkshake during the ride, along with the sun beaming down on me, I'd succumbed.

I can't forget to mention that due to my excitement the night before, I'd hardly slept. All I could think about was how he would take me. Would he be gentle at first and build up to a harder thrust? Would he stall and make me wait, or would he get right to it?

A warm hand touched my shoulder, dragging me out of my sleep.

"Hmm." I shifted a little, peeling my eyes open, trying hard to adjust them to the sun.

"We're here, Kandy." Cane had killed the engine, his gray-green eyes on me. I pulled my gaze from him and focused on the house in front of us. It was nice. Simple.

I don't know why I was expecting a mansion of some sort, or even a house like his real one in Atlanta, but I wasn't complaining. It was still beautiful.

This lake house was a basic two-story home. There were wide, square windows built into the front of the home and a long, cement sidewalk surrounded by pedicured grass leading up to the front door.

"Wanna check it out?" Cane asked.

"Sure." I unclipped my seatbelt as he opened his door and stepped out. He placed a pair of sunglasses over his eyes while I lifted a hand, shielding my eyes from the sun. Walking around the car, he made his way up the sidewalk and to the door.

He unlocked the wide brown door and let me walk in before him.

The house was even more beautiful on the inside. The living room furniture was a light shade of brown, the floors made of dark brown hardwood, the lights letting off a soft, gold glow. The accent wall was made of slightly burnt bricks, and built into it was an electric fireplace. The furniture was gorgeous, the placements perfect, but nothing could beat the view.

As soon as I walked through the doors, it was the first thing to pull me in. The water shimmered with the wind, and I could see a pier leading to a square deck not too far off. Green treetops and sand and boats and water. It was absolutely breathtaking.

"Wow. Do you come here often?" I asked, turning to look at him.

He shrugged. "Not as much as I'd like. Maybe twice a year, if that, and it's always for work. This makes the first time that I'm actually here for work and pleasure, if you will." His eyes flashed as he looked me over. Not once, but twice. I guess it was a good thing I'd worn my jean shorts and favorite belly shirt. He couldn't stop looking at me.

I pressed my lips, feeling the burn in my cheeks.

"We'll have dinner delivered," he announced, finally pulling away to place his keys on the glass table around the corner. "You okay with Italian?"

"I love Italian."

"Good."

Cane headed back outside to grab our suitcases from the trunk and while he did, I made my way through the house, absorbing every feature of every room. Most of the rooms were painted a pale blue and accented with white curtains and white bedspreads. I wondered which room we would be in when *it* finally happened.

Dinner arrived less than an hour later, and we ate at a large table made of white marble. From the table, I could see the lake and the setting sun perched on the horizon. There was a wide window that Cane had opened, the curtains drawn apart, and a soothing breeze passed by us every few minutes. The sky was remarkable, as if made of swirls of pink and blue cotton candy. I loved this time of year most—when the sun would set and the temperature was comfortable. Not too hot, not too cool.

Cane sat in the chair next to mine and asked me questions about college, my majors, my dorm, and the trip I'd taken for my campus tour with Mom, right before the trip to Destin. I knew I wanted to major in English and marketing. I told him I probably wouldn't need much. Mom had gone overboard on our college shopping spree several weeks ago. My room was packed with stuff. There was no way it was all fitting in our car, so she was debating renting a U-Haul or a rental SUV.

I was glad he wasn't making our time alone awkward. I expected him to walk on eggshells around me, but he wasn't. He was calm and collected. He laughed and still flirted with me, but not so much that it seemed forced. I loved this side of him so much more than he realized.

After dinner, I offered to wash the dishes. Cane had poured himself a neat scotch and was sitting on a stool behind the counter, watching me clean as he sipped. I could feel his hot gaze sweeping all over me and became a little nervous.

Perhaps he was contemplating—thinking about ways to get out of this and take me back home. He could have easily made up an excuse, and I wouldn't have been able to do anything about it but complain, which he could easily ignore.

Finally, he made a move and pushed off the stool. I glanced over my shoulder and watched as he picked up his scotch. He came around the counter and stopped by my side. "I have a few phone calls to make but it won't be long," he murmured.

"Okay. That's fine."

"You'll be okay down here for a while?"

I smiled. "I'll manage."

He grabbed my arm gently, stopping me from rinsing the forks. I looked up to meet his glassy eyes, and heat tunneled through me as soon as I locked on them. "You seem on edge, Kandy. You know we don't have to do this," he murmured. "I can take you back with no problem."

My throat worked hard to swallow, like all words had become lodged in my throat. I wanted this to happen. I wanted it so much that the ache was gnawing at every single nerve in my body...but in the back of my mind, I couldn't help but think about Dad and Mom, or how much this would change things between Cane and me. He wouldn't look at me the same afterward. There was a chance he'd think I sucked and wouldn't even visit anymore.

I brushed those thoughts aside. "No, it's fine. I want to stay with you."

He dropped his gaze to the floor, as if in deep thought.

"What's wrong?" I asked.

He thought on it for a bit, then shifted his gaze back up to mine. "I just...I don't know if I'll be able to be gentle enough with you, Kandy. I'll try to be, but if there's one thing I know about myself, it's that I like to fuck.... *hard.*" He blinked slowly, and my stomach clenched, but definitely not in a bad way. "It's been a while since I last had any or did anything..."

"It's okay..." I turned to face him. "I trust you, Cane."

"You shouldn't," he said, and his gaze became all too serious, his lips pressing thin. He finished off his drink without so much as a wince and then took a step back. "Give me twenty. Make yourself comfortable." He turned and walked out of the kitchen.

I watched him go then finished up the dishes. My heart wouldn't stop racing.

His words scared the hell out of me. If anything, they'd felt like a threat, but I knew Cane. He knew when to be in control and when to let loose, but in my situation, it was different.

I was new to him—a young, innocent girl, who didn't know much at all about pleasure or sex. I was certain he'd never had anyone this much younger than him. He didn't know what I could handle—hell, *I* didn't know what I could handle, but I hoped I could manage whatever he had to offer.

32

CANE

It'd been well over twenty minutes since I'd come upstairs.

I paced the room with guilt in my heart that started as a snowball but had eventually rolled into an avalanche, and I couldn't control it any longer. I only had one call to make, and it was settled, but as soon as the quiet swept over me and I remembered why I was here, it tore me up inside.

Kandy...

I'd had a lot of shit thrown my way, and I got through it unscathed and with no problem, but I didn't have it in me to carry this kind of guilt around for the rest of my life. I feared Derek would smell it on me, or worse, notice the changes. I feared I'd distance myself from him and her, just so I wouldn't have to face my backstabbing and secrets.

I wanted to give Kandy everything she'd ever wanted, but giving *myself* to her was a daunting task. She'd sent that text message to me, and I understood where she was coming from, and to be honest, I didn't want anyone else to have her first. I wanted her to myself, no matter how greedy or selfish that made me. I refused to let another man or *boy* take what we both knew belonged to me.

With a sigh, I stepped in front of the tall window and focused on the body of water. It splashed over metal-gray rocks and sand, the docked boats swaying gently. It was peaceful. Beautiful. This was one of the many reasons I liked to come here and escape, because of this view. The tranquil sunset made the rippling body of water glitter in an alluring manner that would make any person want to drop their feet in, or go for a ride on a boat.

I knew I couldn't stay in here forever. She was waiting for me out there, and the last thing I wanted her to think was that I didn't want her...because that would be a fucking lie. I wanted her so damn much that I was sure the cravings would have killed me if I'd allowed them to take over.

If it wasn't going to happen now, it never would. We were alone together with nothing but time, and for some reason, that thought alone was driving me out of my damn mind.

It was much easier to say no before because there was always someone or something to cut us off and prevent us from taking things further, but now that she was alone, with no protection and no disturbances, stopping wouldn't even be on our minds.

I wasn't kidding about what I'd told her in the kitchen. I wasn't gentle or sweet when I fucked. I never had been, which made scarring her my biggest fear of all.

33

KANDY

I was starting to get nervous.

I'd washed the dishes, took my suitcase up to the bedroom he'd told me about, and now I was sitting on the canopied California King bed, running a hand along the cotton comforter. It was blue and plush, the walls a soft gray.

I liked this room the best, and could see why he did, too. The window right across the room gave an elevated view of the lake. I could even see a few houses across the body of water.

Cane was torn. I couldn't believe I'd forced him into bringing me here and having us get to this point. Though I didn't exactly make it an ultimatum, I implied it by making it known that if he left me with my virginity while I was in college, I would probably give it to someone else. I highly doubted I would give it to anyone right away, but things always changed—you never knew what could happen or who I could meet down the road.

Day and night, it was Cane who was on my mind, not some other guy. Sure, I could meet someone in college, hang out with him, and get drunk, but I probably wouldn't let him take it as far as getting my panties off. I'd been touched by Cane on more than one occasion. I had memorized and craved his touch, and knew no one would be able to make every single part of my body spring to life like he could.

I was about to stand from the bed and go back down-stairs, but the sound of his footsteps stopped me. I looked up as they came closer, and then he appeared between the frames of the door. His tie was loosened, the buttons of his dress shirt undone. His belt was gone as well. He looked relaxed, like this was the look he wore after a long day of work.

"Took a while," I said softly, but instantly hated myself for the nervous betrayal in my voice.

"I was thinking." He walked into the room, looking around like he hadn't seen it in a while. He drew in a deep breath and then unleashed it, dropping his eyes to mine. "Let's not jump straight into this," he declared.

I sat up higher. I knew it. He was calling this off. "What do you mean?"

"I mean...let me freshen you up and get you relaxed first."

"How are you going to do that?"

He looked to the right, at the bathroom door, and then lifted a hand to gesture to it. "A bath okay? I have essential oils that I use for myself. Helps me unwind after a long day."

I pressed my lips and nodded "Sure. That sounds nice."

He was pleased, I could tell by the twinkle in his eyes as he shifted his gaze from me to the door. I wasn't sure if it was the idea of bathing me that excited him, or if he was just happy to be able to finally see me naked.

He walked past me to get to the door, pushing it open and walking into the bathroom. Standing from the bed, I made my way to the door too, gripping one of the frames and pressing my cheek to it.

I watched him lean over and grip the silver knobs of the claw-foot tub. He started the water, dropping his hands under the stream to check the temperature. When it was just right, he grabbed a small, purple bottle from the shelf pinned to the wall above it.

"Lavender and chamomile," he noted, smirking at me. I smiled back as he added a few drops to the water. "It will make you feel calmer. Loosen the tension in your muscles. It always soothes me."

"I'll be honest, Cane. I can't picture you sitting in that bathtub," I laughed.

He laughed with me, a comforting noise that didn't make me feel so out of place. "There's a bigger one down the hallway that I use. My tub at home is a California luxury whirlpool. It fits two people." He placed the oil in its rightful place and grabbed another bottle, adding a few drops of it to the water too and creating an instant bubble mixture.

Walking to the cabinet by the shower, he took down a sky-blue towel, similar in color to the walls of the bathroom, and placed it on the towel rack. Going back to the cabinet, he pulled down two white votive candles in frosted glasses, sparked the wicks with a lighter from his pocket, and then placed them on the countertop.

The oils from the tub were already making the bathroom smell delightful, but the lit candles made it romantic. When it was all set up, he came my way, stopping one step short. He grabbed my chin between his fingers, eyes falling to study my lips. "I'll let you get comfortable. Turn the water off when it's where you want it to be."

I bobbed my head and he pulled away, walking out of the bathroom and leaving me to it. I left the door partially open, my belly a swirled mixture of butterflies and excitement. I was truly nervous now. Cane would see me naked. *Completely* naked. A bathing suit wouldn't hide me this time. I would be fully exposed.

I undressed slowly in front of the tub. I looked all around me, from the tub, to the glass-cased shower, down to the stone flooring and marble counters, to the two windows that were a few inches above my head.

I told myself this was okay. I was nervous as hell, but I wanted this, and it was finally happening. I couldn't back out—*wouldn't* back out. With that thought in mind, I dipped a foot into the water. It was the perfect temperature. I climbed into it and sat down, sifting some of the bubbles through my fingers and running them over my legs. I shut the water off when it was just above my chest, and no less than a minute later, Cane was coming back in.

I drew my knees to my chest and smiled at him over my shoulder as he walked my way with a footstool in hand. He placed it in front of the tub and sat. He wasn't wearing his dress shirt anymore. He'd changed into a plain white T-shirt. The shirt revealed everything, from his broad, sculpted chest to the perfect, narrow torso that led down to thick thighs. His tattoos were revealed, and it was always strange seeing them, but only because he usually covered them up. The look suited him, but if I'd seen a man like Cane, the last thing I would have assumed was that he was the millionaire owner of a wine, chocolates, and lingerie company.

"The water okay?" he asked me.

"It's great."

He gave a close-lipped smile and grabbed something that was beside the tub. He lifted up a pink sponge and back scrubber and dipped it into the water.

"I'm going to bathe you. All you have to do is relax," he murmured. But relaxing was hard as hell to do when I was naked as hell in front of him.

I did the best I could. I dropped my legs, and was glad the foam covered most of my breasts. "I know it seems weird and is new for you," he said, running the sponge over my arm. "This is new for me too. Doing this with someone like you."

"You've done this for other women?"

"Only one."

"Who?"

"My mother."

I wasn't expecting him to say that. "Oh."

He was quiet for a beat, focused on sliding the sponge over my shoulder.

"She was drunk," he continued, focused on the sponge. "She'd thrown up all over herself, in her bed—everywhere. I had just come home and could smell it through her door. It was awful. Almost made me want to throw up." He let out a pained laugh. "When I was younger, I remember she would use chamomile and lavender for my baths. I used to have a bit of a temper problem, so she'd run the bath for me, add the oils, let me soak for a bit until I'd calmed down, and then she'd come and help me wash. When I got older she didn't do it as much, but I did miss them."

"Oh. Well, that's nice. Sounds like you really love her."

He didn't respond to that. Instead he swapped the sponge for the back scrubber. "Sit forward a little."

I did as instructed, and he scrubbed my back gently. It was so soothing. He was gentle and careful, but still thorough. "It would be nice to meet your family one day."

"No, it wouldn't." His voice was harsher. "They're not good people to surround yourself with."

"How aren't they? They made you, and you aren't so bad."

He stopped washing my back and pressed a hand to my shoulder, lightly forcing me to sit back. His eyes dropped to my chest and his nostrils flared. It took him a while to blink, but he did eventually. I lowered my gaze to what he'd been looking at before and noticed my light-brown nipples were prodding through the foam.

"Sorry," I whispered.

"Don't be." He ran the sponge over my shoulders and chest, but was careful going between my breasts. His thumb skimmed over my nipple as he worked his way down, and my breath hitched. His throat bobbed.

"My mother is a drunk and an addict. As a matter of fact, she's in rehab right now," he stated. "For the second time in a year, actually. I told her if she gets clean I'd buy her a condo in Charlotte. She wants to move there, open up a bakery soon and start over, but I refuse to invest if she isn't serious about her health or her future." I could tell he was talking about his family to distract himself from looking at me, or thinking about touching me, and I was okay with it. I'd always wanted to know more about his family, and here it was. "My sister is engaged to some shithead drug dealer and lives in Los Angeles with him, so I don't see or hear from her much. He has money, so she doesn't need much from me. Can't forget to mention that he doesn't like me."

"A drug dealer?" I frowned a little, confused. "Why a drug dealer?"

He shook his head. I sensed that he knew the answer, but didn't want to talk about it, so instead, I said, "Well, it's nice to know you still care and think about them."

"I do care…but sometimes they make mistakes. I want to help them as much as I possibly can, but there's only so much you can do for people who don't really want help."

"I guess." I chewed on my bottom lip. "Is your dad still in jail?"

"I'm assuming so, yes."

"You don't keep in touch with him?"

He frowned then, head shaking. "Fuck no."

"Has he tried getting in touch with you since?"

"Yes, but I never respond. What's the point? No person wants to have a conversation with a father who beat them senseless as a child."

Wow. That hurt my heart to hear, and from the sad look in his eyes and the tightness around his mouth, I realized this was hurting him too. Badly. "Cane, I'm so sorry," I whispered.

"There's nothing to be sorry about, Kandy." He shrugged. "It's the past. We live and we learn. He can't hurt me now, and that's all that matters." He dropped a hand into the water, running the sponge over my belly. The lower he went, the more I felt myself clench. "I don't want to talk about that anymore. I'm here with you."

He washed the insides of my thighs, getting closer and closer to my pussy. I looked up and his eyes were on me, like he wanted to see how I would react with him being so close down there.

By the way he stared, so hotly I could feel his gaze heating up my soul, I knew I'd given him the reaction he was looking for. My chest was tight as I held my breath, my fingers balled into fists while trying to control my body.

Cane released the sponge, so that all that was left between my legs was his hand. He slid that same hand forward, pressing a finger to the lips of my pussy. He was right outside the folds, and with one push, he'd have access.

Leaning forward to put his lips to my ear, his breath ran cool over my shoulders and down my chest, making my nipples tight and painfully aware of his presence.

"Your pussy is so soft," he whispered in my ear. I sucked in another breath, to which he said, "Relax, Kandy. Just breathe."

So I did. I inhaled and exhaled, letting the gentle scent of lavender soothe my mind and body. "Close your eyes and rest the back of your head on the tub," he instructed.

I shut my eyes and tilted my head back, the base of it meeting the coolness of the porcelain. I wasn't expecting him to pull his hand away. I wanted him to keep it there, and even whimpered with the loss.

He chuckled softly. "Patience, little one. We have two whole days together. Plenty of time for me to train and play with your body." His fingers were in my hair, running through it. He poured some water over my hair, along with a squirt of shampoo, and then massaged my scalp. He did this for a while, and it felt so good that I wanted to nap while he did it.

He rinsed the soap away and then washed my body again. This time he didn't hesitate with the sponge. He ran it over my breasts, lifted my arms to wash beneath them, ran it up my belly and then down again to get between my legs. He washed me down there and I shifted, sinking my teeth into my bottom lip.

"Breathe," he whispered. "Relax." His voice was calm. Deep. I breathed in and out as he washed me. "Okay?" he murmured.

"Yeah. I'm okay."

He dropped the sponge again so all that was left was his hand. His groan was feral and deep as he spread the lips of my pussy apart. He slid a finger over my clit and a sharp gasp flew out me.

My eyes popped open, my lips parted, ready to form words, but he repeated himself again.

Breathe. Relax.

I nodded, sighing, as he slid his finger down slowly and plunged it into me. The base of his palm massaged my aching clit while his finger thrust in and out.

His eyes locked on mine, hot and hungry, while my lips parted. He immediately dropped his gaze to my mouth. Before I knew it, he was leaning forward, his mouth on mine to claim it.

His hand worked faster, his finger hitting the familiar spot that triggered everything wrong and good inside me. It was a gradual thrust and swivel of his palm, all of it bringing me closer and closer to the edge as his warm, silky tongue devoured me. His lips were in sync with his hand. Every time he would thrust, he'd kiss me. Every time his tongue met mine, he'd groan.

It felt so good.

I almost wanted to cry from the pleasure.

I was close…

Close.

Close.

And then it happened.

Only this time, it was much more powerful than the first time in the den. I came hard, gripping his arm tight. I accidentally bit his bottom lip and he hissed, but didn't draw back.

"Fuck, baby," he growled, but I was still coming and he was still thrusting his finger and palming my clit, making sure he collected every ounce of what he worked hard to score.

He grabbed my face with his other hand, forcing my eyes on him as I panted. "You're so fucking beautiful. You know that?" His lips met mine one more time, his tongue getting a thorough taste of me, and then he pulled away. "Relaxed?" He smirked at me.

I nodded, sitting up sluggishly. "Yes," I admitted breathlessly. "Very relaxed."

After my bath, Cane stepped out of the room to let me get dressed. I shuffled through my suitcase until I found the outfit I'd planned to wear—a sheer black gown that hugged my body. Despite the tightness, it still managed to be comfortable. I'd bought it with the spending money Mom had given me.

I didn't want Cane having any reason to deny me. If that meant dressing like an escort, so be it. I'd bought it for only his eyes to see.

After I rubbed lotion on my legs and arms, brushed my teeth and hair, and checked the mirror a thousand times, the sun was no longer in sight. The sky still had a trace of light far off in the distance, but it was mostly dark now. Cane had lit candles in almost every corner of the bedroom, creating a tranquil atmosphere.

I was ready now. Still nervous as hell, but ready.

I sat on the edge of the bed, crossing my legs. As if he were on cue, Cane came back into the room, still looking amazingly handsome. As if he didn't recognize me, he blinked rapidly before giving me a thorough sweep up and down with his eyes. I pulled my bottom lip between my teeth, my face blooming with heat.

"Too much?" I asked softly.

"No." He took a step forward. "It's perfect."

I dropped my gaze, releasing my trapped lip. "Cane?"

"Yes?" He'd taken several steps closer, his eyes flashing from the candle light.

"I don't want you to think about anything else but me tonight. Okay?"

He looked me over, puzzled for a brief moment. I don't know if he was coming to terms with it, or if my request was unreasonable, but he finally straightened his back and said, "Okay."

After that, his eyes darkened and his jaw pulsed. This was a new Cane, in a completely different light. A darker, more mysterious man. A man who was ready to unleash everything he'd kept bottled inside.

My request, I believe, is what skyrocketed the evening. Before, he seemed to be holding back, waiting for me to let him know that this was okay and that it was all I ever wanted.

Well, it was. I needed this to happen right now. What we had at home had been placed on the back-burner. This was our escape— our moment—so we had to enjoy it. If there was one thing I knew, it was that escape was only temporary. So if this was going to be temporary, I wanted to fulfill myself and get as much out of this as possible.

"So…what now?" I was truly curious. I had no idea what came next. Did I go to him, or did I wait for him to come to me?

Cane's jaw locked. He was quiet for so long that it made me fidget. My pulse skittered, creating a chaotic racket in my ears.

Finally making a move, he took a step to the left and pulled his shirt over his head. As he did, I couldn't help staring at the ink and abs that'd been hidden beneath the thin layer of cotton. He tossed the shirt aside, eyes falling down to mine again. All he had left were the black suit pants from earlier. The bulge between his thighs had grown.

"I want you on your knees," he commanded, voice gruff. This

was a new voice. It held the same deep, demanding baritone he used when he'd had enough of waiting. "If you really want me," he continued, "kneel for me. Right now."

I swallowed thickly, focused on him as I slid off the edge of the bed and fell into place. My knees pushed together when they hit the floorboards, my hands shaky. I don't know why they were shaking. Why was I so fucking nervous? I hoped he couldn't tell.

He squared his shoulders, chin tipped up. "Crawl to me," he ordered, a simple demand that sent chills down my spine. I leaned forward, pressing my palms flat on the floor, my hair falling around my face. I dropped my head to look at the floor, but he grunted with disapproval. "Eyes on me." I picked my head back up, focusing on him, and with that, I could have sworn I saw a hint of a smirk form on the edges of his lips. I crawled on the cold, wooden floors—hand, knee, hand, knee—my heart beating like a drum. "Good girl," he sighed, as if the sight of me on my knees gave him satisfaction.

When I was at his feet, still peering up at him, he lowered to a squat and placed a finger beneath my chin. "You'll do anything for me, won't you?"

"Yes," I vowed.

"Good, because you'll be doing a lot more for me tonight, little one." He stood back up, his muscles flexing.

He shut his eyes for a brief moment and inhaled, and my stomach flipped. Panic swam through me. He was thinking too much about this. I knew what was on his mind. The guilt and secrets he'd have to keep buried once this was done.

"Cane," I pleaded.

He held up a hand, head shaking.

I pressed my lips together, waiting.

Waiting.

Waiting.

"Get on the bed," he finally said. His voice was harsher. He dropped his head to glare down, and I slid back a bit before rising.

I made my way toward the bed, and he ordered me to lie flat on my back. I did as told while he stepped near the bottom of the bed, watching me with intense eyes.

"Have you ever played with yourself before, Kandy?"

His question caught me off guard. "W-what?"

"Have you ever made yourself come with your own hands?" he asked, like the question was a simple one to answer. Like he was asking if I liked cream with my coffee.

I shook my head. "No."

His eyebrows shifted up, surprise in his features. "You've never tried?"

"I've tried but never had anything happen."

Still standing at the bottom of the bed, he grabbed my ankles, lightly dragging me toward him. He was hovering above me when his hands came up to my thighs, shifting the sheer material of my dress up to my waist. I nearly stopped breathing when his hot skin skimmed over mine. He noticed. "What have I told you, Kandy? Breathe," he insisted. Though he'd demanded it, his voice was soothing. His eyes shifted down to my pussy, and he stared for several seconds, unblinking.

I'd shaved this morning, long before Cane came to pick me up.

I was fresh. Bare. Ready. I'd read many articles about what to do down there before sex. I wasn't bold enough to go for a Brazilian wax, nor did I have the money for it, so shaving was the best I could do for now. He seemed pleased, though.

"This," he groaned, running a hand over the smooth mound. A tattered breath shot out of me, and my pulse quickened. "Make sure you're *always* like this when I have you."

His thumb skimmed over the slit, lightly dipping between the lips of my pussy to press on my clit. I gasped, and he'd clearly gotten a thrill out of it because his eyes widened and shimmered.

Straightening his back, he said, "Show me how you'd play with yourself."

My heartbeat became heavier. "I don't know if I can," I said.

"I know, I know." He shut his eyes and released an unsteady breath, like all of this was unbearable—like his patience was wearing thin and all he wanted to do was thrust hard and relentlessly into me. But he kept his composure. He didn't want to rush this. "Show me how you'd play with yourself with me on your mind. What would you do? Where would you want to be touched?" His palm ran up my thigh. "Where would you want to be kissed? Licked? *Fucked?*" His eyes fluttered open again.

I wanted to blink, but couldn't. The look in his eyes was both terrifying and thrilling.

"Cane, I— "

"This is new for you, I know," he crooned. "But I know you. I know you've at least thought about coming for me. *Show me.*"

He wasn't lying. I'd thought about touching myself while thinking about him many, many times, but it never lived up to what I really wanted. I'd stopped a long time ago, telling myself I would wait for his touch and eventually his cock.

I breathed as evenly as possible, dropping my right hand between my thighs and trailing the pads of my fingertips up them.

"Close your eyes and think about me," he instructed, and I hesitated at first, but went through with it anyway.

Shutting my eyes, I let my hand take over. It instantly had a mind of its own. Or perhaps I was eager and so, so tired of waiting. I spread my legs apart so my right hand could find the soft heat between them, while my left hand traveled up to my lips. I lightly nibbled on my forefinger, using my other hand to spread the lips of my pussy apart.

I heard Cane let out a deep and heavy groan, a sound that fueled the most sensitive parts of me. I placed my middle finger on my clit and rubbed it in slow, deliberate circles. I couldn't believe my own touch could shock me so much, but it did, and I let out a shaky gasp, dragging the hand that was between my lips down to my breast. I cupped my breast, still rubbing.

"That's it," he rasped. "Now make yourself *come.*"

I didn't know if I could, had never been able to truly make myself come, but I was determined to try for him. So I kept rubbing and squeezing and kneading. It felt amazing, and the fact that I was doing this to myself gave me a sense of empowerment.

I worked my hips up and down, applying more pressure with my finger. I wanted to see what I felt like, so I slid that same finger into my pussy. Soft. Damp.

"Damn, baby," he rumbled. "Don't stop."

I didn't. *Couldn't.* He was the audience, and I was the performer—wanting to give him my all.

"Oh," I moaned, and Cane gripped the top of my knee with one of his large hands. His touch ignited me, setting my whole body on fire, inside and out. I could imagine the flames running through me like a natural wildfire, burning everything and getting hotter and hotter by the second.

I rubbed faster, slid my finger deeper, repeating the actions over and over again until I felt heat building up in my core. The sensation was out of this world.

My eyes were squeezed so tightly I could see stars. "Oh, God... I think I'm about to—"

Shit. I was close.

So close.

"Cane," I moaned. "Cane!" I don't know why I'd called his name, but he clearly loved it because he gripped my knee tighter. Just as I was about to reach the brink, make myself come like he'd ordered, he pushed my hand away from my pussy. My eyes shot open.

"Wha—"

His head did one simple shake before he grabbed either side of my waist in his large hands, tilted my hips up, and dropped his head between my thighs. His mouth pressed on my pussy to kiss it, and I let out shrill sigh.

"Oh my gosh," I gasped. "Wait...are you sure? There?"

"Yes, I'm sure. And yes, *here.*"

His velvety tongue parted the lips and slid through with ease, licking up and down to get a full taste. A shrill noise escaped me— one I never thought I could conjure up.

"Shit," he hissed. "You have no idea how long I've been waiting to taste your pussy, Kandy." He tasted me again, his tongue doing a slow, torturous, gradual slide from my entrance to the delicate bundle of nerves. "Sweet as fucking candy, baby." He swirled his tongue around on my clit again, gripping my hips even tighter, like he couldn't hold on tight enough.

"Oh my gosh," I breathed. *This was happening. This was really fucking happening.*

From where I lay, all I could see was his head bobbing up and down, licking the forbidden juices away. I couldn't look for long, though. The sensations rocked my body too much. I almost thought I wouldn't be able to handle it. I'd been at the top and ready to fall before he got between my legs, but this had taken me to a completely different height.

"Cane!" I squealed, clutching the sheets, his hair—clutching at anything that I hoped would catch my fall. But there was nothing to catch me. The climax was near, and the fall would come right after it. I knew it—had felt it once before. But not like this. No, nothing like this.

He grunted and ignored my pleas, eating my pussy like I was his last meal. His tongue was both torture and pleasure, pushing up and against my clit, then drifting back down to lap up every drop. He didn't hold back at all. He was still gentle, but if I could compare him to anything, he would have been a hungry wolf. Aggressive. Possessive. In total control.

"Fuck," he cursed, barely resurfacing. "Fuck, baby. You taste so damn good." When his tongue plunged into me, it was a wrap. His silky tongue tipped me right over the edge. My back bowed, and my eyes practically rolled to the base of my skull. I tried controlling my body's reaction, but it was damn near impossible.

There was no way I could control an orgasm this powerful and perfect. My legs locked, and Cane clutched my ass and groaned harder, but didn't stop.

Before I knew it, I was crying his name.

Crying. It.

His name was my only chant. *Cane. Cane. Yes, Cane!*

I trembled with pleasure, wailed with ecstasy. My stiff legs quaked around his head, my pussy clenching tight with the release. It took a while for the fall to happen, but before it, Cane accepted every single drop, drinking me all in like the finest wine.

When I found ground, my whole body was weak. I was loose, to the point where I felt I would spill into a puddle on the floor if I moved an inch.

Cane dropped my legs on the bed and straightened himself again. He was even harder now, his cock practically begging to be set free.

"You're still on birth control?" he rasped.

"Yes," I assured him, still out of breath.

"Good. I hate condoms." He shoved a rough hand through his hair, dropping his gaze to the bulge below. A deep, subtle laugh left him, his head hung low. "I'm fucking crazy. I know it. Look at me." He rubbed his face a little too roughly. "Look how hard I am for you. I can't even remember the last time I've felt like this. This *eager*. Like a teenage boy."

I sat up sluggishly. "Don't stop," I begged.

"Oh, I don't plan to, baby." He grabbed my hand and helped me up from the bed. His hand then pressed on my shoulder, forcing me down until I was on my knees again. "Trust me when I tell you we have a long night ahead of us. I hope you've prepared for it."

35

CANE

Her pussy tasted better than I imagined it would. She was soft, warm, and sweet. Everything I'd hoped she would be. I fucking loved it, but the wait was killing me now. I was trying hard to stay patient and rein in my impulses, but she made me want to lose every single ounce of control. I wanted to get lost inside her—so lost that I didn't have to find my way back.

"Unzip my pants," I demanded.

Never had I been so impatient. I'd had plenty of women in my life, all of them desperate and ready to please me, but none of them were like Kandy. She was ready to satisfy me, but still had her virginity. Her innocence was going to be mine soon.

All mine.

Grabbing at my belt, she loosened it, and then unbuttoned my pants. The zipper was slow to come down. Fucking torture.

"You came hard for me," I murmured, running my fingers through her hair. "Was it everything you imagined?"

"Yes," she sighed.

I grabbed her hair, tugging on it lightly. "Pull my briefs down too."

She did so immediately, rolling them down to my ankles.

Releasing her hair, I stepped out of my pants and then bent over, taking the briefs off. When I stood straight again, my cock was pointed directly at her face. It was so hard that it looked angry—thick at the crown, and glistening at the tip. The sight of her licking her lips as she stared at it set my blood on fire.

"I want to apologize in advance." I sighed and throbbed when her hands ran up my thighs.

"For what?"

"I want to use your mouth, Kandy. I need to *fuck it.* I told you it's been a while since I've done anything, so if I just so happen to lose control and get a little rough, you'll understand?"

"Yeah, I will."

"Good." I stroked her hair and then her cheek when she looked up at me with wide brown eyes. "Good." The pad of my thumb skimmed over her full, pouty lips. "Open your mouth for me."

She licked them before spreading her lips apart. She still peered up with those big, glossy eyes—eyes that made her look so fucking tempting.

I gripped the top of her head, bracing myself as I slowly entered her mouth. Her tongue was warm and perfectly wet. She sealed her mouth around me, and I groaned, shutting my eyes. "Fuck, Kandy." Gripping her head tighter, I drew my hips back. "Remember what I told you when we did this before?"

"To breathe through my nose."

"Good girl. That's all you have to do. Breathe through your nose and focus on pleasing me."

"Okay."

I entered her mouth again, this time thrusting a little deeper. The tip of my cock hit the back of her throat, my sack on her chin. "Shit." Both hands came down to her head, wrapping around it. I needed to come. It'd been a long fucking week, and after seeing her naked and watching her come twice for me, I couldn't hold back anymore. I knew her pussy was soft right now, wet and ready for me.

All thoughts and desires to hold onto control vanished. I held her head like it was my personal fuck-toy, shoving my hips forward.

My one and only goal was to come deep down her throat. So I fucked her mouth, loving the sounds of her gags, easing up when I knew it was becoming just a little too much for her. She didn't like when I eased up. She enjoyed this, probably just as much I did. She held my thighs for support and squeezed when it was unbearable, but never too often.

She liked having her mouth fucked. That I knew for a fact.

"This fucking mouth of yours," I grunted, sliding in again. I glanced down, and my cock was hard as a fucking rock. Seriously, I'd never seen it so hard, so anxious.

Straightening my back, I pressed my thumb on the center of her forehead while the rest of my fingers gripped the back of her head, like holding a bowling ball. Her throat relaxed, but she didn't stop sucking. She shifted her body back and forth, like she had something to prove. My cock looked so big in her mouth. With the girth of it, it could barely fit between her lips, but she made do.

Her eyes had watered up, eyelashes damp. She stared up at me for approval, but I couldn't speak, nod, or do much of anything but watch her when our eyes latched. I watched this young, beautiful, gifted, seductive girl with my cock in her mouth like it'd always belonged there, and I fucking lost it.

"You look so fucking sexy right now," I rasped, body tensing.

I was right there. So goddamn close.

I brought her face closer, slamming into her mouth and aiming for her throat again. Her lips were spread wide apart, touching my pelvis. She breathed loudly, gagged hard, but didn't let up.

"Such a good girl," I groaned. "So damn good, baby."

She moaned around me, and I used my hand to guide her head, moving her mouth forward and backward around my dick again.

The noises she made were unbearable. The suction of her lips was tighter than ever before. I shut my eyes and tipped my head back, still using my hand to guide her head.

Forward.

Backward.

Forward.

Backward.

She was sucking the fuck out of me, moaning with each thrust, sighing when I'd push her head back, like the absence annoyed her.

And then it came.

I came.

I brought her head forward and kept it there. I knew she couldn't breathe much, and I hated how much that thought turned me on. She squirmed and moaned, and I loved it. I loved that she'd completely lost control.

With my cock lodged down her throat, I came, swift and hard, unleashing a feral noise I'd never heard myself make before. There'd been plenty of women I'd fucked, but I'd never made this noise with them. Never gotten *this much* satisfaction from a single face fuck.

"Ah shit, Kandy." There was no denying it. No fighting what was bound to happen. My cum spilled down her throat and, like the good girl she was, she swallowed every last drop with small whimpers.

I finally hauled back, my cock doing a slight spasm when it was free from her lips. "See that?" I groaned, and both of us stared at my sated cock. "You did that because you. Are. *Incredible.*"

And I meant it. She was beyond incredible.

36
KANDY

It was about to happen.

The moment we'd both been waiting for. Cane had already come, but somehow, he was still hard. He fisted his semi-stiff cock and stroked it in my face for a short while before ordering me to get back on the bed.

I stood and turned around to climb on top of it.

"Lie back and get comfortable."

I did my best, but none of this was really comfortable for me. It was all so new. I couldn't believe this was really happening. Really, really happening.

My biggest fear was that it would hurt. I looked at the size of him and knew it would be painful, but Frankie had told me it only hurt in the beginning. Maybe for like two or three minutes. She said after that, it got better, and now she loved sex. I hoped she was telling the truth. I hoped I'd love sex, too.

The candles flickered, the gold glow enhancing the dips and curves of his sculpted body. Cane was completely naked, and he looked absolutely delicious. I wanted to lick him from head to toe, trace his tattoos with my tongue and then take his cock into my mouth again, just for the hell of it. Yes, he looked that amazing.

"You're sure you're still on birth control?" he asked, stepping to the right side of the bed.

"Yes, Cane. I wouldn't lie to you. The pack is in my bag, if you want to check."

"No. It's fine." He scanned my naked body twice, from head to toe. "I believe you." He got on the bed and was between my legs before I could blink again. He leaned forward, resting his elbow outside my head, while his other hand pushed one of my legs up so my knee was almost touching my chest. "I only ask because I need to fuck you raw. I want to feel how wet you are, and how tight your pussy can get around me."

I nodded, but when I felt his cock poking at my entrance, I tensed up and pressed a hand to his shoulder.

"You're so big, Cane," I whimpered. "I'm scared it'll hurt."

"It will," he stated blatantly. His expression was sympathetic. He brought a hand up to cup the back of my neck, while his thumb stroked the apple of my cheek. "I won't lie to you and say it won't, though I'm sure that's what you want to hear. I'm a man, Kandy, and you're a girl who hasn't even been broken in yet. You're so tight down there that you'll have no choice but to bleed a little while I'm inside you."

I winced and my eyes burned. I wasn't fond of pain.

"We don't have to," he murmured, his face serious again. "I can work you up to it a little more before this happens. I don't want to rush you—"

"No." I pulled him closer—so close his lips were almost touching mine. I could feel his heartbeat through my chest. "I know it will hurt, but I want to get it over with, and I want you. *Now*. We won't have another chance like this."

He let out a measured breath. "I want to give you what you want but, Kandy…you look fucking terrified."

"I'm not." I shook my head hard, but I wasn't even sure if I believed myself. "Just a little nervous, but I'll be okay. I promise."

His lips smashed together, and he stared at me like I knew he would—like he didn't believe me.

"I want it," I assured him, and his eyes hardened. The hand he had around the back of my neck tightened.

"I'll take it slow," he responded.

I nodded and held him just as tight.

"Watch my eyes," he breathed. "Just look at me. Don't think about the pain. Think about how it'll feel when you're past that point and finally have what you've always wanted."

"What's that?" I whispered.

He placed a kiss on my upper lip. "Me inside of you."

3 7

CANE

Crazy. That's what this was.

Fucking crazy.

This girl. This *moment.* My chest felt so fucking tight, my heart slamming against my ribcage, but my balls were even tighter.

I held the back of her neck and watched her warm eyes. She was so anxious, her eyes filled with too much worry. She had every right to be nervous. Maybe I was a little too big for her. Maybe she'd bleed more than she was supposed to. I'd never taken a woman's virginity before, so breaking her in and loosening her up was going to require double the work.

But this was Kandy.

My Kandy. My baby.

And as my baby, I knew I had to take care of her.

"Ready?" I asked, shifting my hips upward.

She nodded way too quickly, which proved she wasn't ready for it, but rather ready to get it over with. "It's okay," I murmured.

I started with just the head of my cock, inching it in slowly. She winced, and her fingernails dug into my back. The pain shot through me, but it didn't bother me. She could stab me with her nails until I was scarred for months if it helped. I just knew I couldn't stop.

I slid in a little deeper, and she cried out a little.

"It's okay," I cooed. "You have to relax your body, Kandy. You can't tense up, or it'll hurt more. Understand?"

She nodded.

"You can close your eyes if you want to," I offered, but she shook her head rapidly.

"No. I need to see you." She glanced down, where we were starting to conjoin. I had a several more inches to go. "Keep going."

I clutched the back of her neck, planting my mouth on top of hers. I wanted to do everything I could to distract her from the pain. She brought her hand up and squeezed a handful of my hair while the fingernails of her other hand dug into me again. She whimpered and even said "ow" on my mouth. I was about to pull back, but she held me close, refusing to let go.

"Don't stop," she begged. "Please. Keep going."

Each plunge was slow. Gradual. Her pussy was slowly but surely spreading to wrap around my cock, and though it was probably hurting her, to me it felt fucking amazing. She was way tighter than I thought she would be. Her whimpers softened, but continued. She was tense, but steadily loosening up.

I became greedy, kissing her harder, holding her closer. Her next moan was unleashed and was much louder than the rest, and that's when I knew every single inch of my cock was buried inside her. I lifted my head, my lips almost touching hers. For a moment, I couldn't move.

The grip she had around me was fucking insane. She was so damn snug and wet. "Shit. You're so tight, baby," I groaned. "Don't even want to move. Feels so good like this." I locked on her eyes. "You okay?"

"Yeah," she sighed and nodded.

"Want me to start?"

She nodded again.

"I'll keep it slow." I pressed up on my elbow and lightly shifted my hips. Just that one shift made her hiss. She squeezed her eyes shut for the first time.

"Fuck...Kandy. I can stop if this is too much for you," I informed her again.

"No, Cane. Please." She pulled me down, and my chest landed on top of hers.

She needed time to adjust around me. I slowly moved my hips forward and backward. With each thrust, she would wince or hiss, but I kept going like she'd asked, until finally her hisses transitioned to smooth moans.

"Still hurts?"

"Not as much," she admitted breathily.

"Good." I kept a steady pace, dropping my mouth to the crook of her neck. I kissed her there repeatedly, stroking as gently as possible. I wasn't used to being gentle. Having her tight, virgin pussy wrapped around me wasn't helping my urge to fuck her senseless, but it felt good—too good to ruin the moment with selfish desires.

Well, that's what I told myself, anyway.

With every stroke, I was losing myself more and more. I could smell blood, feel it smearing on my thighs and pelvis, and that alone made me want to turn into a fucking animal because *I* did that. I broke her in and made her bleed. I did, and no one else. It was mine, and not a man on this earth could claim it but me.

"Faster," she begged.

That was all I needed to hear. I pulled up, wrapping her legs around my waist and staring her deep in the eyes as my cock steadily pumped in and out of her pussy. There was blood all over me. All over *her*. I should have stopped and took care of it, but I couldn't.

I kept fucking her, taking away that innocence and soiling my sweet Kandy. Making her filthy and impure, everything I'd desired. She moaned louder, her fingernails sinking into the sheets.

"I need to feel you come around my dick, Kandy. Will you do that for me?" I panted.

"I'll try," she moaned.

"No, baby, you won't try. You will."

I pressed my thumb on her clit, thrusting in and filling her up inch by inch. She moaned even louder, crying my name.

Her pussy clenched around my cock, and I was one-hundred percent sure that she was going to wring me dry.

"Shit." I leaned forward and sucked one of her brown nipples into my mouth before releasing it. "Fuck, you feel so good. So damn good." My teeth grazed over her nipple, eyes darting up to find hers. Hers were squeezed shut, her breaths unsteady. "This is what you wanted, right?"

"Yes," she groaned.

"You wanted me to fuck you like this? Take what's always been mine?"

"Yes!" she cried.

She opened her eyes, and they begged me for something. I wasn't sure if they were begging me to make her come, or begging me to come inside her. Whatever it was, it riled me up and made my blood boil. I lost all control when her big, brown eyes hooked me.

I groaned, slamming my hips forward a little too roughly. She cried out, and I thought I'd hurt her, until she said, "Yes, Cane!" She liked this. The pleasure and the pain. Seeing me like this— above her. In control. Dominating this pussy.

She'd clench, and I'd stay still long enough to feel her cunt throbbing.

"Please, Cane," she pleaded, bringing her hands up to her breasts. "I think I'm close."

Her back had bowed, her nipples taut and thick as she rubbed her thumbs over them. I pressed my thumb to her delicate clit again and rubbed it in small circles.

It was just enough to tip her over the edge.

I felt her sweet pussy tighten around me and then her legs locked, which knocked me off balance and made me collapse on top of her.

"Oh, Cane," she cried out, and with three more gradual, deep pumps, I was coming too. I thought I would be able to control it—last a little longer—but that shit wasn't happening the first time. I'd wanted this to happen for so damn long and now that it was, I refused to hold back.

"*Fuuuck.*" I buried my face in the crook of her neck, clutching her hips.

I should have felt like shit for coming inside her, but I didn't. In that moment, I couldn't think about anything else but how wet and tight she was, how every time I throbbed and knew my cum was filling her up, her pussy would clench to savor it. I came deep in Kandy's little pussy, and for the first time in a while, I felt only pleasure and passion and power. I felt complete and fulfilled, like nothing in this world could stop me.

Coming inside her was something I'd fantasized about and imagined, but actually *doing* it made me feel like a fucking king.

"Damn," I groaned, dragging my lips up to her ear. "You don't know how long I've been waiting to do that."

I picked my head up to look at her, and she was smiling. That surprised me, but in a good way. I was glad I hadn't hurt her. "You have no idea how long I've waited, either," she admitted with a giggle in her voice.

"Fuck," I chuckled. "You've got me stuck, baby. Can barely fucking move."

She giggled again.

I finally found some strength, though my bones felt like they were made of jelly, and pulled out of her. I looked down at the mess we'd created. The sheets were stained with splotches of red, and it was all over our midsections. She sat up and looked down for a moment, before pinning her eyes on me. "I'm sorry," she whispered. I climbed off the bed and grabbed her hand. "Don't be." Tugging on it, I made her come to the edge of it before standing in front of me. I wrapped an arm around her waist, then tipped her chin with my free hand, giving her a deep, smooth kiss. She moaned, bringing a hand up to wrap it around the back of my neck. This kiss was meant to be short and quick, but in that moment, neither of us was willing to let go. I, for the life of me, couldn't stop it. Something had come over me. I didn't recognize this territorial, greedy side of myself, but I refused to put a stop to him.

I don't know how long the kiss lasted. Before I could think things through, I had picked her up in my arms and was taking her to the bathroom. I placed her on top of the counter and finally broke the kiss. Her lips were pink and mine felt raw.

"Let's shower," I murmured. She held my hand, not wanting to let it go, but did so reluctantly when I made way for the shower. I started it up, and soon the bathroom was cloudy with steam. I grabbed her by the waist and helped her off the counter, letting her in before me.

I helped her wash up, running a sponge over her back and over her supple breasts. She took care of the rest while I washed myself.

When she was finished, her dark hair wet, and water trickling over her lips, she peered up at me.

I stared down at her.

It seemed we both wanted the same thing in the heat of that very moment. No words needed to be shared. The blazing lust dripped out of our pores and swirled in our eyes, making it all the more obvious.

She took a step toward me, and I picked her up by the waist, pressing her back to one of the shower walls as she locked her legs around me.

"I want it again," she breathed on my mouth.

She had no idea how badly I wanted it too.

I gave her what we both wanted. I was still slow to enter her, and she still hissed from the discomfort, but not as much as the first time. She had both arms wrapped around the back of my neck for support, and had bitten my bottom lip as I pushed into her.

It only took a few strokes.

A few light moans.

Several heavy, deep groans.

It was something about that shower—the steamy build up, the foggy glass, and the calming stream of water that did me in. Or maybe it was because this time, she was feeding *me*—giving me parts of her I never knew I wanted.

Passion.

Tenderness.

Affection.

Her kisses twisted me up inside in the best way possible. Her mouth tasted as sweet as her name and the shape and curves of her body in my hands was to die for.

In that moment, I realized that this was what she'd been trying to show me all along.

She wanted me to feel loved. Wanted. Appreciated.

And it had worked because that night, I felt everything.

38

KANDY

We laid down together after the shower.

He held me. Kissed me. Cuddled me from behind.

I was wrapped up in his warm arms and, though I was naked and damp, I'd never felt safer. It was the perfect night, and all because he was brave enough to give it to me.

That night, it didn't matter that we weren't meant to be. It didn't matter that he was seventeen years older, or that he was CEO of a million-dollar company and I a soon-to-be college student.

None of it mattered because in that freshly made bed, beneath the white cotton sheets, with his muscular arms around me and his soft lips in my hair, we were one, and I refused to let the harshness of reality ruin our perfect moment.

I don't know when I'd fallen asleep, but when I woke up, it was still dark outside, and I was no longer tangled in Cane's arms. The candlelight still flickered, creating bouncy, bold shadows on the wall.

I was naked, the thin white sheets the only thing covering my body. I slid off the bed and found a black robe hanging on the door, looking into the mirror as I slid my arms into it. My hair was wild, my curls all over the place. They were going to be a bitch to tame in the morning.

I headed out of the bedroom, down a moonlit hallway. From where I stood, I could see the moon through the tall arched window. The view was so stunning. The milky moon was perched there, on the horizon, the water rippling beneath the silky light.

I walked down the hallway, checking each room to see if Cane was in any of them. All of them were empty save the very last room closest to the window.

The door was wide open, this room slightly smaller than the bedroom I was just in. A large desk with a computer on top was in the far left corner, right next to a window that gave the same perfect view of the moon and lake. The seat in front of the desk was empty, but the love seat that was against the light blue wall was occupied.

Cane sat there with no shirt on, just sweatpants, his legs spread slightly apart, with a laptop balanced across his legs. He seemed deep in thought with his eyebrows pinched together and his eyes narrowed as he clicked away at the keyboard.

I could have watched him like this for hours. Shirtless. Tattooed. Muscled. Working. I had no doubt that Cane was passionate about his job. He talked about it every time I saw him. From where I stood, he looked boyish and innocent, like a kid in elementary school would look if he didn't know how to answer a question on the spot.

I was about to go back to the room and let him work, but before I could make a move, the typing stopped and he tilted his head, catching sight of me.

"Did I wake you?" he asked with a low, soothing voice.

"No. I just woke up and saw you weren't there." I held a hand up. "It's okay. I can go back to sleep. I don't wanna bother you."

"You're not bothering me." He shut the laptop and placed it on the stand beside him. "I'm having a hard time concentrating right now anyway. Come here."

My heart drummed. I tightened my fingers around the lapels of the robe, making my way toward him. I was about to sit beside him, but he shook his head and caught my waist, twisting me around so that I was facing him, and lowering me until I was on his lap.

"You belong *here*," he murmured.

I smiled, unable to ignore the warmth gushing through me, down to an area that was now sensitive and raw. "Good thing I like it here."

He scanned my face before asking, "Why are you really awake?"

"I don't know." I shrugged. "I always wake up around this time for some reason. At home I'll usually go downstairs for water or juice or something and then go back to sleep."

"Yeah. Now that you mention it, I do remember hearing someone in the kitchen around three in the morning when we were in Destin."

I put on a soft, bashful smile. "It was most likely me." I chewed on my bottom lip for a brief moment before asking, "Why aren't you sleeping?"

He let out a weary exhale, like he was stressed just thinking about it. "I was sleeping for about two hours. Then something came up with work. My assistant has handled most of it so that I don't have to rush back, but I'll have to get there eventually."

"Oh."

"To be honest, I can't remember the last time I slept a full night."

"No?"

"No." He thought on it, looking past me. "Probably before Tempt started. I'm a napper." He smirked. "I nap throughout the day, work all morning and night. My body is used to it now. Took that short snooze with you and then got back up to work. It's all I can really think about these days."

"You really love your job." It was a statement, not a question.

"Very much." When he said that, I was almost jealous of his job. He treated it like a baby—he was proud of it and refused to let anyone mess with it. I was slightly envious, but admired him even more because of it.

"That's a good thing," I said. "Not many people care about their jobs."

"What makes you want to major in English?"

My lips twisted for a moment as I pondered. "I don't know. I really love writing, and in school one time, we had to go over someone else's paper and edit it, which was fun to me. While everyone else hated it, I was thrilled. Ever since that conversation we had at the baseball game, I've also considered modeling. Is that weird?"

"Not at all. You'd make a beautiful model."

"Shut up," I laughed.

"I'm not kidding." His eyes were serious, but his soft smile remained. "You're beautiful, Kandy. Don't let anyone tell you otherwise."

"Thanks." I blushed. I could feel it all over my face. My neck.

Cane gripped my hips, lowering his eyes to the robe. "You look good in that."

"Your robe," I noted.

"Yeah." His fingers trailed up the cotton. When he reached the top lapel, he slid it over, revealing my left shoulder and breast. My nipple instantly tightened when the air hit it, and as his eyes drank me in, he sucked in a sharp breath, like he couldn't believe what he was looking at. Like seeing me bared before him was so good it hurt.

He used his other hand to push the fabric away, and both my breasts were exposed, my nipples pointed at him.

I had to fight the urge to cover up. This was all so new to me—

being completely naked and revealed—but he loved it as far as I could tell. I had a feeling not only did he get off on my nakedness, but also the vulnerability of the situation.

"Lift up for me," he murmured, his voice a little more gravelly.

I lifted my hips, and he dropped his hands to lower his sweatpants and pull out his beautiful cock. It was stiff and thick, and even with only the moonlight as leeway, his size was still daunting.

Cane gripped my hips and brought me forward so that my entrance was directly above his dark crown. I swallowed hard, wrapping an arm around the back of his neck.

"I told you I would teach you things," he mumbled. "Right now, I'm going to teach you how to ride me."

"I'm afraid I won't be that good at it," I whined.

"I'll guide you. Just do what feels right."

His words calmed me. I bobbed my head, and he held my waist with one hand, dropping the other to grip the base of his cock. My body shuddered when I felt him at my entrance, then slowly he lowered me, filling me up inch by slow inch. I tightened the arm I had around the back of his neck, sucking in a sharp breath as I tried adjusting around his size. It stung again, the pain spreading between my thighs, but it wasn't as painful as the first or second time.

"Breathe, my sweet Kandy," he cooed. The hand he had on my hip came up to the back of my neck. He slid it up until his fingers were tangled in my frizzy hair. Those same fingers brought my head forward to press our foreheads together. The hand that had been guiding his cock came up to my waist, and he used it to shift my hips forward and back.

"Ride it," he growled on my mouth. "Fuck me like you've always wanted to fuck me." I clenched around him, and he felt it, groaning deeply, breathing raggedly through his nostrils. "Your pussy belongs around my cock, baby. You know that?"

I shook my head, trying to find the rhythm and keep it there. He was so big inside me, making me feel fuller than ever before.

"Talk to me," he groaned. "Let me hear your voice."

"It feels really good," I confessed. "So good."

"Yeah? You like having me inside you?"

"Yes," I breathed.

"How long have you wanted to fuck me like this?"

"For so long. *So long.*" I wrapped both arms around the back of his neck, and he dropped his hands to my waist, guiding my hips again.

"Fuck," he groaned. He squeezed my ass, like he couldn't hold on tight enough. I was getting a little better at it, rocking front to back then sideways and up. I was sure he was enjoying it. He'd dropped his hands to my ass to squeeze it, then sucked on the bend of my neck, burying himself deeper. "Don't hold back on me, baby. Moan for me. Let me hear all the sexy noises you can make."

So I did, because truthfully, I *was* holding back. I didn't want to sound stupid or like an amateur porn tape. I had no idea what I was doing, and I was sure there were other women that were ten times better and more experienced than me. Women like Kelly.

The thought of her sent a wave of jealousy over me, but she didn't have him right now. I did.

He was mine.

All mine.

He was buried deep inside *me*, not her, and that thought alone gave me all the satisfaction and empowerment I needed.

I rode Cane's cock faster, and harder, moaning in his ear, sliding up and down on his thick, hard, beautiful cock. My fingers got tangled in his dark tresses, my pussy clenching his length.

"Yeah, baby. Just like that," he groaned.

I swiveled my hips, lowering my head to kiss him. I needed his lips. I needed all of him. I wanted to breathe him in, wrap myself up in him. I wanted all of Quinton Cane. Every single trace of him.

So I fucked him, just the way he wanted me to.

I rode his cock, even while feeling his body grow tense and his cock harden and throb inside me. I rode him until he was grunting and squeezing and cursing under his breath. I rode him until he was thrusting upward while forcing my hips down to get as deep as possible, making me scream his name and beg for more.

And then, before I could take in a full breath, he was groaning. "Ah! Shit, Kandy."

He was coming.

Coming for me.

Inside me.

All for me.

I caught his bottom lip between my teeth as I came too, moaning into his mouth as we both shot up to heaven and floated right back down to earth.

I breathed raggedly against his mouth while he panted. His eyes slowly drifted up to mine.

"How the hell am I supposed to let this go?" he mumbled on my lips.

"You don't," I told him, gripping his face in my hands. "Don't let me go."

He stared up at me, and I saw the guilt swim in his eyes but chose to ignore it. I was glad when he pushed up on one arm to stand, bringing me up with him. He slipped out of me, but held me snug to his body, walking out of the office to get back to the bedroom.

He laid me down on the bed and then curled up behind me. I sighed, loving every moment of this. I loved it so much that it pained me to know that, inevitably, this would come to an end. Our time together would soon be interrupted with real-life shit.

I wanted more nights like this. More moments to cherish. I craved more time with him, but knew I couldn't have it. At least, not in the way I really wanted it.

"You know that when we get back, things won't be the same," he said, low in my ear, running his palm over the top of my arm. "There's your mom and dad. There's work. College. Distance. *Life.*"

My eyes burned just thinking about it. "I know," I whispered, and I hated that my voice cracked.

"I just...I don't want you to hold on to this for too long. Okay, Kandy? The last thing I want to do is disappoint you by not being there when you need me. As much as I'd like to be selfish with you, I know you deserve to live your life. Meet new people. Do new things."

"I know, Cane. I understand."

"No, baby," he said, laughing so deeply it made my belly flutter. "You don't understand. You won't for a while, honestly."

"Just promise that you won't avoid or ignore me. Things will change, yeah, but don't let it be for the worse."

He was quiet for several seconds. All I could hear was my pulse in my ears, trying to find a steady rhythm again. "I won't avoid or ignore you, as long as you promise to behave when we're around your family."

I turned over, pushing my pelvis into his and sliding into his arms. "I promise."

He kissed my forehead. "Good." Stroking my cheek, he let out a deep sigh, looking over me to the window. "I haven't felt this good before. Complete like this. It's a strange feeling."

"How so?"

"To be in bed with another woman and *not* want to leave? With Kelly it was just a quick fuck and separate showers. We'd lie in bed together but not for very long, and even while I held her like this...I didn't really *feel* anything. But with you..." He trailed off, dropping his eyes to mine. The moonlight made his shimmer, and I saw more green than gray this time. "I feel everything, and I don't understand it. Being with you is fucked up, we both know that, but...it feels so fucking right. And sometimes I hate how right it feels. If it felt wrong, it'd be much easier to let go. End it."

"I feel the same way," I confessed. "If only we both felt the same way you did with Kelly. A small connection. Maybe it would be a lot easier."

"Maybe."

I pressed my lips, a sudden guilt sweeping over me. "Why'd you have to be my dad's best friend?" I laughed, but the laugh hurt my chest and my heart. "Why couldn't you be a stranger I met on a bus or a plane or even in a dirty bathroom?"

"Why'd you have to want me so damn bad?" His laugh was deep and sweet and made my belly flutter. "And why did I have to want you just as much?"

"I don't know," I mumbled. My eyelids became heavy again, my whole body sated. It was amazing how content he made me. I'd never been so settled in all my life. "I don't think we'll ever know. I just know that it's hard as hell to fight it."

He was still stroking my cheek. His touch was comforting. I loved it—being caressed and held like this. I felt safe and whole and my body oozed with warmth and pleasure. I didn't want to be anywhere else but in his arms.

"Well, one day," Cane whispered, just as I was drifting off to sleep, "fighting is what you'll have to do to save yourself from me."

I fell asleep before I could respond.

39

CANE

I watched her sleep until slivers of gold spilled over the horizon and the sky transitioned from a silvery, midnight blue to an orange-y haze.

I'd never seen anyone sleep so peacefully. My family hardly ever slept, and if they did, it was because they were shit-faced and had passed out. Being around someone this good for so long was strange to me.

I truly couldn't figure out what made Kandy so different, though I'd thought about it many times. For a while, I thought that maybe it was because she was my best friend's daughter. I'd watched her grow up, spent many years around her and her family, which created an automatic bond.

Maybe it was because she understood me, too. She gave me what I needed during all the right moments, and received just as much from me.

But the biggest reason that hit me was that I knew I wasn't supposed to want her. Our illicit time together gave me a thrill, even though that thrill could turn out to be my downfall.

If there was one thing I knew about myself, it was that I liked to torture myself. Sometimes I felt like I needed the punishment, especially when things in my life were going too well. I would rather punish myself than let the universe fuck me over.

I loved Kandy. I loved that little girl so fucking much. It started as something innocent and friendly, and blossomed into more. It hit me like a train when I realized how I felt for her. Before the night Derek was shot, she was just...Kandy. Just a girl. My best friend's daughter, a friend, and nothing more. But after that, I saw her in a new light. She wasn't a little girl anymore, I realized. She had breasts and full hips, and a beautiful, fresh face. Her creamy, tan thighs and ass had filled out so much. I noticed all those things and began to want her.

All I could think about was Kandy Jennings after that. At work. At the gym. While I traveled. Even in those rare moments when I dreamed. It was always Kandy.

She deserved so much better than this. I wasn't the right man for her, and deep down, she knew that, but she wanted me anyway. Once this weekend was over, blissful moments together like this would never happen again.

I loved my best friend. Loved him like a fucking brother. I owed him *everything*. I couldn't ruin our foundation or keep stabbing him in the back like this. Our friendship was too strong and our bond ran way too deep, and at the end of the day, Kandy was still his little girl—a sweet, young, beautiful girl who, one day, would get over me. I had no idea how I was going to move past her, especially when the future meant seeing her over and over again, but there would be no choice.

She was going to school. The distance would separate us and she'd eventually find a guy her age.

I would continue building Tempt, work my ass off, travel, and stay on top of my empire. I'd worked so hard for my company. I couldn't let it collapse after everything I'd been through. Kandy was a distraction, but in just days she'd be gone and Tempt would still be here.

I loved Kandy to death, but I couldn't let my love for her—or my lust for her body—stop me from achieving my goals. Eventually, we were going to have to let this shit go, no matter how hard it would be in the end.

40
KANDY

I woke up the next morning feeling like a different woman.

I was sore down below, but it was a sweet soreness—the kind of achiness that came with fractions of bliss and satisfaction. I wanted to cling to this feeling forever.

I rolled out of bed with a smile. I couldn't fight it, no matter how hard I tried. I freshened up, tied my hair up in a top bun, and changed into a blue maxi dress.

I checked my phone and there was a missed call from Mom. She'd paid for long distance so she could check in with me. I knew she'd worry if I didn't call back, seeing as I refused to answer the phone yesterday, so I sat on the bench in front of the bed and dialed her.

"Hi, sweetie!" she chimed after answering.

"Hey, Mom." I smiled, realizing how much I actually missed her voice. "How's Paris?"

"Oh, honey. It is a dream. Your dad and I are about to go have dinner at a restaurant with a view of the Eiffel Tower."

"What? I'm jealous! That sounds amazing!"

"Hey, sweet cheeks!" Dad yelled in the background.

I giggled, and though he couldn't hear me, I said. "Hi, Dad."

"I wanted to call and check in, but I also wanted to tell you to be on the lookout for a package. It should be arriving sometime between today and Monday." She blew a breath, as if she were exasperated. "This whole thing with work."

"Work? What happened?"

"Well, my boss did something that wasn't very pleasant or respectful. I'm starting a case to get out of my contract early at the firm. He was a bit too pushy with me several days ago."

"No—I believe what you're trying to say is he's an asshole!" Dad yelled distantly. "He tried to come onto your mother. He tried to kiss her! He's lucky she calmed me down!"

I gasped. "What? That jerk!"

Mom let out a sigh. "I know. Your dad could see right through him. I could tell he was being flirty, but I didn't think he'd actually be that bold. I mean, the man has a wife! He's insane!"

"So does this mean you'll have to find another job?" I asked, worried. Mom loved her job. Dad and I always told her she should have just opened up her own firm. She always said she wasn't ready to do that yet.

"Well, that's the good part of all of this. Cane said he knows someone who is willing to give me a position at their firm as soon as everything is settled. It's a much bigger firm too! Highly respected and recommended."

"Aww, that's great!" It really was great to know that. It was a good thing Cane was in our lives. He always knew how to help.

"Well, we're about to go. Make sure you keep an eye out for the package, okay, honey? I miss you so much!"

"I miss you more!"

She made a kissing noise, said "Bye," and then the call ended.

I smiled down at my phone for a moment, and then looked all around me.

I wasn't home. I was in a place I shouldn't have been, and the guilt gnawed at me, inside and out. I wasn't going to let that bring me down though. I had to enjoy the next twenty-four hours with Cane and cherish every golden, luxurious moment.

With that thought in mind, I left the bedroom, walking barefoot down the hallway and the staircase.

Music was playing from somewhere, and I instantly recognized the voice. Childish Gambino. Frankie loved him, and after listening to him stream out of her speakers, his soulful voice grew on me, so much so that his songs filled every playlist I had. Knowing Cane actually liked him too made me realize that maybe we weren't so different after all.

As Gambino sang about *staying woke*, I made my way around the corner, the funkadelic voice getting nearer. The kitchen was occupied, much to my surprise. A man in a white chef jacket and black pants was standing in front of the island. The countertop was covered in foods like muffins, thick strips of bacon, eggs, pancakes, sliced fruit, and coffee. His hair was a deep shade of gray, his face chubby and rosy.

He spotted me and smiled. "Oh. Good morning," he greeted, and then he stepped back, grabbing some glasses from the cupboard and placing them on the countertop too. The man dusted off his hands, walked to the open door, said something, and then turned around, coming my way. "Enjoy."

I watched him go then swept my gaze over the food before making my way toward the drawn double doors that led out to a deck overlooking the lake. Soft gusts of wind made the white curtains billow, some of it running over my skin and shifting the loose tendrils of my hair. I spotted the noise-maker—a Bluetooth music player built into the wall, along with speakers. When I made it to the door, I pressed my cheek on it and tried hard not to sigh.

There he is.

Cane was sitting in a cushioned chair, his legs spread slightly apart, and his cellphone in hand. He was staring at the lake, eyes narrowed, and I couldn't blame him. The view from the deck was breathtaking, but very bright with the sunlight bouncing off the water.

A female's voice was coming out of the phone and he was nodding repeatedly as she spoke. He wore a white T-shirt, but it did nothing to hide his chiseled body.

"That's fine. As long as the percentage remains the same or increases, it should be okay until I get back." As if he could feel someone watching him, he turned his head to the right and found me. His eyes appeared greener beneath the rays and sparkled as they ran over the length of me. Maybe I wasn't imagining it last night. They were greener. Was Cane one of those people who had eyes that changed colors during certain temperatures or even certain moods? I'd learned about that in school. It was possible.

He picked up a white mug and brought it to his lips, his eyes trained on me as the woman on the phone continued her business chatter. There was a familiar hunger in his eyes, but also a deep adoration I'd never seen before. I blushed as he sipped.

"Is that acceptable, sir?" the voice went on.

"Perfectly fine, Cora," he responded. "I'll see you tomorrow afternoon."

"Sounds great, sir," Cora said. "Enjoy your getaway."

"Believe me," Cane gestured with his hand for me to come to him. "I will." He ended the call while watching me walk his way. My smile spread even wider, my heart racing. "Look at you," he sighed. "Glowing."

I bit back a grin, sitting on his lap. "I wonder why."

"Oh, I know why." He wrapped a hand around me, pulling me close. He smelled good. Fresh, like he'd showered again this morning. Cane was an early bird. I needed to make a mental note of that because I loathed mornings. The only reason I was up that morning was because I wanted more time with him. "You okay? I didn't get too rough last night, did I?"

"No." I shook my head, lacing my arms around his neck. "Not at all. It was perfect, Cane."

"Perfect?" He cocked a brow. "Sure that's the word you wanna use?"

I giggled. "Yes, because it's true. It was perfection."

With a boyish smile, he asked, "You hungry?"

"I could use a hot meal."

"Good." He rubbed my back. "I had a local chef I know send one of his people to bring a few things from his restaurant. Go grab something to eat."

I nodded, pushing off his lap and going into the kitchen. I grabbed one of the plates and topped it with pancakes, apples, and bacon. After pouring myself a mug of coffee and tucking the bottle of warm syrup beneath my arm, I headed for the deck, taking the seat next to his.

"Is Cora the assistant you were talking about last night?" I asked, pouring syrup on my pancakes.

"No, Cora is my secretary. My assistant's name is Deon. He's good at his job."

"Cora knows about your little getaway?" I asked with a smirk.

"I told her before I left that I would be here for a few days. Told her I needed some time to think."

"Ah." I bit off a piece of the apple slice.

"Wasn't a lie. There are a lot of things to think about." He put his hand on top of mine, and I stopped eating, dragging my gaze up to his. I noticed there weren't any hard lines around his eyes, per usual. His eyes were softer than I'd ever seen them before. "I've been thinking about you all morning, Kandy. How the hell are we going to keep doing this?"

"Doing what?" My heartbeat quickened, beating in my ribcage.

"Act like this was just a time to get whatever this is out of our systems? Because I'll tell you right now, I haven't had nearly enough."

I pressed my lips. "I don't know." Sitting back, I crossed my legs and looked to my right to focus on the body of water. "Like you said, I'll be in college soon. We won't see each other as often as we do now."

"But when we do? Then what? Did you think about that?"

"We just...see what happens, I guess. Who knows? Maybe what we feel now will go away. Maybe we'll change and become friends again, like we were before I came onto you that night..."

He sat back, pulling his hand away to scratch the tip of his nose with his thumbnail. "Maybe," he said. He sighed, looking over the rail. "But something tells me this won't just go away—that the time and distance will only make us want each other more when we see each other again."

"We'll do better. We just can't fight it like before. You know how crazy and irrational I can get when I want you..." I dragged my teeth over my bottom lip. "I hate fighting what I want, especially when it comes to you."

He sat back, running the pads of his fingers over his temple and forehead. "But all of this is so fucked up," he mumbled. "So fucked up."

"Cane—"

"No, Kandy. Don't say anything. There's not much that can be said when we both know it's true. This is all so very fucked up. Having breakfast with you like this? Spending a whole weekend with you? Having *sex* with you?" He dropped his hand. "You don't know this, but when I think about Derek, I think about him facing a psychotic man with a gun, that psychotic man being my worthless father. I think about him being brave enough to stand in front of that threatening, menacing man, and taking him down to save my mother, who could have been killed that night, but survived. She got out alive because of Derek. Honestly, I don't know what the hell I'd do without her. Yeah, she can be delusional and has her issues, but I love her. I...*shit*. I *need* her, Kandy. That's why she's in rehab for the second time, because I want her to do better, and I'm tired of losing her to the drugs." He sighed and my throat thickened with emotion. "As a kid, I used to pray she'd get better. I promised her and myself that I would get her help when I could, so she could be the woman I knew and loved as a child. The one who protected me and put my sister and me first. The one who left my father without one look back—back when she was clean and honest and full of life. Before he found her again and fucked up her life. I know she's still in there, and now that I can help her I'm fulfilling that promise, but I can't help thinking about how I'm breaking the trust of the man who gave us another chance to rebuild our relationship. A man that I owe *so much* to."

My eyes were hot, the truths truly setting in. Whatever appetite I thought I had completely vanished.

He huffed. "But then there are moments like this, when I'm around you and feel on top of the world. Moments like this are when I wonder—why? Why does it have to be *you* that I feel so much for? Why does it have to be so complicated, like my life isn't already complicated enough?" I felt his pain and conflict with the raw crack of his words. "Why do I have to choose between my best friend and what my heart and mind really desires, after sacrificing pretty much *everything* in my life just to get to where I am today?" His eyes glistened, red-rimmed, and my heart both swelled and ached for him. "At the end of the day, I know what I'll have to do. It's just going to be hard to fall through with it."

"Cane...I-I'm sorry," I whispered, grabbing his hand. "I swear, I'm so sorry. I wish I felt something else too. I feel awful keeping this secret from my dad—especially after hanging out with him last week. I felt like shit that day and swore I would avoid you, but here I am. I don't know what it is about you. I've felt it since I was a little girl—this crazy connection that is impenetrable and special. I know it's wrong to want you, but when I see you or I get the chance to be around you, all of that wrongness disappears." I sniffled. "I—I don't know. It's hard for me to explain. He always says how he's so proud of you and all you've accomplished, and that you deserve it more than anyone. He talks about how you helped him get through his recovery with baseball or basketball games, or quick beers at the bar you guys met at, and I literally hate myself. But then there are moments like this, when we're alone, like you said. You're right next to me. Touching me. Seeing me for who I *really* am...and there's nothing I want more than you. It's like nothing else matters when we're together."

"I know," he sighed, a weary, painful noise that made my heart ache and bloom. Did this really hurt him that much? To the point he couldn't choose—*wouldn't* choose? To the point he would leave us all behind if it came down to it? God, that thought scared the hell out of me. I didn't want him to leave. I wanted him around forever. I wanted him to always be one phone call or drive away. To be honest, I just wanted him to myself.

Cane leaned forward and stroked my cheek. He wiped a tear away, a tear I didn't even realize had been shed. "It's funny," he laughed, a genuine one that seemed to come from deep within him. "I can handle everything about my job. When there's a deal that has to be made, I'm down to do it, and I usually come out on the winning side. I've traveled all over the world. I've met some of the richest men on the planet, sold hundreds of bottles of wine to them in less than five minutes with a good pitch, and it was all so simple to me. But when it comes to you?" His head shook and dropped. His dark lashes touched his cheekbones, and I'd never seen him look more vulnerable than now. "I have no clue what to do with you. Wanting you is a beautiful challenge, Kandy Cane, and though it's complicated, I don't want to figure this one out anytime soon. As selfish as it sounds, I want this challenge to last for as long as it possibly can. I love the spontaneity of what we have—the satisfaction I get when I see your smile, and the comfort I feel when your skin touches mine."

"Oh my God!" A laugh bubbled out of me, and I swiped my tears with the back of my arm. "How is a girl ever supposed to get over you when you talk to her like this?"

He grinned, cupping a hand around the back of my neck and bringing me forward to place a warm, smooth kiss on my cheek.

Bringing his head up and pressing his forehead to mine, he said, "I don't know, but what I do know is that we're a fucking mess."

He was so right.

We were a mess.

A wild, beautiful, perfect mess, and that made me the happiest girl ever.

41

KANDY

For the rest of the morning, Cane worked on his laptop while I sunbathed on the deck. He was in the chair beside mine, and every time I rolled over, I caught him staring at me, like he was deep in thought.

"What?" I'd laughed.

"Nothing," he responded quickly, but gave a boyish smile that proved he was thinking about way more than *nothing*.

We ate sandwiches on the deck for lunch, and for dinner we settled with ordering pizza, which was more than okay with me. Cane had music playing after dinner, and we pretty much danced the pizza off. He'd twirl me quickly, and I would giggle, and then he'd reel me into his arms, bend me backwards just a little, and place a warm, soft kiss on my lips or the hollow of my neck.

He was so romantic, and when I told him he was, he denied it. Said he was just being himself, whatever that meant.

By nightfall, we were all over each other again. I mean, how was I supposed to resist?

"You're gonna wear me out," Cane teased as I gripped his hand and led the way upstairs.

I smiled over my shoulder, making my way to the master

bedroom. I couldn't wait anymore. We'd been teasing and flirting all day, but I needed him again. I wanted to feel his warm body on top of mine, his lips all over me, his mouth in the special places only he was allowed to touch.

Cane shut the bedroom door behind us and then walked around the room lighting the candles he'd had on the night before. He turned to face me after sparking the last one, and pulled his shirt over his head with a small smirk. I was sitting on the bed, my shirt now off, only wearing a bra and shorts.

"You're eager," he noted, walking my way.

"I am," I murmured when he stepped between my legs. His hands dropped to hold my waist, and he tugged me close, both of us releasing shaky breaths. The tip of his nose skimmed over the arch of mine, trailing down to my lips and then up my cheekbone.

"I want to try something different tonight," he murmured on my mouth.

"Yeah? What's that?"

"I'd rather show you." He pulled away and told me to turn around and crawl to the middle of the bed. I turned and crawled, feeling his eyes on my backside. He ordered me to stay on all fours, so I did.

The bed dipped behind me, and his fingers found the waistband of my shorts, gently pulling them down. I lifted both legs to help him get them off.

All that was left was my panties and bra. Cane let out a deep, coarse groan behind me as he gripped one of my ass cheeks. He squeezed it with a sigh, and the bed dipped even more as he fully climbed on top of it. I felt heat behind me, and when I glanced over my shoulder, his face was near my behind.

He nuzzled his nose between the crack of my ass and I let out a gasp. This was different...and I was surprised that I liked it so much. Having him invade my personal space this way and take control? New. Different. Exciting.

He ran his nose up and down, and I felt the heat of his mouth near my pussy. Was that why he was doing this? To tease me? Get me worked up?

"You always smell so good," he rasped. He brought his face forward with a sigh while pushing my panties aside. In an instant, his hot mouth brought me to life. I gasped as he kissed my pussy from behind. He kissed it again with a guttural groan, and a trail of goosebumps swept over my skin.

His hand came up to press between my shoulder blades and he pushed me down until the right side of my face was on the bed.

"Relax for me, Kandy Cane," he mumbled, and that name—his sultry voice—automatically calmed me.

"I need you soft and wet, so I'm going to eat your pussy just like this. That okay?"

"Yes," I breathed. I was tight, so raw and exposed. All I wanted was for him to take care of me, ease the tension in my body, and smother me with heat and dominance and power.

I waited for what felt like an eternity as he got off the bed. I heard rustling and figured he was taking off the rest of his clothes. The bed dipped again and his palm ran over the curve of my ass.

"You look so good like this," he crooned. "Spread open, your pussy ready to be used. Are you ready for me, baby?"

"I am," I sighed. I was so damn ready.

His face was even closer, and a finger ran through my slit, making my entire body shake.

He chuckled lowly. "So sensitive," he teased. The heat of his mouth was closer to that area again. I could feel his breath streaming between my thighs, gentle as it ran over my sex. The warmth of his tongue was next, and it lightly curled over my clit. A sharp gasp flew out of me. I knew it was coming, but didn't expect it to feel so amazing.

I moaned and shifted a bit, but Cane held my hip to keep me in place. His nose was almost near my untouched hole, and I don't know how, but it felt so damn good.

"Stay just like that, baby," he ordered, and his tongue ran

through the slit and up to my clit again. "Let me eat this sweet pussy of yours." His tongue plunged into me this time and he gradually withdrew, sliding it over my swollen core again. I couldn't help the moans that flew out of me. He held my hips, licked, sucked, and plunged. It all felt so good, especially with his face so close to my ass. His tongue slid up so high that it almost neared the puckered hole again, but then it came back down, and I whimpered. He chuckled.

"I won't go there yet." Those were his final words before he finished me off. His tongue was magical, relentlessly lapping me up from behind until, finally, I came.

"Oh, Cane!" I squealed. He savored every drop.

"Mmm," he groaned. "Fuck, baby. I love the taste of your cum." He pulled back and sat up, but remained behind me. Something hard poked me and I knew what it was right away. Sliding a finger inside me, he groaned and said, "Oh, yeah. You're ready for me."

I shifted on my knees, adjusting my hips up, ready for him to take me. Placing a hand on the small of my back, he thrust his hips forward, allowing only the tip of his cock to touch my entrance.

"It may hurt a little in this position," he mumbled. "If it's too much, tell me to stop and I will." I could hear how breathless he was. He was probably hoping I *wouldn't* tell him to stop.

He inched forward, and while he did, I felt *everything*. His thick crown pushed into me, and I clutched the sheets, squeezing my eyes shut. I breathed when he told me to, and he pushed in a few more inches.

I accepted the pleasurable pain, knowing there would be a reward by the end of it. His size became easier to adjust around, but at this angle and with his girth, he felt so much bigger than before. I felt full already, and he wasn't even completely inside me.

"Okay?" he breathed.

"Yes."

"Good." He thrust his hips forward, giving a powerful shove that made my toes curl. "I want to see how much of me you can handle." He pushed forward again, one of his hands getting tangled in my hair. He wrapped his hand around the ends of it, forcing my face off the bed. I moaned louder, and he stroked deeper, his skin clapping on mine. "Can you handle that?" he asked, and though I couldn't completely, I bobbed my head because I refused to admit any weakness when it came to him.

He held my hair tighter, grunting as he gripped my waist with his other hand and slammed forward again.

I whimpered and he leaned forward to kiss my spine, as if that kiss would make up for such a powerful drive. The grip in my hair went slack, and I looked over my shoulder at him. He was staring right at me, and when our eyes latched, he slammed forward again. And again. And one more time.

"Fuck, baby," he rasped when I let out a louder cry.

He was being rough. So rough. It was startling at first, but I couldn't deny this. This was what I'd been waiting for—this side of him that had been hidden, patiently waiting to rear its naughty, twisted head. This was what he liked: rough, hard sex. Sex that made me breathless and weak while his cock grew harder with every primal thrust.

Something stung my ass next, and I realized it was his hand. It was hot in that area, and he spanked it one more time. "This beautiful, perfect ass," he grunted. "I've wanted to fuck you like this for so long, Kandy. *Shit.*"

He stopped working his hips to flip me over, but as soon as I was on my back, he was inside me again, burying himself so deep that my back arched, and I gasped for breath.

"Oh, shit," he rumbled. "You are so fucking wet for me, baby." He grabbed my legs and lifted them, putting his hands on top of my kneecaps and working his hips forward and backward. He picked up his pace, fucking me faster. *Faster.*

"Cane!" I screamed. I was so loud, but couldn't control it, and he knew it. He knew it because his eyes flashed in the gold, flickering light, and his nostrils flared, like it made him even hotter to hear me desperate, calling his name. He kept rocking those hips, this time dropping his hands to wrap them around my throat. His grip was light, but slowly he applied pressure.

In that moment, I thought maybe there *was* something wrong with me. Maybe I was a crazy masochist who loved pain. Maybe something in me was broken, for relishing the frisson of fear combined with overwhelming pleasure.

When he did that, wrapped his large hands around my throat and took my life in his hands, I was struck dumb with lust. The loss of control drove my body wild. My moans were chaotic and my hips shifted up and down with every thrust he provided. His eyes were bolted with mine, and with one simple command, I witnessed fireworks.

"Come," he commanded, cock buried deep, his hands still around my neck. "Come for me, Kandy. Come all over my dick, baby."

His voice, his cock, his *hands*—it was all too much. My mind and body couldn't handle it. I couldn't hold on much longer. I was shooting up higher and higher, toward the stars and the moon— so high that I almost couldn't breathe, couldn't speak. Couldn't think.

Cane pulled his hands away, and with one powerful, full drive of his hips, I came. I came hard around him, clenching him to me like I was afraid he'd stop and not let me finish. My back arched and my pussy pulsing, soaking the entire length of him.

"Oh, yes, baby. Just like that. That's exactly what I wanted," he rasped. But he didn't stop. He kept going until his body tensed and veins appeared on his neck and forehead.

Suddenly he jerked back and collapsed seconds later, his mouth crashing down on mine, and his teeth sinking into my bottom lip.

"Oh fuck," he groaned. "About to come." He jerked his cock rapidly between our sticky bodies, his hot cum squirting all over my belly and pelvis. After his release, he finally set my lip free and dropped his head, burying his face in the crook of my neck. "I'm sorry if I hurt you," he whispered.

"You didn't."

He picked his head up, finding my eyes. "You enjoyed it?"

"Probably more than I should have," I admitted with a silly smile.

He grinned, lowering his mouth to mine again. He kissed me softly. Once. Twice. I clenched and sighed. "You're a dream, Kandy Cane."

"I am?"

"Yes." He pressed his lips together. "If only I could stay in this dream forever. I'd make you mine in every way."

I sighed. "I don't want us to wake up."

He blinked slowly and looked away. By the wrinkles that'd formed on his forehead and around his eyes, I could tell he was thinking about something he shouldn't have been. He finally looked at me again, pushing up on one hand. "Let's shower and watch a movie. Any movie you want."

I grinned, but didn't ignore his sudden change of conversation. Now wasn't the time, I knew that. So I nodded. "That sounds fun."

We took a hot shower, and in there, I dropped to my knees and sucked his beautiful cock until he came again. I couldn't get enough of him, and I'm sure he couldn't get enough of me either. I loved the way he tasted—the way he felt in my mouth. I loved when he stroked my hair and looked down at me with soft eyes, his mouth slightly parted, like he was weak for me—would *always* be weak for me, and had no control over that. I loved everything about this man. I wanted to please him in every way possible.

We dressed in comfortable clothes and went downstairs to his living room to watch a movie. I picked an action movie and, I don't know what exactly triggered the sensation, but I was instantly reminded of Dad. We'd watched this exact movie together before.

The thought of my dad made me want to cry, and as if Cane sensed it, he tipped my chin and forced me to look at him.

"What's wrong?" he asked.

"It's nothing."

"Don't lie to me." His face was stern, as well as his voice. "What are you thinking about?"

I pressed my lips together, twisting my fingers around each other in my lap. "Dad."

He blinked down at me but I looked away before I could see the guilt sweep over him and cloud his eyes. My bottom lip trembled, and I couldn't hold it anymore.

I cried.

I cried because this weekend was so perfect and real and amazing.

I cried because, after tomorrow, it would be over and I wouldn't have Cane to myself anymore.

I cried because I loved Cane so very much, but I loved my dad too. I didn't want to hurt my father, so I knew sacrifices had to be made, and as if Cane knew it too, he pulled me to his chest, stroked my hair, kissed the top of my head, and cooed to me. "It will be okay, Kandy Cane. I promise, you'll be okay. You'll get over me soon and everything will be fine."

But he didn't know that. He had no damn clue. I would be broken without him. Something would be missing—a piece of myself would be forever lost unless we connected again.

We wanted each other so badly, but our love for my dad outweighed those desires. Our love for him was the reason this weekend would only happen once in our lives. We couldn't risk ruining our reality, and we also didn't want to lose each other. In order for that to happen, a change had to be made. I could want him all I wanted, but I couldn't *have* him. He was never going to be mine.

That was my reality, no matter how much it hurt me to know.

He knew it and I knew it...so no, I wouldn't be okay.

42

CANE

As hard as it was to do, we ate our last breakfast in paradise together then took our time packing up and putting our bags in the car.

I wasn't ready to go, but I knew I had to get her home. I'd called Derek, and he told me he would be back the next day and I was their ride from the airport. The sooner I had Kandy home and safe, the better.

On the way back, our fingers were entwined, the wind running through my hair and stirring her brown strands up. I had the windows down, the sunroof peeled back, both of us wearing sunglasses while French Montana and Jeremih sang about the unforgettable to an island club beat. It was the best I'd ever felt, sitting in that car beside her, with her hand in mine.

With every passing minute, my heart ached, knowing I'd have to let her go for good. Going back to reality was going to be hard, but this was life, and unfortunately, my life was never fucking easy.

As bad as I felt, I was glad that it was *me* she was going through this with and not some other man. I had the small comfort that her first time had been safe and consensual, and I knew she'd gotten pleasure from it. A lot of women couldn't say the same.

I knew I wasn't going to get over her, but at this point I had no choice but to try to let go. It was going to be a tough battle—internal warfare—but letting go of love was something I'd done before. I'd done it repeatedly with my mother and sister.

I could do it again.

43

KANDY

When he kissed me goodbye, the weight of our non-existent future was lifted temporarily. For a split second, I forgot about reality and only thought about his lips and how soft they were, how perfect they matched mine. How amazing he smelled. How he groaned when he tried to pull back, but came in for more, like he was parched and couldn't satisfy his thirst.

I don't know how long we kissed, or who stopped first. I do remember holding his hand for a while, the rims of my eyes burning because I didn't want to let go.

"Don't," he murmured. "You'll be fine, Kandy Cane. I promise. I'll still be here."

That much was true, but it didn't help. Still, I sucked it up like a big girl. I didn't let my tears fall while I stood in front of him on the porch, but as soon as I made it up to my bedroom and tossed my bags in the corner, I curled up on my bed and shed the tears that'd been begging to be unleashed.

It lasted for a while—about a good fifteen minutes—until my phone chimed and a message from him popped up.

Cane: You better not be crying.

278

At that, a laugh bubbled out of me and I sent him a quick response.

Me: I'll be okay.

Cane: I know you will.

I fell asleep a short while later, my eyes dryer and my smile faint.

The next day, I called my best friend. She'd been waiting to hear the details ever since I got home.

"Tell me every-fucking-thing," she demanded. I heard noise in the background, a scraping noise like furniture was moving.

"What's going on there?"

"Oh, my roommate is rearranging the furniture. Said she doesn't like the layout. Whatever that means," she muttered. "Anyway, go! Tell me everything! Was it as good as you hoped?"

"Oh my gosh, Frank," I let out a joyous sigh. "It was...*ugh*. I don't know how to put it into words." I paused for a moment, and I knew the wait was killing her because she groaned. "It was better than I imagined it would be. He was gentle, but also rough and dominant. He knew exactly what to do to make me come." I blushed at that, looking at myself in my bathroom mirror. "I didn't want those two days to end. Ever."

"If I were you, I would have stayed longer. Screw everything else. That man likes you just as much as you like him. Hell, he probably loves you now that you've given it up to him."

I laughed. "I don't think so."

"Was he big?" she probed.

I busted out laughing. "Huge, Frank. I was almost scared of it."

"Holy shit!"

"Can you please not curse like that around me?" I heard someone shout in the background.

"Dude, fuck off!" Frankie snapped, her voice distant. "Don't like it, request another fucking roommate, Polly!"

I giggled. Frankie could be such an asshole sometimes. "You'd better stop or Polly's going to smother you with a pillow while you sleep," I sniggered.

"Not if I get to her first. Gah, she's so uptight. Damn prude. "

I walked out of the bathroom when I heard a car door shut. Pushing my curtain back, I saw Cane's car in the driveway. Mom and Dad were walking toward the house with suitcases, and Cane's car was going in reverse. Was he not coming in?

"Hey, Frank, I'll text you, okay? My parents are here."

"Okay. Please do so immediately before I strangle my roommate."

I promised before ending the call and tossed my phone on the bed. I hurried down the stairs and as I rounded the corner, Mom and Dad were walking through the door.

"Hey, baby!" Mom squealed.

"Baby girl!" Dad bellowed.

I smiled at both of them, rushing into their arms. They hugged me at the same time.

"How was the anniversary?" I asked when they let me go.

"So good," Mom sighed, and beamed at my dad.

Dad returned a smug smile, and that was enough for me to know they'd fallen in love all over again—not that they weren't before. It was just stronger now. I was glad. They needed that time to reconnect and learn about each other again.

"I see my house is in tip-top shape," Dad said, walking past me and scanning the house.

I rolled my eyes. "There were no parties thrown here, Officer Jennings. Take a chill pill."

They both chuckled. Dad came my way, planting a kiss on the top of my head before walking to the kitchen. Mom followed after him, letting out an elated sigh about her package on the counter, and when they were gone I walked to the living room to look out of the window. Cane's car was nowhere in sight. I don't know why that bothered me so much.

I shouldn't have been worried though.

That same night, he sent a text to check on me.

The next morning, he sent another, wishing me a good morning. He sent me cute messages that whole week, and they always made my day. He'd even sent emoticons, because I'd told him he was lame for not using them. This continued for a solid week and then it just...stopped.

I always waited for him to text me first. I knew he was busy, and I didn't want to bug him, despite how badly I wanted to hear from him.

The first day of no messages, I thought nothing of it. I assumed he had his hands full with work and couldn't get to his phone quickly enough.

But then another day passed and nothing.

On the third day, I began to worry, so I sent him a text to ask if he was okay. The bouncing dots popped up to show he was about to respond and I waited...and waited...

Nothing.

44

KANDY

He's busy. He's a CEO. His hands are full. That's what I told myself, though deep down, I was finding it hard to stick to. Fortunately, Mom came to my room with good news, just two days before I was about to head off to college.

Cane was coming over for dinner.

As soon as I got the news, I hopped off the bed and rushed to my closet to find something nice to wear. I went with a soft pink dress that made my boobs look bigger and my waist narrow.

I hadn't heard from him in five days. I didn't know if he'd had a trip out of state or what, but since he was coming over, things were going to be okay. I would see him. Even though I was curious why he hadn't checked in, that was all that mattered.

I straightened my hair and did my makeup, taking my time on the wing of my eyeliner. While adding my mascara, the doorbell rang, and Dad called my name, which meant my time for getting ready was up. It was time to greet our guest as a family, like we always did.

"Don't give too much away," I told my reflection. "He's just a friend. A friend. Nothing happened."

I drew in a breath and nodded at myself before going past the stacked boxes and bins in my room to get to the door. I made my way down the stairs and stepped around the corner just as the door swung open.

He was the first thing I saw. His hair was freshly trimmed and appeared like it was lightly fingered with gel. He had a bottle of red wine in his hand and held it up when Dad greeted him. Dad accepted it, and they did their brotherly handshake and hug.

I stood a few steps away, breath dwindling, my legs locked, as he stepped through the threshold and smiled at Mom before giving her a hug.

When he was done with her, all that was left was me.

His eyes met mine first…but they weren't soft, per usual. They were hard and distant. Cloudier than they were the week before. I frowned instantly. These weren't the same eyes that I'd last seen. These weren't the soft, mostly green, sincere eyes that looked at me with nothing but love and adoration. They were gray and unreadable. I blinked rapidly as he looked away to peer over his shoulder.

And then I saw her.

She came through the door with a short red dress on, her makeup flawless, and her hair half-up, half down. She gave my parents a hug around the shoulders with a smile and chimed, "So good to see you guys!"

When I saw her, my heart fucking failed me.

I wanted to swallow, but couldn't. I wanted to run, but knew I wasn't allowed to overreact. I wanted to slap the shit out of Cane right where he stood, but knew it would have started a shitstorm that he apparently wasn't worth. I hated that I couldn't do anything but stare and look helpless. My eyes became hot and prickly, and I dropped my head when Cane met up to Kelly's side.

"Wanna help me get the dinner set up, sweetie?" Mom asked. I looked up at her and nodded, and I swear I wanted to cry on the spot. My heart hurt so much. My stomach was in knots. What was going on? Why was he doing this to me? Why was she with him? He wasn't hers; he was mine!

How could he...

"Yeah," I said to Mom, and followed her to the kitchen, doing my best to ignore the conversation Dad was having with Kelly and Cane about his new line of wine coolers.

While I helped get the food on the table, I tried wrapping my head around what was going on. I had no answers or solutions. I knew we were only supposed to be friends, but why did he go back to her so quickly? Was it that easy for him to get over me?

Kelly and Dad came into the dining room, and Kelly complimented how great dinner looked, as always. I rolled my eyes and didn't even give a fuck if she saw.

"I'll go check on the chicken," Mom called.

"Oh, I'll come with you," Kelly said. She and Mom went to the deck to check the grill and Dad headed out with them, winking at me on the way. I forced a smile at him, and as soon as they were out of sight, I hurried out of the dining room and rushed out the front door.

Cane was standing beside his car with a cigarette pinched between his lips. He'd just gotten off the phone, lowering it and staring down at it with a grimace.

"What the *fuck*, Cane?" I hissed before the door could even shut behind me. He looked over his shoulder with a continued grimace, but when he caught sight of me, his eyes softened for the first time that night. "Why is she here?" I demanded. "Why would you bring her back around after what we did? And so fast—you couldn't wait two more days until I was gone?"

"Kandy...please, just go back inside." He shoved rough fingers through his hair. "I'm not in the mood for this shit tonight."

"No—fuck that, Cane. You tell me why you would do something like this? You haven't answered my calls or texts in days. You've been completely ignoring me after checking in with me every day, and then you show up with *her*? I mean, I know I'm inexperienced, but was it so bad that you had to go back to *Kelly?*"

Cane's head shook, his jaw tight and flexing. "Just move on from me, like I told you to do." He tossed his cigarette down and stepped on the butt of it with the tip of his shoe, then walked around me to get to the door.

"Cane!" I wailed after him. "Talk to me!"

But he didn't. He kept walking and didn't bother looking back.

"Please," I begged, but my voice had cracked and was much softer than before. He was walking through the door before I could blink my tears away. The tears stung and my throat thickened. I couldn't believe this. He seemed so into me—so determined to hold onto me and keep me as his...but then *this* happens?

I bit back tears as long as I could, looking around my neighborhood, feeling like everyone was watching. I couldn't cry out here, and I didn't want Mom or Dad to see me, so I rushed into the house, where Cane was nowhere in sight, and hurried for the stairs. Before I could make it to the staircase, though, the downstairs bathroom door swung open and stopped me in my tracks.

Kelly walked out with a gasp, holding a hand to her chest. "Oh, Kandy, I'm so sorry—"

"I need to get to my room." The tears were becoming harder and harder to control, so I lightly shoved my way past her and ran up the stairs. I didn't give a fuck if I was being rude. Fuck her. Fuck them both.

"Kandy?" she called. "Is everything okay?"

I ignored her. As soon as I made it to my room, I let my walls crumble. I sat on the edge of my bed and curled over. I felt a pain in my stomach I'd never felt before—an ache that I knew would never dull or be soothed unless a certain someone came to fill that aching hole.

But that person was an asshole.

He was a heartless bastard.

He never gave a fuck about my feelings.

He got what he wanted and then disappeared. And not only that, he shoved another woman in my face. It was like the two days we spent together meant absolutely nothing to him.

The tears were salty and hot, and I tried hard to muffle the sounds so that, if someone were to pass, they wouldn't hear me. Instead, I drew my knees up to my chest, buried my face into my thighs, and bawled. I cried so hard I couldn't breathe, and truthfully with my thighs in the way, it wasn't easy.

I believe five minutes passed by before I heard someone knocking on the door. I jerked my head up with a gasp and waited to see if the person would go away. They didn't. There was another knock on the door.

"What?" I called.

"Kandy, it's me. Kelly."

I frowned then. I didn't want to see her right now. I was angry with her, when I honestly shouldn't have been. She didn't know about Cane and me. She didn't know that he'd stolen my virginity with pretty words and lies and was now treating me like a piece of shit. Now that I thought about it, I would have been better off giving Carl my virginity. At least with him, he wouldn't have been so quick to walk away or ignore me.

"Can I come in?" she asked, and I sighed, swiping the tears off my face, though I was sure it wouldn't cover up the hurt.

"I guess," I mumbled.

The door pushed open and Kelly walked in with wide eyes. "Are you okay?" she asked.

I pressed my lips and shook my head. "I'll be fine."

"Boy troubles?"

I shrugged.

She was quiet for a moment, watching me. I avoided her eyes. I hated crying in front of people. Hated it. I didn't like anyone seeing me weak or vulnerable...no one besides Cane, obviously.

Kelly finally made a move by shutting the door quietly and then taking a step closer my way.

"Problems with Cane?" she asked, and that caught me completely off guard.

My brows drew together when I picked my head up to meet her eyes. I expected to see a soft, sincere expression, but instead her eyebrows were knitted too, her entire face tight and stern.

"W-what?" I asked.

"You heard me," she said. Even her voice sounded different—sharper, without the soft touch of a southern accent she'd had previously.

"I don't know what you're talking about, but I'd like to be left alone right now."

She tilted her chin with an agitated sigh. Pulling her white clutch from beneath her arm, she opened it and took something out. She then tossed the object my way. It was a pair of panties. *My* panties.

I dropped my legs in a flash, pushing off the bed. "Why do you have these?" I demanded.

"No, Kandy. I think the question is *why were your panties in Cane's suitcase?*" She cocked a brow.

I had nothing to say. I was speechless. Utterly and completely dumbstruck. Kelly huffed a laugh, tucking her clutch beneath her armpit, and took a step to the side. She gave my room a sweep with her eyes, walking around like she had nowhere else to be.

"The thing is that I knew you liked him. I've always known. I see the way you look at him, like you're waiting for something to happen. You are head over heels for him, and I get that. I mean, Cane is a handsome man. And wealthy too. He has this way of making a woman feel...*wanted.*" Her eyes sparked as she took a step toward me. "For a while, I thought it was one-sided, but then the beach happened...and I noticed the way he looked at you, and

I'd never seen it before. He looked at you like he wanted fuck you all over that house. I noticed how protective he was of you. I even noticed when you two would disappear at the same times...and then I remembered our last night there, when he called me by someone else's name." She pressed a hand to her chin and tapped it, as if she were deep in thought. My palms were slick, my jaw slack as I watched her. "Bits, that's what it was. *Bits*. I had no idea who Bits was...until I heard him call you by that name the next morning. But still," she continued, "I ignored it and gave him the benefit of the doubt. I mean, what would Quinton Cane, a thirty-five year old man with a million-dollar company, want with a girl who is nearly half his age? It just didn't make any sense, so of course I just considered myself crazy and figured your little crush on him was getting to my head. He did pay you much more attention than me, and he asked a lot of questions about you, but I'd considered it nothing. I needed time to think, so I eventually got back to my senses and paid him a little visit a few nights ago. He wasn't home yet, so I decided to wait for him...and that's when I noticed the unpacked suitcase. And that's when I found those in the side pocket." She pointed at my panties on the bed. "I remember them very well. Pink with red hearts. I picked them out for you when we went on our little shopping spree in Destin. Remember?"

Her eyes were hard on me. I'd never seen her like this—almost vicious, like she wanted to rip my throat out.

"Kelly, I—I swim at Cane's house almost every other day. I used his shower and probably just forgot to grab my panties."

"Oh, Kandy." She made a *tsk* noise. "You poor, sweet girl." She came closer, but was still staring me down. "I may seem like the nicest, most oblivious woman ever, but trust me...I'm not. I notice *everything*. Just like I've noticed how much Cane admires you—how badly he wants to keep you in his life—I've also noticed how riled up Derek can get when he's tested. I know the extremes he would go for his daughter. You are his world, and Cane is his best friend. If he found out that Cane touched you in that way...well, he would never look at him or you the same again. He would despise Cane...quite possibly ruin his life and career. And for you...well, the trust would be broken, don't you think? Your parents won't see you as their sweet, innocent, beautiful girl anymore. They won't know what to do with you."

My chest grew tighter. Fuck, I could hardly breathe. I stumbled back when she neared me, her back straight. "Cane had one rule to follow tonight and that was to not talk or look at you. No alone time with you. No running off to be alone, just to see if you would follow. None of that. He is to *never* be alone with you again. I told him that if it happened, I would tell Derek and Mindy everything they don't know, and trust me, the last thing Quinton wants is to lose his friends, the few people who truly accept him for who he is. He also doesn't want his life ruined over a teenager."

I tried to swallow, but it felt like I was swallowing glass.

"So the same goes for you, sweetie. If I see you so much as *look* at him in that way, talk to him in that way, or even touch him when you walk by, I will inform your parents. Your father won't be happy, and just may end up doing something that will ruin both Cane's and his own life. His career will be tarnished, and your mother will be left to deal with a *filthy*, desperate daughter she can't handle, and a husband with a short temper. Your perfect little life, with your perfect family, will be torn apart." She stabbed two stiff fingers into my chest. I gasped sharply, tumbling backwards and landing on top of the stuffed toys in the corner.

Kelly smirked and shook her head. "Look at you. *Pathetic.* And you really thought he would give everything up for you? You're nothing but a secret to him, Kandy. A memory. Go to college and live your life, and stop trying to ruin mine. Make it easier on yourself and forget about him, because I'm sure he's already starting to forget about you."

With that, she spun around and walked to the door, yanking on the doorknob with a twist and walking out.

45

CANE

This was for the best.

I loved Kandy, I really did, but there was so much on the line—so many opportunities laid out before me.

My friendships.

My company.

My family.

My life.

Giving in meant all of what I'd tried to keep buried would come crashing down on me. I had to play my cards right.

You hate me now, but you'll understand soon.

You'll see…

It was for the best.

46

KANDY

There were too many questions running through my head—too much heartache for me to bear alone. I had one more day left in Georgia, and I needed answers. Immediately.

During dinner, I couldn't even look at him. The worst part of it was that I had to sit and watch Kelly touch him and pretend everything was okay. I had to sit in the midst of laughter and joy while my heart felt heavy with gloom. Cane didn't look or interact with me at all. After dinner was over, I went straight to my room to soak my pillow.

After thinking about it all night, I realized that I didn't care about Kelly's threats. I could go to him without her knowing. He wouldn't tell her I showed. I wanted him to tell me to my face that he was already over me, without her threats lingering above us. It was the only way I could accept it and move on, like I should have been doing before.

If I could hear the truth from him, then I'd let it all go. I'd forget, like he told me to.

With that in mind, I got dressed in jeans and a nice blouse, but didn't bother with any makeup. I didn't have the energy, and my eyes were too damn puffy from crying to even bother. I was glad both my parents had to work that morning, but they'd promised they would be back later that afternoon to help me finish packing and getting ready.

I grabbed my keys and headed to my car. When I got behind the wheel, I searched my GPS for Tempt's address. Once found, I started the car and drove off.

Though it was only a twenty-five minute drive, it felt like an eternity. All these thoughts roamed through my brain, intertwining and colliding. Some of them screamed for me to spare my heart and go back home. Others told me to keep going and get answers.

When I spotted the tall building, I parallel parked in front of it, then sat there a moment. Was I really about to do this? Was I that desperate for answers?

After shutting off the car and yanking the keys out, I found out that I was. I pushed out and headed straight for the spinning doors. There was a woman at the front desk, but she was occupied, so I went for the elevator before she could spot me.

When it chimed and the doors opened, she looked over at me. "Hey! Excuse me!" she called, but I ignored her, tucking my hair behind my ear and rushing into the elevator. I jabbed my thumb into the button to make the doors shut, and then stared at the numbers. Cane was the boss. If he was going to be anywhere, I assumed he would be on the top floor or somewhere near it. I pressed the highest number—15—and my belly dropped with the lift.

The numbers ticked by so damn slowly. I chewed on my fingernail as I anxiously waited.

Finally it stopped. The doors pulled apart, and this floor looked completely different from the first one. This one had floors made of dark gray marble, and at the end of the walkway was a desk. It was vacant. I stepped off, and the elevator doors closed behind me. It was quiet.

Too quiet, almost.

I took several steps forward, hearing something behind the door ahead.

A voice. His voice. *He's here.*

I sped up my pace and went to the door at the end of the hall. It was halfway open, and through the crack, I saw Cane pass by with a white button-down on, the sleeves rolled up to his elbows. "I need that delivered by tonight, Cora. No—it can't wait until morning. They guaranteed it would be ready tonight, and I want it there. We will be too busy tomorrow to even deal with that. Good. Thank you for handling it."

He ended the call with a hard sigh. I blinked slowly, watching him sit on the edge of his desk and scroll through his phone. Now was my chance to talk to him. He was alone. Cornered.

I pushed on the door with the tips of my fingers and it let off a slight creak. Cane picked his head up with a frown but when he caught sight of me, his eyes widened and his lips parted. He placed his phone down and pushed off the desk.

"Kandy—what the hell? What are you doing here?" he demanded.

But I ignored him, pushing the door closed behind me and running into his arms. He caught me before our bodies could clash too hard, and I was glad. So glad. He held me tight in his arms instead of pulling away, and my tears were instantaneous. I buried my face into his chest. "Why?" I asked, voice muffled. "Why? I don't get it."

He made a noise that got trapped in his throat. "Kandy," he murmured, and I could hear the agony in his voice.

I picked my head up, meeting his eyes. "What does she have on you? I don't get it. What did you do?"

He pressed his lips. "You don't want to know," he answered, and his eyes immediately turned dark and filled with guilt.

I wanted to know. I really did, but it hit me that we were alone. All alone, just like we were at the lake house, and in the den the very first time we attempted something. We were best when we were alone. Just us. Uninterrupted.

"I wanted to see you before I left," I whispered.

He stroked my hair. "I'm glad you did."

"I'm never going to forget about you, Cane, and I know you aren't going to forget about me either. I don't care what she says."

He unleashed a hard and heavy breath. "I'll figure this out," he said with his lips in my hair. "I swear."

"By the time you do, you don't think it'll be too late?" I looked up again.

"I hope not, Kandy Cane."

I smiled a little. I put my focus on his lips, how full and supple they were. I missed those lips. I missed everything about him. His scent. His touch. His beautiful, sculpted face. The ink that stained his arms and peeked out from beneath the collar of his shirt.

"Can we?" I begged. "One more time?"

He blinked down at me with a pained expression. "Kandy…"

"Please," I begged again.

He shut his eyes for a moment, inhaling through his nostrils and then exhaling. When he opened them, they were softer. Understanding.

He lowered his head and brought his hands up to cup my face in them, and when his mouth met mine, my cold blood ran warm again. Anxious, I tangled my fingers in his hair and pulled at the buttons of his shirt. I was sure I'd ripped it. Buttons clanked on the floor, but I didn't care and neither did he. He reached down to pull my shirt over my head, our kiss breaking for a just a moment before we were smashed together again.

Picking me up, he turned for the love seat that was against the window and laid my back down on it, climbing between my legs and unbuttoning my jeans with haste. My panties were next, and while he slid those down, I fumbled with his belt, button, and zipper.

We were both free from the waist down. His shirt had been

torn open, hanging loosely over his arms. He stared down at me, eyes sparking from the sunlight pouring in through the wide window. I stared up at him, the most beautiful man I'd ever laid eyes on, and my eyes burned again, but I didn't want to cry. Not yet.

I grabbed his arm and yanked him down, draping my arms around the back of his neck. One of his went under my back and slid up to grip back of my neck, the other holding my waist.

He looked at me again, and though my tears flowed abundantly and my heart was crumbling into pieces, I told him what I wanted.

"I want you to make love to me." Those words—all I'd ever wanted.

He watched my face for several seconds. "Kandy..." His voice broke, but I shook my head and kissed him. I needed this. I didn't want him to speak anymore. This was hurting enough. My chest ached and my mind raced and buzzed. With a grunt, he entered me, so deliberately that I had no choice but to whisper his name and beg him to complete the stroke.

His thrusts were full and deep. So deep that I was sure I'd feel his imprint days after, and yet he was so gentle that my heart and belly fluttered.

"Don't ever think I don't love you," he said in my ear. A full thrust. More tears. "I fucking love you, Kandy. Love you more than words."

But this had to happen.

Letting go had to happen.

So I cherished this moment, right in his office, beneath the beating, yellow sun, surrounded by papers and leather. I ignored the burn of the leather on my backside, focusing on the strokes he provided. This was his final parting gift. With our tongues tangled and tied, and his body conjoined with mine, I knew he was telling the truth.

He loved me.

SHANORA WILLIAMS

He was making love to me.

I cried.

I *came*.

Euphoria and heartbreak. It was a strange combination, one I wouldn't wish on my worst enemy. Knowing this person could make you feel so amazing, but also knowing this same person held the power to break your heart.

If that wasn't love, I didn't know what was. I was young and naive, yes, but my heart knew what she wanted. She'd known it for the past nine years. I was in love with Quinton Cane, and that was never, ever going to change.

Cane held me tight when he released, and even after, when the rest of his body had gone lax. He ran his fingers through my hair, panting rapidly as he tried catching his breath. Lines of liquid fire ran down to my ears.

"This hurts," I sobbed. "It fucking hurts, Cane."

"I know," he breathed. "Fuck, I know, Kandy. I'm so fucking sorry. I told you I'll fix this. I swear—just give me time. Things will go back to normal when I—"

I shook my head, forcing my hands between us to push against his chest. He had no choice but to lift up and when he did, I slid from beneath him and grabbed my jeans. I tugged them on and then slid my feet into my flip-flops. Cane picked up his pants as well, pulling them over each leg.

"Kandy," he persisted.

"I have to go," I muttered.

I grabbed my shirt and pulled it over my head. Before I could get to the door, he caught my hand and whirled me around. He didn't leave time for me to protest. His mouth claimed mine and our bodies connected again. Molded. A perfect match. A match that would never be.

"Don't forget me," he begged.

Begged.

Cane had begged, probably for the first time in his life. I met

296

his eyes and the rims of them were red and glistening. "Don't walk out like this. Let me at least take you to dinner, a movie?"

I shook my head. "No. It's okay. I have to get home and finish packing. Dad should be there soon. Besides, I don't want you to get into any more trouble than you're already in."

He blinked, lowering his gaze. He grabbed my hand and clutched it, and for a moment we stood there just breathing. Thinking. *Breaking.*

I really had to go. I couldn't do this—stand here and hurt. I couldn't have him, and the sooner I let this go, the better off we both would be.

Reluctantly, I pulled my hand away. He was hesitant to let go too, but he did. I had so much to say to him as I walked to the door, but none of the words were willing to come out. All of them became lodged in my throat, so I forced a smile at him instead— smile that cut me up inside like jagged edges of broken glass.

"Don't forget me, Kandy," he said again, taking a step toward me, but I had already turned my back to him and walked out of the office.

The door closed...

Cane and I were no more.

47

KELLY

I hated that sneaky bitch.

I hated everything about her. I'd known for a while that he was messing with her. His odd and overprotective behavior made it so damn obvious, but I kept a level head and considered it a phase.

Surely, he will get over it and realize he needs a real woman, I thought. *He's just having fun. Remember he told you that he didn't get to have a lot of fun as a teenager?* My nice side pleaded with me, begging me to show sympathy and mercy. She was fucking wrong, and I will never listen to that side of me again.

I thought winning Kandy over and playing girlfriends would get her to back off, but it didn't. Hell, I had even hoped that my little story about how he helped me at the club would have worked, but it didn't. I'd made that story up, and she seemed to eat that shit right up, but it wasn't enough for her to move on, I suppose. Hell, he didn't even own a club, but I ran with it.

To be honest, I discovered Cane in a psych ward, where he was handling a mother who was screaming at the top of her lungs about how badly she needed a shot of heroin. She was wrestled down and drugged, hauled away right in front of him.

See, I knew his secrets, and he trusted me with them, but only because he didn't know how *vicious* I could be when my limits were tested. He also didn't know the real me.

He'd tested me repeatedly, stomping right over me, seeing me as only a woman who wanted him and nothing more. To be truthful, he was ruining my plans now by wanting her. Enough was enough.

She thought she could just waltz in and steal the show, take what was mine? She was fucking wrong.

I knew I couldn't just go by a pair of panties. For all anyone knew, they could have been any woman's panties, and I would have looked like a fool pulling out pink underwear and flashing them, screaming they were an eighteen-year-olds.

So I did what I had to do—what my mother had trained me to do—so that I would never end up with a divorce or be abandoned. I wired Cane's office.

I made up some bullshit excuse to his staff about how Cane wanted his office redesigned while he was out of town, had a few men come in, and they bugged it. Microphones. Hidden cameras in the lamps. I would be able to see everything, and he didn't know it.

He didn't want me, I knew that, but he had the money I needed, and the business that would help me skyrocket and grow my brand even more. Millionaire Wine, Chocolate, and Lingerie Seller, and Classy Interior Designer. I could see it like a package deal waiting to happen...but there was one thing standing in our way.

That little slut, Kandy.

I gritted my teeth as my personal investigator rolled over the film of them fucking on the leather love seat that I fucking selected personally. I couldn't see their bodies, thank fuck, but even a blind man would be able to tell what they were doing from the noises they made.

"Turn it off," I snapped, pushing to a stand and grabbing my bag. "Can you make copies of that?"

"Yes, ma'am," he answered quickly.

"Good. Make ten of them, and give two to me right now."

He bobbed his head and started clicking at his keyboard. My copies were made in no time, and when he handed me the USB flashdrives, a thrill shot through me—one I hadn't felt in ages. I loved the power I possessed. These USBs would end it all and leave him with no choice but to be with me. I slid them into my purse and walked to the door.

"Where are you going with that?" he asked, brow cocking. "My watermark is on them, you know? You have to pay for it."

"Don't worry, Hank. You'll get your money plus more once I know my plan has worked."

48

CANE

I hated that I couldn't see Kandy off on good terms, but even if I had been capable of it, I wouldn't have been able to. I had a negotiation party at my house that I'd been planning with Cora for a solid three months. Everything was already in place. I'd never seen my home so clean and organized. Gold lights, ice sculptures, decorations. Waiters stood in the den with trays of wine and hors d'oeuvres, waiting for the guests to arrive.

This was going to be a big deal for me. If I could get Mr. Zheng to accept my offer, I would have a Tempt warehouse opening in Tokyo in no time. I'd be able to sell my products there, expand my brand. It'd taken me years to get him to even talk to me, and now that I had him in my palm—in my city—it was time to seal the deal.

I got my suit tailored and fitted that morning, and by six I was dressed for the occasion, ready to take on the night. The party started at eight, but around seven, some of the guests were arriving. I greeted every single one of them at the door, keeping my chin up and doing my best to ignore the heaviness that weighed on my chest.

That heaviness was guilt. Fucking guilt, man.

It wasn't just about not getting to see Kandy off, but about the way she walked out yesterday. She didn't look back. She was already prepared to let me go. I saw the pain in her eyes, tasted it in her tears. She was going to be hundreds of miles away, and I was going to miss the fuck out of her.

I had to handle Kelly before even trying to talk to Kandy again. I needed her out of the fucking picture...but that was going to be hard to do with all she knew about me. I thought I had her on a leash. I was so wrong. Until I figured something out, I needed to do whatever I could to make her keep her fucking mouth shut. If that meant pretending to be a couple, so be it.

I walked up to Cora, who was standing in the hallway with a clipboard. "This turned out nice," I said as a few guests walked by with drinks already in hand.

"I told you it would, sir." She looked up at me over the bridge of her glasses.

One of the assistants came our way, and notified us that Mr. Zheng had arrived.

"Time to get my game face on, huh?"

"Yes, sir, it is." Cora walked to the door and I stood in place. Mr. Zheng walked through the threshold, a heavyset man with dark hair and warm, fawn skin, and I went to shake his hand.

I'd never met Mr. Zheng in person before, only chatted with him through phone calls and emails. He was a pleasant man, very serious with a dry sense of humor, so it was a good thing I knew how to handle that. Even though things seemed to be going great, I hadn't brought my A-game for the night. I felt like everyone could tell, especially my future distributor. I swiped drink after drink, trying to tame my frazzled nerves.

If only I could get her off my mind. If only it were that simple...
Fuck.

Still, I did my best, giving compliments when necessary, but not overdoing it. This was my job. My life. I could stumble, but I couldn't fall. Falling made me weak, and I vowed to never hit the ground again.

During a small conversation with Mr. Zheng, I spotted Cora across the room, scanning the area. When she found me, she pushed through the crowd, murmuring her apologies. Meeting up to me, she gave me a perplexed expression. "I'm sorry to interrupt you, Mr. Cane, but there is a Derek Jennings at the door for you, and he's not on the guest list."

Derek's name caught me completely off guard. I hadn't invited him or even told him that I would be home. *Shouldn't he be with his family right now?*

I excused myself from Mr. Zheng and his wife, telling them to try more of the new wine that was floating around on trays. Adjusting my gold tie, I walked out of my living room where music by a live band played, and down the hallway that led to the door.

Cora stood in front of the half-open door waiting for me. She heard me coming and rushed my way.

"Do you want me to call the security guards at the gate?" she asked, panic in her eyes.

"What? No. The men at the gates know Derek. His name's on the visitor list for the house." I looked at her with a slight frown. "What's going on, Cora?"

"He just...well, I know he's your friend, sir, but he seems a little unstable right now. I think he's drunk. His car is parked on the front lawn and he's been walking around, ranting and demanding that he needs to see you. It's making some of the guests uncomfortable."

I narrowed my eyes and pulled them away from hers, going for the door. When I drew it open, I spotted Derek standing in front of one of the guest's cars, staring at his reflection. "Derek?" I called.

Nothing but his head and neck moved as he peered over his shoulder, but his eyes didn't meet mine.

"Derek, what's going on, man?"

He turned around, and as he did, I noticed his hands were clenched into fists. I slowed my pace, running my eyes all over him. From the glossy look in his eyes and the sweat that dotted his forehead, it was clear he was drunk. "Did you drive?" I asked calmly. I knew how he could get when he was drunk, and it was clear he was upset about something. When he drank, he always talked about his past. His anger would sometimes get the best of him. Something was wrong.

He took a step toward me. "I'm not drunk," he lied. I could tell he was lying. His words slurred together. He took another step forward, stumbling as he came up the stoop.

"Look, D, let me call someone to get you home," I insisted, reaching for him, but he shoved my hand away before I could touch him. I frowned. "D, what the fuck, man?" I snapped. "I have business guests here. This is important. I'm trying to be patient with you, but I don't have time for this shit tonight. All right?"

"Oh, you don't have time for my shit?" He scoffed, letting out a belly-deep laugh. "You—you don't have time for my shit?" He continued, laughing like it hurt, and my frown deepened. I looked over my shoulder at Cora who was standing by the door that was halfway open. She was worried now, her cellphone in hand. I shook my head at her, and she lowered it, still panic-ridden.

Facing Derek again, I asked, "Do you need to talk about something with me? We can talk in private."

"Oh, trust me," he growled. "Trust me, Cane. I have a lot to fucking say to you. Mr. Big CEO!" Derek ran a hand over his face, so roughly that I thought he would hiss with pain. He then brought the hand up to his forehead, using the palm of it to smack himself repeatedly.

"Derek!" I barked.

"Fuck!" He roared.

I rushed toward him. "What the fuck is your problem? Why

are you even here? You're supposed to be getting ready to take your daughter to school in the morning!"

He took a step sideways, breathing raggedly. "You know, on the drive here, I kept trying to figure out exactly how I could get to you. I kept wondering what I could possibly do to ruin your fucking life and your trust, just as much as you've ruined mine." His nostrils flared, and he lunged toward me, and that's when I figured out why he was here.

The anger was written deep in his irises, his teeth bared, hands like shackles.

He knew.

"Kandy," he seethed, wrapping a hand around my throat and squeezing tight. "My *daughter!*"

"D-Derek," I wheezed, clawing at his hand, trying my damnedest to shove him off, but he was built like a fucking machine. Though we were nearly the same height, he had more mass and body strength on me. I was no match for him.

"You fucking pussy! Fucking my *daughter* behind my back! My little girl! I should fucking *murder* you right now!" He snatched something from his waist and pressed it into my temple. It was warm, like he'd been holding it only seconds before facing me. He pressed the barrel of the gun to my head, and I heard a shrill cry behind me. "Maybe I will, huh? *Kill* you? I mean, out of all the people…all the men in this world…" He breathed through flared nostrils like a heated bull. "You, Cane?" His voice came out broken and tears lined the rims of his eyes, like he hated this just as much as I did, hated seeing the pain in my eyes, knowing I couldn't breathe, but also knowing that Kandy was more important than any of those feelings.

He finally released my throat, shoving me away from him. I landed on the grass, breathing raggedly, my gelled hair hanging over my forehead now as I held up an arm. He staggered backward, sliding the gun back into his holster.

"Derek," I wheezed, but I couldn't get up. Why the fuck

couldn't I get up? My legs had given out on me. My heart was beating out of my goddamn chest. He was my friend—my best fucking friend—and he had just put a gun to my head. I deserved this. I did. I knew it...but never thought it would come to this.

"You have *no idea* how badly I want to end you right now, but for the sake of my family, I won't." His jaw clenched, and his head shook slowly as I regained steady ground. He turned his back to me and started to walk off, but I made a foolish mistake.

"Derek, wait. It's not like that! You know me, man! Kandy is—" I grabbed his shoulder to try and stop him, get him to hear me out, but he turned in a flash, lifting his arm and slamming his fist right into my face.

"*Fuck you,* Cane," was the last thing I heard before the back of my head hit concrete and all I saw was black.

BREAKING
Mr. Cane

NEW YORK TIMES BESTSELLING AUTHOR
SHANORA
WILLIAMS

BREAKING MR. CANE:
THE HEART-POUNDING FOLLOW UP TO *WANTING MR. CANE*!

KANDY

I was left broken, my heart beating a little bit harder in order to survive. I'd tried picking up the pieces, but when it came to Cane, it was hard to let go.

The way we touched was special and we promised to never forget one another. I had him right in the palm of my hand—thought everything was perfect—but in the blink of an eye, he was gone, leaving me with no choice but to pretend that what we had never existed.

CANE

She was off-limits to me, but I pushed the boundaries anyway. Now, I was stuck between a rock and a hard place, my career slowly but surely slipping out of my grasp, and ghosts from my past returning to make things much more complicated.

My love life had never meant so much to me until I met Kandy. After being knocked down and left stranded, any sane man would have stayed far away, but I wasn't sane—not by a long shot.

I knew reality was harsh, and the universe had all the odds stacked against us. Despite it all, *nothing* was going stop me from making her mine again.

And if someone tried, they were going to have to go over my dead body first.

AVAILABLE ON JULY 12TH, 2018!
EBOOK PRE-ORDER AVAILABLE!

MORE BOOKS BY SHANORA

NORA HEAT COLLECTION
CARESS
CRAVE
DIRTY LITTLE SECRET

STANDALONES
TEMPORARY BOYFRIEND
100 PROOF
DOOMSDAY LOVE
DEAR MR BLACK
FOREVER MR. BLACK
INFINITY

SERIES
FIRENINE SERIES
THE BEWARE DUET
VENOM TRILOGY
SWEET PROMISE SERIES

Most of these titles are available in Kindle Unlimited.
Visit www.shanorawilliams.com for more information.

Feel free to follow me on Instagram! I am always active and always eager to speak with my readers there: @reallyshanora

<u>CONNECT WITH ME!</u>

FACEBOOK GROUP: Shanora's Sweethearts
Twitter: @shanorawilliams
Instagram @reallyshanora

Visit www.shanorawilliams.com for more book information and details.

Printed in Great Britain
by Amazon

60312112R00178